The Day Will Come

The Day
Will Come

Judy Clemens

Poisoned Pen Press

First Edition 2007

10 9 8 7 6 5 4 3 2 1

Library of Congress Catalog Card Number: 2006940929

ISBN: 978-1-59058-299-2   Hardcover

Poisoned Pen Press
6962 E. First Ave., Ste. 103
Scottsdale, AZ 85251
www.poisonedpenpress.com
info@poisonedpenpress.com

Printed in the United States of America

For Jim Clemens
Brother, Friend, Musician

Acknowledgments

As always, it took many people to bring this book to life.

Todd Novak, lead singer and songwriter of The Cowlicks, regaled me with more stories than I could fit into this book. Maybe someday I can use them all. Without his knowledge and the willingness to share his experiences, the Tom Copper Band would not exist. Check out his band at www.thecowlicks.com.

Dr. Lorin Beidler offered suggestions for the medical subplot in the story, and Tami Forbes was generous with her time and answers to what I'm sure were unusual questions.

Investigators Chris Jackson and Toby Jenkins of the Lima Fire Department took time out of their busy schedules to answer my many questions about fire code and emergency planning.

David Wright, poet and author of A Liturgy for Stones, among other works, took a look at the Tom Copper Band's song lyrics to make sure they didn't stink. You can read about him at www.dwpoet.com.

Detective Randall Floyd and Officer Jim Mininger of the Telford Borough Police Department answered my questions about law enforcement with generosity and detail.

And of course the farmers helped out, as they always do. Marilyn Halteman and Paula Meabon offered anecdotes and details about spring life on a dairy farm, many of which they will see in the book.

Eileen Tague, sound technician extraordinaire, made sure I didn't make too many gaffs in the Tom Copper Band's sound system.

Janet "San" Powell donated to charity to become a character in this book. It is my hope that she enjoys seeing herself in print!

Thanks to all of those who read early drafts: Todd, Tami, Paula, Phil and Nancy Clemens (my parents), and Steve Smucker (my hubby).

Writing about Stella is a privilege and a whole lot of fun. Thanks to all of the folks at Poisoned Pen for continuing to make my dream come alive, as well as the booksellers who make the finished product available. I must thank my family, who make do without me while I head off to book signings, for being patient and supportive. And, of course, a huge thank you to all of the readers who are able, for some reason, to find it in their hearts to love someone as prickly as Stella Crown.

Darkness holds us fast this night
His teeth are bared
His knuckles white

But sometime soon the Day will come
We'll feel Her fire
We'll greet Her sun

The Day will come
My love, my own,
The Day will come
The Day will come

—The Tom Copper Band

Chapter One

"So who'd you see last, Stella?" the guy asked, as familiar as if we'd known each other for years instead of five minutes in the concert line. His T-shirt had the most recent Kenny Wayne Shephard tour emblazoned on it, so I figured I knew his own answer to the question.

"Haven't gone to many shows lately," I said. "Cash shortage. These tickets are gifts from my friends over there." I hooked my thumb toward my live-in farmhand, Lucy, and Lenny, her fiancé and my biker buddy. "They're getting married next Saturday, and I'm her..." I cleared my throat. "Her maid of honor."

"Cool," the guy said. I think his name was Fred. "So who'd you see last?"

Back to that. "Would've been Bad Company, I guess. When they were in New Jersey last year. Awesome concert."

Fred nodded. "I was there, too. Can't remember a whole lot of it, though. Too much beer." He smiled, revealing a mouth of missing teeth. "Probably won't remember much of this one, either, once I get inside."

Lovely.

A breeze whipped down South Street, and I shivered, clutching my elbows to my sides. The sun wasn't offering any help, unable to find us in the shadow of Club Independence, and for a moment I wondered why I'd left my cozy dairy farm for the cold concrete of Philadelphia. I turned to share some body warmth with my boyfriend, Nick, only to find him standing off to the side, his gaze fixed on the sidewalk.

"You all right?" I asked.

He didn't respond, so I stepped toward him and rubbed my hands up and down his arms. He raised his head, and I frowned at the lack of color in his cheeks. "You okay? You haven't been yourself today." Or the two previous days, if truth be told. Usually energetic and fun, Nick had spent most of this visit popping Tylenol and drifting off in the middle of conversations.

He rubbed his eyes with a finger and thumb. "Sorry. I thought that nap this afternoon would help, but now I can't shake my headache. And my eyes are acting funny."

I looked into his baby blues, concerned to see how bloodshot they'd become. Slipping my hands inside his leather jacket, I pulled him close. "You want to go home?"

"No, no. I'll be all right." He put his arms around me and rested his cheek on the top of my head. "Besides, Lucy and Lenny paid enough for these tickets I don't want to waste them."

"If you're sure."

"I'm sure."

A group of Harleys eased up and idled by the curb. The lead rider, an older guy in chaps and a leather skull cap, checked out the line. "This where Tom Copper's playing?" he yelled.

"You got it," Fred, the toothless beer drinker, yelled back.

"Where do we park?"

Fred pointed east. "End of the road. Public parking lot."

The rider saluted and led his group off in a roar of shotgun pipes.

A man with a Club Independence Security shirt planted himself by our section of the line. "No cameras will be allowed in the building," he said, projecting his voice. "No recording or video equipment. All such devices will be confiscated at the door, to be returned at the conclusion of tonight's concert. Thank you." He moved down the row, and began his spiel again.

"Hey, guys," Lucy said. "Line's moving."

"About time," I said.

I detached myself from Nick and followed Lucy and Lenny in the slow trek toward the front door. Not any too soon either, if the bluish tinge to Nick's lips was any indication. I hadn't thought it was *that* cold.

"Thanks again for getting these tickets, Luce," I said. "I'd heard they were completely sold out."

Lucy smiled. "Yeah, well, it's a little easier when you know the sound guy."

"And when the band's playing at your wedding in a week," Lenny added.

Nick tripped over something—a crack in the sidewalk, maybe—and I grabbed his hand. He grinned sheepishly, but didn't show me his pearly whites. I didn't smile back.

"Here's your tickets," Lenny said, pulling papers from his wallet.

I took them and handed one to Nick. "You're sure you want to stay?"

He gently squeezed my fingers. "Yes. I'm sure."

I studied his face. "Okay. I'll stop asking."

"Coat open, please, miss."

I faced the security guard and unzipped my leather jacket, holding the sides out so he could see I didn't have any explosives strapped to my stomach or a gun holstered on my belt. He impersonally scanned the rest of my body and patted my jacket pockets.

"Thank you. Next."

I stepped aside as Nick got the same inspection, the man a little more forward with his checking of a male patron.

"Whew," Nick said when he reached me. "I was afraid he'd confiscate my cell phone, since it can take pictures. Guess they figure if they start that they'll have a couple hundred to deal with."

"Just try not to take too many photos of the girls serving the beer."

He laughed, and we stepped toward the door.

A man with a mane of jet black hair and a great arch of a Roman nose reached out to take our tickets, scanning the bar codes and handing them back to us. "Enjoy the show." Beads of sweat shone on his forehead, and I shivered once more as the cold from the outside clashed with the lobby's heat.

"Stella!"

I glanced around and found Lenny's bright red hair on the far side of the foyer. He waved his beefy arm and we pushed our way through the crowd to where he and Lucy waited with a guy in a Tom Copper Band T-shirt.

"Hey, Jordan," I said.

Jordan Granger, one of my eight "adopted" Granger brothers, was living out a childhood dream as the Tom Copper Band's sound man. A young-looking guy in his mid-thirties, he'd told many stories of being mistaken for an intern or groupie at other concert venues. Fortunately for the band, his technical knowledge was on a much higher level. He jerked his head toward the auditorium. "Want to meet the guys?"

"Really?" I looked at Nick. "You up for it?"

"Sure. Let's go."

"We'll get a place for the concert," Lucy said. "Think you can find us?"

I hesitated. "You don't want to meet them?"

"Already have," Lenny said. "When we signed them up to play for our reception."

"Right. Okay. We'll find you somehow. Any idea where you'll go?"

"Not on the dance level, if you don't mind," Nick said.

Lucy looked at me and I lifted a shoulder.

"All right," she said. "We'll try to find a good place a little farther from the speakers."

Jordan bounced on the balls of his feet. "Ready?"

I gave a thumbs-up. "Let's go."

We walked around the edge of the lobby, exiting through a far door into a warren of hallways and weaving around until we reached another door that said *Back Stage Access—Authorized Personnel Only*. I guessed being with Jordan made us okay.

Swinging the door open, Jordan collided with a pair of women coming through the other way. Once they backed up

I could see they each wore a Tom Copper Band T-shirt like Jordan's, but were otherwise opposites: one was tall and dark with lots of makeup and jewelry, the other short and blonde with only a hint of mascara. In one area they were unsurprisingly alike: both, being young and female, immediately slapped their eyes on Nick, who did a good impression of a GQ model even with his bloodshot eyes.

"Get those cables taped down, Annie?" Jordan asked the blonde.

She tore her eyes from Nick. "I promise no one will be tripping over them."

"Good. Thanks." He gestured to us. "Come on."

The two women stole one more look at Nick before disappearing out the stage door, and we followed Jordan.

"Got some new groupies," I said to Nick. "And you're not even a rock star."

He grunted. "Too young. Besides, I like my women to have visible body art."

I laughed, and he reached a hand up to rub the back of my neck, where my steer head tattoo sits proudly under my short hair.

Jordan led us through one more door, where the sound of animated conversation greeted us.

"So there we sit at this diner in New Orleans," a guy was saying, waving a bottle of Red Stripe beer, "and I'm about to take the first bite of my po' boy when Tom here grabs it out of my hand and digs into it like he hadn't had anything to eat for two days."

A man sitting on a sofa barked a laugh, covering his face with his hands. "Oh, Tom!"

"Well, I practically hadn't." Tom Copper's long hair and goatee were familiar, the same as on the band's album covers. "Those southerners seem to think the ultimate vegetarian meal is a grilled cheese sandwich with a side of iceberg lettuce. They were about to serve it to me again and I was desperate."

"So I ate his stuff," the first guy said.

Tom moaned. "And I ended up being sick for two days."

The man on the sofa laughed again.

"Hey guys," Jordan said. "Can I introduce you to someone real quick?"

Conversation stopped and all eyes landed on us.

"Hey, Jordan, man," Tom said. "You know your friends are our friends."

"Sure." Jordan waved a hand at me. "This is Stella Crown. Practically my sister. And Nick. He's with her. From Virginia."

Tom walked over, his hand extended. "Howdy, Stella. Nick from Virginia. Glad you could join us."

We shook, and he pointed around the room. "That guy, giving me grief, is our bassist, LeRoy. He might be a smartass, but he's got good chops."

LeRoy laughed, his teeth white against his cocoa-colored skin. "Pleased to meet you."

"That there's Donny, our guitarist."

We waved at Donny, a skinny, balding man with a tattoo of a bull on his forearm. His guitar hung around his neck, and he stood in a corner where he'd been practicing when we'd walked in.

"And Genna, who does vocals for us."

Genna, a pretty, pixie-like woman probably in her late twenties, smiled at Nick and me, not letting her eyes linger on Nick. Instead, her eyes flicked toward Jordan before she turned and snatched a baby carrot off the buffet table behind her.

"The guy on the couch," Tom said, "is Parker, used to be our drummer."

"I left them to find normal folks to hang around," Parker said, grinning.

"Oh, shut up," Tom said. "You're the one who chose to come by tonight and get another dose of us."

"He likes us!" LeRoy said in a high voice. "He really likes us!"

They all laughed, and Parker shook his head in mock disgust. Like the other guys, Parker looked to be in his early to mid-thirties, but while the band was dressed in carefully chosen performance clothes, Parker wore new jeans and a striped short-sleeve shirt.

"I'm a teacher now," he said to us. "One of those respectable types."

I nodded, thinking they all looked respectable to me.

"Well, thanks," Jordan said. "We'll leave you alone to get ready."

"We are ready," Tom said.

"You mean you've done your meditation?" LeRoy asked. He closed his eyes, chanting something unintelligible.

"See what I mean?" Tom said to us. "I don't get no respect."

LeRoy and the rest of the guys hooted. Genna, after another quick glance at Jordan, left the room through a door on the other side.

"What's up with her?" Tom asked Jordan.

Jordan shrugged and turned back the way we'd come. I gave one last wave to the band and followed Jordan into the hallway.

"They're crazy, but nice," he said.

I laughed. "They seem like fun."

"They are."

I wanted to ask him about the woman, but figured he'd tell me if he wanted to.

"Check this out," he said. He took us through another door marked *Stage*, and suddenly we were in the wings, standing behind heavy black curtains, the noise and smoke from the dance floor drifting our way. "As long as you can't see the audience, they can't see you. So don't worry."

"Are those the cables that girl was taping?" I asked, pointing at a line of duct-taped wires. "What was her name? Annie?"

"Yeah. Somehow they got loose and Donny, the guitarist you met back there, tripped over them during sound check. Could've been bad."

Urgent whispered voices drifted toward us from the other side of the black curtain, getting louder until they were directly opposite us and we could hear a low voice. "I swear to God, if you don't cut it out I'm gonna wring your fucking neck!" A man stormed past us and out the stage door.

Jordan sucked in a quick breath, and a number of emotions washed over his face. We waited, not speaking, until whoever was on the other side of the curtain exited a different way. I looked to Jordan for an explanation of some sort, but he wasn't giving any, his face closed and tight.

"Well, come on, then," he finally said.

We left the stage, Jordan taking us back toward the door we'd originally entered.

"See you after?" I asked.

He shook his head. "Probably not. I gotta break all this stuff down and get it out of here. There's a touring dance troupe coming through tomorrow and these things belong to the band, so we don't want them getting mixed up with another company's equipment."

"Thanks for the introduction," I said. "It's fun seeing those guys close up."

Jordan flashed a smile, the first one I'd seen on him that night. "Sure. They're good people."

Before we got to the door it opened and a man strode through, a walkie-talkie squawking in his hand. He nodded at Jordan as he strode by, his eyes passing over Nick and me with a quick appraisal.

"That's Gary Mann," Jordan said when the man had gone. "Owns the club. Nice guy. Keeps the building up to code, which is more than I can say for a lot of these places." He held the door open for us. "Enjoy the concert."

"We will," I said, but checked out Nick's response, seeing how he hadn't said much of anything backstage.

Nick tried out a smile. "Thanks, Jordan."

"You bet."

The door closed behind Jordan as he turned and walked away.

I looked down the hallway. "Think we can find our way out of here?"

"I guess we'll have to try."

After a few minutes of trial and error we found a door to the lobby, and from there discovered a set of stairs leading to the second level. Lucy and Lenny had said they'd avoid the main floor, so we started our search a level up.

There were no chairs in the club, and pushing our way through the standing crowd took some effort. Eventually we made our way to a small clearing at the front of a platform and were able to turn around and scan the faces.

"There," I said.

Lenny's red hair again acted as a beacon in the thick smoke, and Lucy waved frantically beside him. I held my hand up to let her know I'd seen her, and tried to figure out the best way to get one level up to where they stood.

I grabbed Nick's wrist and pulled him toward another set of stairs, only to be stopped by a small woman who stood immobilized, intimidated by the bulky, Harley-shirted men blocking her way.

"Gotta be assertive," I said in her ear.

She looked up at me.

"Like this." I stepped toward the men, raising my elbow and my voice. "'Scuse us, guys. Coming through."

Without a hitch in conversation the men shifted enough we could battle our way past their stomachs, only to find the way closed off by a scantily dressed waitress serving beer.

I leaned back into Nick. "Got your camera?"

He wrinkled his nose. "Too skinny."

"Boy," I said. "You sure are picky."

But of course I was glad.

We'd almost made it to the stairs when Nick jerked to a standstill, yanking me backward.

"What?" I said.

He didn't answer, so I followed his eyes not to a cocktail waitress but to a couple situated at the front of one of the viewing platforms. The woman stood behind the man, her hands on his shoulders. He sat in a wheelchair, leaning forward onto the railing to peer down on the dance floor. He pointed at something, and the woman bent over to follow his finger.

"Nick?" I shook our clasped hands.

He whipped his head toward me. "What? Oh, sorry. Let's go."

We made our way up the stairs and over to the space Lucy and Lenny had carved out in the mass of people.

"Good spot," I said. We were at the front of our level, the stage in plain view. The crowd below teemed with energy and sound, which looked like fun, but we had a prime spot to see without having to stand on tiptoe.

"We had help," Lucy said.

She pointed over her shoulder and I saw yet another of my Granger "brothers."

"Jermaine!" I said. "What are you doing here?"

He smiled, his teeth setting off his dark skin, just like LeRoy, the band's bass player. "Got a call this morning asking if I could fill in on the security team." He indicated his Club Independence Security T-shirt. "Guess somebody came down sick and they needed another body. Jordan suggested me and I got the gig."

"Cool."

"Yeah. Well, gotta go make sure nobody's blocking the exits. Have fun."

He pushed himself away and disappeared into the throng.

"Nick okay?" Lucy yelled in my ear.

We both looked at him, and I shrugged. "Don't know. But I'll get him situated." Pulling on his elbow, I leaned him backward against the railing, where he could get some support before he keeled over onto the dancers below. "You want something to drink?" I asked him.

"Wouldn't mind some water. This smoke isn't helping my head any."

"The smoke's why I didn't bring my purse," Lucy said. "Last time I took it to a concert the cash in my wallet even stank."

"I'll see if I can grab a waitress," I said.

One came by just as the crowd started to roar. The roar faded when everyone saw it was just Jordan, fixing one more cable. "Two waters, please," I said to the waitress.

"And a Coke," Lucy added.

The waitress, definitely not too skinny—perhaps even a bit plump for the outfit—took our order and left.

The crowd started to roar again, and this time was rewarded with the appearance of the band. LeRoy and Donny took their places and were joined by another guy who sat behind the drum set.

"Hey," I said to Nick. "Isn't that the guy from backstage?"

He shrugged.

"The one who said he was going to wring somebody's neck," I said.

Nick shook his head. "I don't know."

It was. We'd met the *old* drummer backstage with the band, but not the new, so it made sense this guy would've been in the wings.

The crowd erupted into an even louder cheer as Tom Copper made his way on stage, holding one hand up in greeting, the other on the neck of his guitar. He swung his hand down in two exaggerated circles and the band launched into a song. One of their trademark tunes, "River Love," a favorite of this Philadelphia crowd.

The river rages
The waters flow
Past twinkling lights
The Schuylkill's show
But tell me baby
Tell me true
Can you feel our love
The way I do?

A laugh bubbled up inside me, and I pumped my fist in the air, the thrill of the bass guitar vibrating my ribs. The song climaxed with Copper's well-known guitar solo, and dancers on the lower level air-banded along with him, eyes closed in rapture. The song ended with three strong chords, and Copper stepped forward, his face shining with energy.

"Good evening, Philadelphia!" he yelled.

The crowd responded with an even louder cheer.

"It's always good to play here at home in the City of Brotherly Love!"

Another roar, punctuated with screams and squeals of girls in the front rows.

"You ready for some more music?" Copper asked. "You sure?"

He laughed, and the drummer banged out the first four beats of the next song. The crowd cheered as Genna, the female vocalist, grabbed a microphone and the band launched into yet another Philly favorite, "Lust on Ice."

The set was over far too soon, the forty minutes flying by in a whirl of sound and lyrics, but Copper promised they'd be back in ten minutes for another round.

"They're amazing!" Lucy said. Her eyes shone with excitement. "I can't believe they're playing at our reception!"

Lenny smirked at me, and I elbowed him. "Good thing you've got deep pockets."

He chuckled. "They ain't that deep. But deep enough to give my girl a special wedding present like this."

"What do you think?" I asked Nick. "Like their stuff?"

He smiled. "It's great."

I looked at him. "But you feel like crap."

"Yeah. I think I'll go try to find a quieter spot for a few minutes. Or at least one with a little less smoke."

"Good luck with that. Remember they're starting again soon. You don't want to miss it."

"I'll be back."

"Want me to get you another water?"

"Sure. Thanks."

My throat was dry, too, but I figured the waitresses would be busy serving the beer drinkers. I fought my way to the bar at the back of our section and pushed up to the counter. A few minutes later I was back in our spot with Nick's water and a Coke for me.

"Seems like they should be starting," I said to Lucy. "Hasn't it been longer than ten minutes?"

She shrugged. "Don't know."

"Come on!" a guy behind us yelled. "We gotta get the baby-sitter home before midnight!"

Lucy grinned. "I guess that's a yes—they are running behind."

I looked around, hoping Nick could find his way back to our spot, but didn't see him anywhere. If I'd had a cell phone I would've called him, except it was so loud in there he couldn't have heard me, anyway.

In another ten minutes the band still hadn't appeared, and the crowd started rumbling. Jordan and the short blonde girl came on stage to fuss with knobs and cables, but they soon left, and the crowd started chanting: "Tom Copper, Tom Copper, Tom Copper…"

The chant exploded into a cheer when the band members loped on stage, waving and smiling.

"Sorry about the delay, folks," Copper said. "Just a few bugs in the sound system. But now we're ready to rock. Are you ready to rock?"

The band dove into a tune in unison with the crowd's cheer, and led us back into the world of rock and roll. Nick still hadn't returned, and I hoped he wasn't collapsed somewhere down below. I was trying to decide whether or not to go find him when the music lurched to a stop. The crowd on the dance floor changed from a mass of rhythm and cheers to a riot of chaos and shouts.

"What's happening?" Lucy asked.

I squinted down into the crowd, unable to understand any of the voices drifting up to me. I leaned further over the railing and finally heard some clear words, which pierced my brain like the harsh feed from a microphone.

"A bomb!" someone shouted. "They're going to blow up the building!"

Chapter Two

An elbow dug into my back, and I tipped forward over the railing. I scrabbled for a handhold on one of the iron rungs, but before I could find one someone grabbed the waistband of my jeans and hauled me back up onto the platform.

I squeezed Lenny's arm in thanks, and kept a hold of it as he moved forward. His other arm encircled Lucy's waist, a wad of her shirt bunched up in his fist to keep him from losing her. All around us people screamed and pushed, and my fear of being trampled was close to overcoming my fear of being blown up. I pulled on Lenny's elbow, and he glanced back at me.

"Do you see Nick?" I yelled.

A head above most people around us, Lenny took a quick look around.

"Nope," he shouted back.

I gritted my teeth, my chest tight. Lenny and Lucy both watched me, waiting.

"I guess let's go," I finally said.

We allowed ourselves to be swept into the crowd, Lenny guarding Lucy from falling under panicked feet or into drunken paths. I held my own behind him, taking what protection I could from his back and my elbows. A few steps further on we reached a standstill, and my face smashed into Lenny's back as the crowd behind me kept moving forward. A surge of claustrophobia struck me and I took a few deep but shaky breaths with my eyes closed.

"What's happening?" I yelled when my dizziness cleared.

"Can't tell," Lenny shouted over his shoulder. "Something's causing a bottleneck."

A man to the side of me began climbing over a group of people in front of him, his eyes wild. The crowd threw him to the side, and he went flying, knocking over several others.

Lenny stiffened, and I fell forward as he lunged ahead. My hand still had a death grip on his arm, so I went with him.

We fought through the crowd toward the top of the stairs, where a man in a wheelchair blocked the opening, a woman hanging onto the chair's handles, trying to keep the chair from plummeting down the stairs. The man clenched the stair's railing, his knuckles white from the strain. It was the same couple Nick and I had seen earlier, although this time they weren't enjoying the view. People stepped over the man, using the chair as a footstool, while some screamed obscenities at him for blocking the path. It was obvious to me he had no chance of getting out of the way, or even moving.

Lenny pushed ahead, and when he reached the man he shoved his way in front of the chair, grabbing the man around his waist and heaving him over his shoulder. Lucy took the woman's arm while I got the chair and tried to push it to the side.

"Over here!" a man yelled. He was about Lenny's size, and between the two of us we got the chair above our heads. "We can throw it over the rest of these folks!"

"Count of three," I yelled back.

He counted and we pushed, heaving the chair over the crowd. I heard the chair crash and hoped we'd cleared the people.

The man nodded and we were swept along with the tide rushing down the stairs. I had no chance to look again for Nick, and had completely lost Lenny and Lucy in the throng.

The lobby wasn't as chaotic as I expected, with security staff strategically placed and shouting directions toward the outside doors. The exit signs shined brightly, and we headed toward them as a herd of cows rush toward their evening feeding.

A final burst of panic sent my pack of concert-goers through the front doors into the night, and the cold breeze blew a surge of energy into my bones. I scrambled away, not stopping until I'd cleared the crowd, which reached out into South Street and down the sidewalk. Cop cars were parked haphazardly on the sidewalk, lights flashing on the surrounding buildings. Police officers, firefighters, and various others attempted to funnel the crowd down the street, probably toward that parking lot Fred the beer drinker had steered the Hogs toward before the concert. Anywhere to get us away from the building in case it really was going to blow.

Some people huddled together, their fear turning toward excitement at the thrill of the threat. I wasn't there yet.

I scanned the crowd, trying to spot Nick or Lenny's red hair, but between the flashing lights, milling crowd, and darkness I became disoriented.

"Please move along, ma'am," an officer said crisply. His uniform was pressed and clean, and he looked about the age of Zach, my fourteen-year-old farm helper.

"I'm looking for my friends," I said.

"We're sending everyone down the street to the parking lot. You can rendezvous with them there."

Rendezvous. Great.

"My friend's sick, and he's trapped in there."

"We'll find him, ma'am. We've got technicians and officers headed in as we speak."

I couldn't claim I was either of those, and seeing how he looked ready to nudge me on down the road, I turned away.

The wind whipped around me again, making me shiver, so I zipped up my coat and crossed my arms over my chest as I trudged down the street with the straggly group. I kept my head up and my eyes moving in case I saw Nick, but had no luck. I hated leaving him behind, but knew that sharp-eyed cop would catch me if I tried to sneak back.

The parking lot was full of cars and displaced concert-goers, and several car alarms shrieked, most likely from being bumped by someone trying to find a place to stand. I walked as quickly as I could through the lot, hoping for a glimpse of a familiar face. I was rounding a corner when a large woman barreled into me, sending me onto the seat of a Fat Boy.

"Whoa, watch it, sister." A man in a leather skull cap hustled up to the bike. The same guy who'd stopped to ask Fred where to park before the concert.

I pushed myself off the bike and rubbed my side where I'd smacked the crash bar. "Sorry. Got shoved."

He didn't answer, but fussed over the bike like I'd gone after it with a mallet.

"Look okay?" I asked.

He started, apparently forgetting about me already. "Yeah. Yeah, everything looks fine."

"Good. Hey, you haven't seen a guy, real big, lots of red hair?"

He shook his head. "You lose your people?"

"Got separated in the club. Can't find them out here."

"Hmm." He pursed his lips and studied me, taking in my leather jacket and motorcycle boots. I guess I passed the test, because he shouted, "Hey, Loader!"

A man about the width of the Fat Boy waddled over to skull cap man. His expression was flat, his eyes dull.

"This here lady lost her folks," the guy in the skull cap said. "Give her a hand up to look around, will you?"

Loader nodded, revealing no thoughts or feelings about the request, and knelt on the ground. I looked at him, then back at the first guy.

"Well, go ahead," Skull Cap said. "Climb on."

"You're kidding."

"You want to find your friends or not? He won't drop you."

I wasn't worried about being dropped. I was worried about being creeped out. But how else was I going to find anyone in this chaos?

"Well. Okay." I swung my leg over Loader's shoulder and he pushed himself up, like a camel. Suddenly I had a new view of the parking lot, and a slew of people peering up at me, surprise on their faces.

"Any luck?" Skull Cap asked.

"Not yet."

"Go ahead, Loader. Give her a ride."

"I don't—" I began, but was cut off when my steed began to move.

Slowly we made our way forward, the crowd parting like the Red Sea before us. It was too dark to see well, and I found myself blinking often to keep my vision clear. If I hadn't been so worried about Nick I would've been much more concerned with people seeing me up there. As it was, I had to make use of my resources.

"Stella?"

I swung around at the call of my name, Loader fortunately so well-grounded there was no fear of tipping over.

Lenny looked up at me, amusement in his eyes.

Lucy stood beside him giggling, her hands on her hips. "What in the name of Pete are you doing up there?"

"What do you think I'm doing?" I held up my hands, not quite sure how to communicate with Loader, who had yet to say a word, or even grunt. I patted him on the head. "Uh, Loader? Can I get down?"

He knelt, allowing me to slip off his shoulders.

"Thank you for the…um…ride."

He nodded, his face as blank as before, and turned to go, on-lookers scurrying out of his path.

"Where did you find *that?*" Lenny asked.

I waved off his question. "Any sign of Nick?"

Lucy shook her head, concern in her eyes. "We've been looking. For both of you."

I surveyed the area. We stood next to Lucy's Civic, about twenty feet from a streetlight and a tree with a dead limb sticking out the top. "You guys going to stay right here?"

Lucy shrugged. "Don't know where else we'd go. They're not letting anybody leave."

"Not that we could get out if we tried," Lenny said.

"Then I'm going to hunt around for Nick."

"Shouldn't have let your bulldozer take off," Lenny said.

"His name was Loader, not Dozer. Anyway, I could get up on you."

Lenny winced. "Normally I'd do it, but I wrenched my back something good carrying Norm out of the building."

"Norm?"

Lenny and Lucy glanced behind them to Lucy's car, where the man from the wheelchair was sitting, the woman beside him.

"Oh. Norm. He okay?"

Lucy nodded. "Just scared. And exhausted."

As he had a right to be. "Okay, I'll be back."

I headed away, searching the faces for Nick's, but couldn't find anyone who even approached his clean shaven state. Shaved heads, sure, but most faces were covered with beards or week-old scruff. Harley T-shirts, flyaway hair, round beer bellies. They were all there. But no movie star blonds in clean jeans.

When I'd made a full circle and reached the entrance to the parking lot I spotted several ambulances with paramedics treating those injured in the rush out of the building. It was at the third one of these I found Nick, sitting on the back ledge of the vehicle. I bee-lined a path to him, stopping only when I could reach out and put a hand on his shoulder.

He blinked slowly and looked up at me, his eyes glassy.

"Nick? What's wrong?"

"Can't find anything wrong, ma'am," the paramedic said. "I pulled him out of the crowd because he looked dazed, but his vitals are fine, and he says he wasn't bumped on the head."

"He's been weird like this all night." I squeezed Nick's shoulder. "Haven't you, Nick?"

He sighed. "I'm sorry. I don't know what's wrong with me. I'm just so tired."

A man with a B.B. King T-shirt strode up to the ambulance, a woman in his arms. "Help me out here? She's got a nasty cut on her leg."

Blood seeped through the denim around the woman's calf, and I winced.

"We should go," Nick said. "I'm in the way."

"Hang on," the paramedic said. "I've got room for her over here. You wait till you feel ready before you get up. Don't want you passing out. I'd just have to help you all over again." He smiled to soften his words, but the look he gave me said to keep Nick on his butt for a few more minutes.

I leaned against the side of the ambulance. "Stay put, Nick. We'll just hang here for a bit."

So we watched the people go by, some still panicked, some laughing—whether from nervousness or drunkenness I wasn't sure—and some peeling off from the crowd to visit one of the ambulances.

The man in the B.B. King shirt came back several times, in each instance carrying or leading one of the injured to an ambulance. His manner was so professional and efficient I figured he must've been an off-duty cop or firefighter. He was dropping off a woman at the ambulance next to us when another man ran up to him.

"You seen Bobby?" the man asked, his voice reaching us ten feet away.

The guy shook his head. "Huh-uh. He missing?"

"I can't find him anywhere."

The B.B. King guy made sure the woman was in the hands of a paramedic before taking off back toward the club with the man.

"You know who that was?" I asked Nick. "He looked familiar."

"We've seen him bringing people to the ambulances."

"No, not the B.B. King guy. The other one, who just ran up."

"Oh." His forehead crinkled. "I guess his face did look—"

"We saw him tonight, didn't we? At the club?"

His face cleared. "Backstage. He was coming in when we were going out."

I smacked the ambulance. "The owner. Jordan told us his name, but I forget it."

"Well, I sure don't remember."

A couple struggled up to the ambulance, the man leaning on the woman for support. Nick hopped off the ledge to make room, and I grabbed his arm. "You sure you're all right?"

"I'm not limping or anything, like that guy. Let's go."

We'd gotten about twenty feet away when a cop stepped into our path, a pad and pencil in his hands. "You folks at Club Independence tonight?"

Why else would we be in that parking lot? "Yessir, we were," I said.

"Anybody else talk to you tonight? Cops, I mean? Since the evacuation?"

"Nope."

Nick shook his head.

"Can you tell me what happened?" the cop asked.

I shrugged. "I don't know. We heard there was a bomb."

He tried again. "I mean what happened with you. We're taking care of the other stuff."

"Oh, well, I was on the second level platform when the music stopped. Somebody yelled up to us that there was a bomb, and we all started clearing out. It seemed like chaos, but I guess most of us got out okay."

"No casualties that we're aware of," the cop said, pride coloring his voice. "And we're pretty sure everyone's out."

"Impressive." I jutted my chin at Nick. "He was somewhere else."

The cop turned to Nick. "Sir?"

"The bathroom on the lower level. It wasn't till I was making my way back up that I ran into mobs of people trying to get out."

He scribbled on his pad. "And neither of you heard anything else about the bomb? Or saw anything suspicious?"

We shook our heads.

"Can I get your names and addresses, please? For follow-up?"

We gave him what he wanted, and he moved on to the next clump of folks.

I looked above our heads and pointed toward the tree with the dead limb. "That's where we're headed. Lucy and Lenny are parked under there."

"Lead on."

We found them where they'd promised, Lucy with a blanket from the trunk wrapped around her shoulders while she sat in the front seat and talked with Norm and the woman. Lenny stood by the front of the car with Jermaine, who must've been done with his security detail.

"Hey," I said.

Jermaine lifted his chin a fraction. "Hey, yourself."

"You look beat." I took in his slumped shoulders and sweat-soaked security T-shirt. He had to be freezing in the chilly air.

"Spent the last hour herding freaked-out folks, trying to keep them from trampling each other."

I nodded. "Cop told us no one was killed in the rush to get out?"

"Not that we know of. Lots of injuries, but no pile-ups, thank God. Mann keeps the club in good working order and up to code, plus the security staff is well-trained. I had to pass a test before he gave me the job tonight."

I looked at Nick. "Mann, that's his name." I gestured over my shoulder. "We saw him not too long ago at the ambulances, looking for somebody named Bobby. Know him?"

Jermaine shook his head. "Nah. But then, I don't know many of the staff. Not by name, anyway."

"You all done for the night?"

"Supposedly. The official cops have taken over now, and we're not even allowed back in the building. I called Vernice to let her know what was happening, just in case she saw it on the news."

"You call home?" I asked Lenny. "Let the baby-sitter know you'd be late?"

He shrugged. "Lucy might've."

"I've got a phone," Nick said. "I'll ask her." He walked over to the car door and leaned in. Lenny followed.

"Stella! Jermaine!" Jordan strode up to us, his face a tight mask of anxiety. The two girls we'd seen backstage trotted along behind him. "You see any of the band?"

I shook my head. "No, but I haven't been looking for them."

Jermaine held his hands up, palms to the sky. "They weren't my responsibility. Don't know where they got to."

Jordan stuck his hands in his pockets, craning his neck to see around Jermaine. "I found Tom Copper, along with LeRoy and Donny. They're set up pretty well down at the other end. But I haven't found Genna."

"The female singer?" I asked.

"Right. You met her backstage."

I studied his face, remembering how Genna had avoided looking at Jordan.

"She's probably with Ricky." The dark-haired girl cracked the gum she was chewing like a cud. "Where else would she be?"

Jordan's expression made it obvious her words had no soothing effect. "I need to know she made it out."

"The cops told us everybody's out of the building," I said. "She's probably stuck in this crowd somewhere."

"Yeah." He didn't sound convinced.

A phone played the first few bars of INXS's "Pretty Vegas" and the dark-haired girl reached into her coat. "Hi," she said. Her eyes flicked to Jordan. "He's here, but she's not. Huh-uh." She looked around. "Under one of the streetlights. I don't know. South, I guess."

"Dead tree limb," I said, pointing.

She repeated our location into the phone. "Okay. We'll wait." She closed the phone and stuck it back in her pocket. "Ricky's on his way here. Says he's close."

"Genna's not with him?" Jordan's voice cracked.

"Nuh-uh." She cracked her gum again. I fought the urge to smack her on the back and send the gum flying. Or down her throat.

"Who's Ricky?" I asked.

Jordan glowered. "The band's drummer."

I raised my eyebrows. Ricky was the guy making neck-wringing threats before the concert. "Why would she be with him?" Jordan didn't answer.

"He's her boyfriend," the gum-cracker said.

I looked at Jordan, who avoided my eyes by studying the crowd, arms crossed over his chest.

"So who're you?" I said to the girls.

The dark-haired girl stopped her mouth mid-chew. "I'm Marley. This is Annie."

The blonde's mouth flickered, as if she were trying to smile but couldn't quite do it.

"What do you do with the band?"

"Oh, we're not official," Marley said. *Crack, crack.* "We just hang out."

Annie's eyes narrowed for a second before her expression ironed out. "I help Jordan with the sound."

"That's right. Jordan said something to you backstage about taping a cable."

"There you are!" The drummer was suddenly there, forcing his way through the crowd and ending up nose-to-nose with Jordan. "Where's Genna?"

Jordan's nostrils flared. "I can't find her. I assumed she was with you."

"Well, she's not."

It wasn't clear whether the spikes in Ricky's black hair were there by design or situation, but they stood up in wild peaks. His thin and angular face highlighted nearly black eyes, and his leather vest, with nothing underneath, made me shiver. He'd obviously chosen it for the concert—and it looked good, I had to admit—and not for a chilly night in a parking lot.

"So why aren't you looking for her?" Jordan asked.

"What do you think I've been doing?"

"Have you called her cell phone?"

Ricky waved his phone in Jordan's face. "For the last half-hour. She's not answering." He thrust the phone into Jordan's stomach. "Here. You call if you think I can't do it good enough."

"I don't want your phone." Jordan pushed his hand away. "But if you're not going to look for Genna, I will."

Jordan's expression made no bones about how he felt toward the drummer, and I hoped Jermaine and I wouldn't have to jump in between them.

"Fine," Ricky said. "Let me know the minute you spot her."

"I'll be sure to do that." Jordan's usually sweet voice dripped with sarcasm, and I watched with surprise as he stomped away.

Jermaine met my eyes with his own, which opened wide with interest.

"I bet Genna just took off," Marley said.

Ricky snorted. "Not without her lap dog." He watched Jordan leave, and I shook my head at the venom in the drummer's voice. He had a few jealousy issues to work out. Not that he might not be right about it.

A cop made the mistake of approaching our group just then. He'd barely opened his mouth when Ricky started into him.

"My girlfriend's missing and nobody in this lame-ass police force will help me find her."

If I'd been the cop, I would've laid Ricky out cold. The officer, however, had more self-control, and actually took a respectful step back. "We're doing our best to make sure everyone's out of the building, sir. Perhaps you could start by giving me your name?"

In fits and starts the officer pulled the information from Ricky, taking down Marley and Annie's info, as well. I told him the cops already had my name, and pointed him back toward Lucy and Lenny.

"We'll do our best to find your friend, sir," the officer told Ricky. "Until then, you just have to sit tight and maybe she'll find you."

Ricky turned away from him, scanning the crowd. He didn't seem to care so much about Genna's safety as about making sure he found her before Jordan did.

The cop, realizing he'd gotten everything he would from us, headed back toward the Civic.

"What about you two?" Ricky said to the girls. "You see Genna?"

Marley shrugged. "Before the concert. Not since."

"And you?" Ricky's eyes bored into Annie, and she huddled tighter in her sweater.

"Saw her backstage. Not after the bomb threat, though."

"Hmphf." He turned back to the crowd, glowering.

"Looks like the place is clearing out a bit." Lenny appeared at my shoulder. "Cop said we can leave if we can get out."

I looked at the car, where Nick now sat in the driver's seat, one leg sticking out the door, his head leaning on the headrest. His eyes were closed.

"We probably should." I looked at Jermaine. "You'll stay with Jordan?"

"Sure. What're brothers for?" He flashed a quick smile. "He rode down with me, anyway. I'll get him home."

"Norm and Cindy's car is down the aisle there," Lenny said, pointing. "We're going to drop them off. You mind following us on foot?"

"Nope. Can Nick go with you, though?"

"Oh, yeah." Lenny's forehead wrinkled. "What's up with him, anyway?"

I shook my head. "I have no idea."

"Okay, so I guess Lucy can drive them down, and Nick can ride. I'll walk with you."

"Peachy." I turned toward Ricky and the girls, but they were already slipping into the crowd, Marley hanging onto Ricky's elbow, Annie sticking close behind.

I couldn't help but hope Jordan found Genna first.

Chapter Three

Five-o'clock rolled around pretty fast the next morning. I silenced the alarm with a quickness that surprised me, and slipped out from under the quilt, doing my best not to fall on my face from exhaustion.

After pulling on some jeans I tiptoed down the stairs, disgusted at the smell of smoke still hovering around my body. We'd gotten home so late I didn't have the energy to take a shower, but now I regretted it. Even the cows would probably turn their noses up at me this morning.

I peeked into the front room, where Nick had taken over the sofa. He'd fallen asleep on the way home from Philly, and I'd practically carried him into the house before dumping him as gently as possible on the couch. His face, from what I could see of it in the darkness, looked relaxed and peaceful.

I walked back through the house to the kitchen, where I poured a bowl of Cheerios and ate it while watching the early morning news. The bomb threat at Club Independence received headline status, after a story about a Philadelphia Mafia multi-homicide, and I recognized scenes from the night before, with the cop cars and fire trucks filling South Street.

The anchor, fresh-faced and handsome—Kevin Something—was speaking. "Last night we reported that the Club Independence security staff was able to evacuate the building with no fatalities after a bomb scare at the concert of one of Philadelphia's favorite musical sons, Tom Copper. The successful clearing of the building marked an extraordinary occurrence in these days when club fires and bombs mean multiple trampling deaths, caused by panic and fear. We are saddened to learn this morning that a body has been found in the building, apparently a victim of the chaos. More from our correspondent on the scene, Maria Gomez."

I stopped eating as the screen split into two pictures—one the anchor, one the reporter on South Street. Milk dripped from my spoon into my bowl, and my mouth hung open. The cops had been so proud the night before of their casualty-free evacuation, and the paramedics calm and confident.

"A tragic development, Kevin, but true," the reporter said. "Officials tell us a body has been discovered in Club Independence following last night's bomb scare, but the identification of the victim will not be released until family has been notified. Cause of death has not been disclosed, nor has the location of the body in the building."

Behind the reporter stood the club, clearly seen now the fire trucks were gone. A few vehicles still dotted the street, the only recognizable one a police cruiser.

I set my spoon in my bowl and watched, horrified.

"When can we expect more details on this, Maria?" the anchor asked.

"Officials hope to locate the victim's family this morning, and have a cause of death by later today."

The anchor set his face in an expression of concern. "And what do they expect to discover?"

"At this point, Kevin, they have not offered an explanation. But no matter the cause, the much-anticipated concert with Philadelphia's local favorite, the Tom Copper Band, has resulted in a death. We will keep you up-to-date as details become available. Until then, this is Maria Gomez, reporting from location on South Street, in Philadelphia."

"Thank you, Maria. We heard also from the owner of Club Independence, Gary Mann."

A video of the man I had seen backstage and again at the ambulance site came on screen. His eyes were sunken above dark bags, and his voice came out husky and drained of emotion.

"I don't know how to talk about this," he said. "We pride ourselves on keeping our security staff educated and well-oiled. We thought we had succeeded last night in preventing any deaths, and I'm sick at this latest discovery. Nothing like this has ever happened before, under my ownership."

That video segued to another, the words on the bottom of the screen denoting the Commander of the Bomb Squad as he stood behind a podium at a press conference.

"Club Independence was as ready as it could've been," he said. "Despite the tragic loss, discovered late last night, I commend Gary Mann and his staff for a job well done, and extend my thanks to the entire Philadelphia police and firefighting force."

A garbled question was thrown at him from the floor.

"Yes," he said. "There was an actual explosive device. It was designed to be detonated by remote control, but we were able to disrupt the bomb before it was used. We are fortunate to have an efficient K-9 team, which hit on the bomb directly upon entering the building."

The video ended and I once again watched Kevin-the-anchor's expressive face. "In addition, the police have asked us to put out a call for a Robert Baronne, Club Independence's office manager. He has gone missing since the concert, along with the evening's proceeds. It has been confirmed that the body discovered in the building is not that of Baronne, and officials are treating the disappearance as a kidnapping." Baronne's picture flashed onto the screen, and I sat back as I recognized the mane of dark hair. Baronne had taken our tickets at the door the night before, and wished us an enjoyable evening.

I also remembered Gary Mann, the owner, and his worries about "Bobby" when he approached the man at the ambulance. Robert Baronne—assuming he was "Bobby"—had already been missing within an hour of the evacuation. I wondered just how much money he'd been in possession of, and who would've known how to get to him through the security staff. If, indeed, he had been kidnapped and not taken off to some island with the money. I turned my attention back to the TV, where a phone number was flashing for those with any information.

"So a concert ends in tragedy," the anchor said, Baronne's image above his left shoulder. "A death and a missing staff member. But hundreds are alive through the efforts of our safety officers. A job well done. We will inform you as more details come our way. In other news, the Phillies have added a surprising name to their line-up—"

I hit the power button on the remote and the TV flickered off. While I'd been milling around in the parking lot last night, someone was dying, or had died. And the bomb had been real. If the threat hadn't been called in, if it hadn't been taken seriously, if we hadn't been evacuated so quickly... I shook my head, not wanting to think of the devastation that could've happened.

In the kitchen I dumped my soggy Cheerios down the drain. Nothing like an unidentified body and the smell of second-hand smoke to ruin your appetite.

Queenie, my collie, met me on the front step, her nose twitching when she caught my scent.

"Sorry, girl," I said. "I promise to shower after milking. And they weren't my cigarettes. Really."

She trotted ahead of me, obviously wanting to avoid my stench by staying upwind.

The familiar and much more pleasant smell of the barn greeted me as I wandered down the aisles of the parlor, saying hello to the cows, who had already claimed their stalls. We had yet to let the cows outside this spring, waiting until the temperatures had reached steady warmth and I had a chance to mend the pasture fences, so they chose a stall for the winter and pretty much stuck to it. Between Queenie and me we got the girls clipped in and settled, and I switched on Temple Radio, their usual favorite classical music station.

I was spreading out hay when headlights flashed through the windows. I listened as a door shut, and as the big dually truck reversed out the drive, then turned to greet Zach Granger, Jordan and Jermaine's nephew and my weekend and summer farm helper. "Morning, Zach."

He sauntered my way, hands in his pockets. "You were at that concert last night, right?"

"Yeah." I stopped pulling hay when I saw the look on his face. "What is it?"

"You know that body they found in the building?"

A lump formed in my throat, and I suddenly knew what he was going to say. "Oh, God, no," I said.

He nodded. "It was that girl singer from the band. Her name was Genna."

Chapter Four

"Where's Jordan now?" I asked.

Zach shook his head. "Home, I guess. Why?"

He obviously had no idea that Jordan would be devastated by this news. Hell, I wouldn't have had any idea, either, if I hadn't seen his face the night before when he talked about her.

"Just wondered," I said. "Since he's part of the band."

He shrugged. "Want me to get started milking?"

"Sure. I'll take care of the feed."

I watched as he casually walked off to fill a bucket with soapy water, having unknowingly delivered news more shocking than he had expected. I stood unmoving, wondering if I should call Jordan or Jermaine, or what exactly I should do. My hands were suddenly pulled forward, Pocahantas tired of waiting for her hay. I yanked the clump apart and scattered it in front of her, my thoughts miles away.

A glance at the clock told me it was only five-thirty. Too early to call Jermaine's house, for fear of waking Lavina, their one-year-old, but I assumed Jordan would be up.

"I'll be right back," I called to Zach.

He waved without looking up from the spigot.

In my office I punched Jordan's number into the phone but was rewarded only with several rings and his answering machine.

"Jordan," I said after the beep. "I'm so sorry to hear about… the news. Give me a call if I can do anything." I hit the flash button and called Granger's Welding on the very slim chance

Jordan—or any of the guys—had gone to work that early, but reached their answering machine, as well. I stared at the phone, then went back out to the parlor. I stood at Zach's elbow while he ran the wet cloth over Cinderella's udder.

"They know anything else about how Genna died?" I asked him.

He glanced up. "Not that they told me. I guess she was trampled, or something. You know, everybody trying to get out."

I thought back to the evening, with its chaos and panic. The closest I'd seen to trampling was the bottleneck at the top of the stairs when Norm's wheelchair got stuck, and the guy trying to climb over the people next to me. Besides, wouldn't the band have had a close exit backstage?

"Nothing else?" I asked.

Zach stood up and skirted around me to drop the cloth in the bucket. "I'm telling you, I don't know much. Just that she's dead. Why?"

I looked at him, thinking if his folks didn't tell him about Jordan's relationship with Genna, I shouldn't, either. Maybe his parents didn't even know. And maybe I was making something out of nothing.

"Just curious. Since I was there, you know."

He looked at me like he wanted to say, "Whatever," but was smart enough not to. I went back to feeding the herd, and he grabbed the milker to stick it on Cinderella's teats.

By the time we'd finished milking and cleaned the stalls I was really feeling the late night and the strain of knowing about Genna.

"Thanks, Zach," I said, smothering a yawn. "I'll get your paycheck to you by Wednesday."

"Sure. No problem."

We walked outside, where I stretched my back and did some neck rolls. "Want to come in and get a bit of breakfast while you wait for your mom?"

He looked at me. "You know, thanks. But I think I'll wait."

"My food not good enough for you?"

"It's not that." He grinned. "It's just…you really stink."

I made a face and swatted his shoulder before leaving him laughing on the lawn with Queenie.

Inside, I took off my boots and made sure I wouldn't be dragging any straw or cow crap through the house on my clothes. In the old days, before I had roommates, I would've just stripped at the washer. Modesty definitely had its drawbacks, no matter how necessary it was. Ever since Lucy and Tess had moved in the summer before, I'd been revamping my behavior. A bit, anyway. In a couple of weeks I could go back to my old ways. Lucy and Lenny would soon be off on their honeymoon, and Tess would be hanging with me for one last week, since she still had school. Then they would both move to Lenny's townhome in Perkasie. I'd be alone again in my creaky old farmhouse, except for those weekends Nick came up from Virginia or I could get away to Harrisonburg.

"Wow, that smells great," I said, peering in the kitchen door. I was surprised my stomach was making hungry noises, after hearing the news about Genna. "Baked oatmeal?"

Lucy looked up from the counter, where she was slicing strawberries into a bowl. Her hair, wet from the shower, had made a semi-circle of wetness on the collar of her shirt. "Thought we could all use a little sustenance after last night." She stopped slicing and searched my face. "What is it?"

I leaned against the doorjamb and crossed my arms, sticking my hands in my armpits. "They found a body in the club last night."

She sucked in a breath. "I thought they got everybody out."

"I did, too."

"Who was it?"

I pinched my lips together. "Remember the female singer in the band?"

"The one Jordan was looking for?"

I nodded. "Genna."

Lucy's eyes filled. "Oh no. What happened?"

"Nobody knows. Zach told me they think she was trampled, but nobody said anything about that on the news, and the cops would've found a pile-up right away."

She stared at me. "You think it was something else?"

"It must've been. Exactly *what*, I don't know."

We stood there, looking at each other, until I changed position and my smell wafted up to me, reminding me how rank I was.

"I have time for a shower before eating?" I asked. "Please?"

"I would appreciate it. The oatmeal needs a few more minutes in the oven, anyway."

I peeked into the front room to see Nick still comatose. I tiptoed over to make sure he was breathing, and when I assured myself he was, went upstairs to the bathroom. Tess was just coming out, her hair disheveled and her princess nightgown wrinkled.

"Hey, Punkin," I said.

She wrinkled her nose. "Eww. You stink."

Ah, the honesty of a nine-year-old.

Twenty minutes later I smelled like Lever 2000, not trusting the girly stuff I'd received as a birthday present to cut through the nastiness. I washed my hair twice and was keeping my fingers crossed that it did the trick.

In my bedroom, I ripped the sheets off the bed, along with the mattress pad and pillowcases, and tried not let them touch my clothes on the way downstairs. By the time I'd stuffed them into the washing machine and started the load, I was hearing Nick's voice in the kitchen.

"Nick stink, too?" I asked Tess when I entered the room.

"Yuck," she replied.

Nick laughed. "All right, I get the hint. I'll take my turn now."

He pushed himself up from the table, and I gave him the once over. His color had returned somewhat, but his eyes were still criss-crossed with red.

"How're you feeling?" I asked.

"A bit better, I guess."

"You still heading home today?"

"Yeah. Once I get breakfast."

"You'll be all right to drive?"

"I'll be fine."

I wasn't sure I believed him, but I let it go.

On his way past me, he stopped and spoke quietly. "Lucy told me about the singer. Jordan going to be okay?"

"So you saw it, too?"

"What? That he loves her?"

I nodded. "And I'm pretty sure it was mutual."

He sighed. "I thought so, too. Poor guy."

He left then, and I sat down to eat. No matter how bad I felt for Jordan, I still got a good helping down. I had to take the cooking while Lucy was around.

After breakfast Lucy headed out for her chores. I stuck around and kept Nick company while he ate his oatmeal.

"I called home and had Mom get me a doctor's appointment," he said.

I looked at him. "You think you caught a virus somewhere?"

He lifted a shoulder. "I have no idea." He looked at his hand, opening and closing his fingers. "I just feel so…weird."

"You'll let me know what you find out?"

"Of course."

"And you're sure you'll be all right driving?"

He covered my hand with his. "Like I said, I'll be fine."

I remembered how Jordan looked when he couldn't find Genna the night before. The nervousness. I felt it now, and I wasn't sure why.

I pulled my hand out from under Nick's and walked over to the window. Queenie and Tess were in the side yard playing tug-of-war with an old sock, Queenie dragging the girl in circles. I watched as they played, and Nick brought his empty bowl over to the counter. He put his arms around my waist and rested his chin on my head, watching the dog and girl.

Lucy walked past with a shovel and garden rake over her shoulder, laughing and calling out something to her daughter. Queenie, sensing something new, let go of the sock to follow Lucy. Tess landed on her bottom with a thump and looked at the sock with confusion. I couldn't help but chuckle at the expression on her face, and Nick laughed softly in my ear.

"I'm gonna brush my teeth and head out," he said.

I turned around, and he let his hands slide with me, keeping me within his arms. "You'll be back for the wedding?" I asked.

"The rehearsal, actually. Lucy invited me to the lunch, and I figured since I have a free place to stay…"

I raised my eyebrows. "She's putting you up?"

"Yeah. In some old farmhouse, with a cranky farmer."

"Cranky? Who're you calling cranky?"

He leaned in to kiss me and I enjoyed it for a few moments until he broke away.

"You going to check on Jordan today?" he asked.

"As soon as you're gone. I wonder if his family has any idea that they were…whatever they were."

"He certainly didn't tell us."

"Huh-uh. And I don't know if his family's even met the members of the band."

He gently slapped my hips. "You'll take care of him."

"We'll see if he wants taking care of."

Nick went upstairs to get his stuff together, and I opened the hall closet to pull out my leather chaps. I'd been riding lots of times already that spring, but not yet without the chaps. That spring breeze could cut through jeans in a heartbeat. My leather jacket, which I'd left on the porch, still stank to high heaven, so I pulled out my denim one and hoped it would do the trick. With the added layer of my leather vest I should be okay.

"Well, I'm off," Nick said. He slung his duffel bag over his shoulder and dangled his truck keys in the other hand.

"I'll walk you out."

After a hug from Tess, a lick—or three or four—from Queenie, and a waved good-bye from Lucy, Nick settled in the driver's seat of his Ranger.

"You'll call?" I said.

"I'll call."

"All right."

"I love you," he said.

"Love you, too."

One more kiss and he was down the driveway and off south to Virginia. I stared after him, hoping the empty feeling in my stomach was more about Genna than whatever was going on with Nick.

Carrying my chaps and jacket, I walked through the dry grass to the garden plot, where Lucy knelt in the tilled garden, planting green beans.

She glanced up. "You going somewhere?"

"To check on Jordan."

She sat back on her heels. "Let me know if I can do anything to help."

"Will do. You'll be here for the milk truck?"

"No problem."

"Thanks." I began walking away.

"Stella?"

I turned back. "Yeah?"

"You'll be home in time for our appointment?"

"What?"

Her eyelids lowered, and I wondered what I'd done to deserve a glare like that.

Then I remembered.

We had an appointment at the bridal shop. I was going to be Lucy's maid of honor in a week, and we still didn't know what I was wearing. I'd put it off for so long Lucy was starting to worry I'd show up wearing my newest jeans and cleanest T-shirt. In fact, I'd almost asked if that would be an option.

I swallowed. "What time's it at?"

"Eleven. And we can't be late."

I looked out over the field, where tiny shoots of corn lay in perfect green lines. "I'll be here."

She turned back to the garden, and I knew I'd better be back in time, or I would become the latest addition on her shit list.

In the garage I put on my chaps, vest, and jacket, and freed my Harley from the chain that locked it to a hook in the garage floor. The 1988 Low Rider and I had been through a lot together, from rebuilding the front end, to last summer's accident, to a complete refurbishing of more bike parts than I could count. The black and chrome were now relieved by blue ghost flames and the words "Daddy's Princess" on the tank. Lenny's handiwork.

Once I pushed it outside I flicked a rag over the main body of the bike and stepped back to admire it in the sunshine. A beauty, if I did say so myself.

The ride to Granger's Welding was pleasant, the leather of my chaps, gloves, and vest keeping me toasty in the spring air. I pulled into the gravel lane with care and parked out front, setting my helmet on the ground.

Peering into the interior of the shop, I could see the silhouette of a very large man at the welder, and stepped out of the sun to get a clearer view. He glanced up and moved back from the machine, putting aside the piece he was working on. Pushing his safety helmet off his head, he used one hand to take it off, the other to adjust the handkerchief he'd tied around his head to keep the strap of the helmet from digging into his skull, seeing how he had no hair to protect it. His eyes were rimmed with red, and his cheeks were sucked in to his teeth.

"You heard?" Jermaine finally said.

"Yeah. Jordan here?"

"Nope. Just me. Jethro's out at a special job in Chalfont. I wouldn't be here, either, if this job didn't have to be done by this afternoon."

I leaned against a table and tipped my head back, my gaze drifting toward the high ceiling. "So where is he?"

"Jordan? Philly. He refused to leave last night until he found that singer." At the tone of his voice I brought my eyes back to him. "Stella, I didn't *know*." He yanked off a heavy glove and rubbed his face roughly.

"You mean about Jordan and Genna?"

He nodded abruptly. "You did?"

"Just last night. I never knew she existed before then as something other than a voice on an album. But there was obviously some kind of tension between them, even though—or maybe because—she already had a boyfriend."

"The asshole drummer guy."

That about summed it up.

"So what happened last night?" I asked.

He took off the other glove and tossed them both on the table beside me. "I stuck around while the parking lot cleared out and I finally found him arguing with some cops in front of the club. He was desperate to get inside and look for her, or see a list of people they'd talked to who had come out of the building. They weren't having any of it, and before we knew it, there were cops and paramedics scrambling into the club. By the time we heard there was a body, Jordan was about freaking out. It was all I could do to keep him from rushing in and getting taken down by the police. When they came out..." He stopped for a minute, his face carefully controlled, and I looked away. "When they came out and said they'd found someone, Jordan knew it was her. They wouldn't let him anywhere near the scene, but when they brought the body out they had him take a look and he... God, I can still see his face. Still as stone. Scary as hell."

Oh, Jordan.

"But they don't know how?"

He shook his head. "Not that they were telling."

We stood together quietly for a moment.

"So Jordan's still down there?" I asked.

"Yup. Refused to come back. Said he'll bring the train back, or he'll get some other ride."

"You know where he is?"

"Last I saw him, he was sitting in the lobby of the police station. Said he wasn't leaving till they told him what had happened to his fiancée."

Chapter Five

"His *fiancée?*"

Jermaine held out his hands. "I'm telling you, that's what he said. When I mentioned it to Ma this morning, she about flipped."

I could just imagine the Granger matriarch being shelled with this kind of news. "What did she do?"

"Set about trying to find out where he was and what exactly he was doing."

"And did she find him?"

"Nope. She actually searched his house."

I raised my eyebrows.

"I know," Jermaine said. "Anyway, she tried calling that cell he uses for work, but it's turned off. The cops said he's not at the station anymore, and they don't know where he went. Ma even called Tom Copper, who said he'd call the rest of the band and get back to her if he found him."

"So Jordan's out there by himself."

Jermaine let out a sigh. "I'd go to him if I knew where to go."

"Yeah. Me, too."

I stood up, brushing dust from my rear. "You hear anything else about the bomb?"

"Just that there was a real one. Set to go off by remote." He reached over to grab his gloves off the table.

"Yeah. I heard that on the news. And about the missing club employee. Robert Baronne? You know him?"

"Not really. He was the front office guy. Took care of the money and tickets. Contracts, too. Wait a minute. You were asking me about a Bobby last night. The same guy?"

I nodded. "Did you see him after the concert?"

He picked up his safety helmet and positioned it over his head. "Wasn't looking for him."

"Yeah. Me neither." I headed toward the front door. "You'll let me know if you hear from Jordan?"

"Sure will. Where you gonna be? Home?"

I glanced at the clock on the wall and made a face. "For the next little while I'm going to be at the bridal shop, trying on dresses."

A short laugh escaped Jermaine's lips.

"Don't even start," I said.

"Oh, I ain't startin'. But I'd love to be a fly on *that* wall."

"Bridal shops," I said, "do not have flies."

Mustering what dignity I could, I jammed my helmet on my head and fishtailed out the drive.

Lucy was waiting for me in the living room, flipping through a copy of *Redbook*.

"I'm here," I said.

She didn't look up. "I didn't doubt you would be."

Uh-huh. And my neighbor's bull was now producing milk.

I hung my leathers and jacket in the closet. "You ready?"

"Just have to call Tess down from her room."

"I can do that."

"I'll get her. You might want to take a minute to wipe off the bugs who lost their lives on your face."

I stalked to the downstairs bathroom and swiped at my cheeks and forehead with a washcloth. The woman hadn't even *looked* at me, and she found issue with my appearance. But then, no doubt the saleslady at the bridal shop probably would have, too, since there really were several spots of bug guts to be removed.

The three of us were soon belted into the Civic—it was Lucy's deal, so she could use up her gas—and on our way to Harleysville.

"What color dress are you getting, Stella?" Tess asked from the back seat.

I looked at Lucy. "Well?"

She grinned. "Pink? Fuschia?"

I growled.

"We'll just see what they have, honey," Lucy said, looking at Tess in the rearview mirror. To me she added, "I asked them to pull everything in your size that's modest, simple, and as unfrilly as they come."

"Great. Can't wait to see what they have."

She laughed, but I really didn't see what was funny about the situation.

"Jordan didn't call while I was gone, did he?" I asked.

She sobered up. "No."

When we finally made it through the light at the intersection of Routes 113 and 63 I wasn't exactly relieved, since that meant the dress shop was only a few minutes away. I took a deep breath, focusing on the fact that I was doing this for Lucy. Lenny, too, I supposed. He'd been my friend for as long as I could remember. Not that he'd give a rip what I wore to the wedding.

"Can we get pizza afterwards?" Tess asked.

Lucy shrugged. "Sure. If Stella's a good girl trying on dresses."

"Can't we just skip the dresses and go straight to the food?" I asked.

"Now, now. Don't be a party pooper."

"A wedding pooper!" Tess shrieked, giggling.

Lucy swung into the parking lot of Marlene's Bridal Shoppe and shut off the car. "Ready?"

"For lunch," I said.

"Grump." She opened the door and got out, Tess doing the same.

I decided I'd better get my ass in gear if I wanted that pizza, so I followed them up the stone walkway to the front door that played "Here Comes the Bride" when we opened it.

The interior of the shop—oh, sorry, the *shoppe*—was everything I feared it would be. Lace, ribbons, bows, lingerie, garters, veils, elevator music, cake toppers… And those didn't begin to compare to the vast array of gowns. Wedding gowns, mostly, which threatened to suffocate or perhaps just eat anyone daring enough to wander further into the store.

"Ms. Lapp!" A young blonde woman wearing a linen suit— *bright green*, of all things—and a widely displayed mouthful of teeth welcomed Lucy with open arms. "We're so glad to see you again. And Tess, of course. How lovely to have you along." She turned to me and the bionic smile lost a bit of its power. Whether it was my tattoo, my seen-better-days jeans, or the scowl on my face I wasn't sure.

"This is Stella," Lucy said. "Stella, this is Allison."

"Uh, hello Stella." Allison tentatively reached out her hand and I decided I might as well shake it.

"So what do you have for us?" Lucy asked, her eyes twinkling.

"Well…" Allison's eyes darted from me to the back, where the dressing rooms lurked. Now that she'd seen me, she was obviously uncertain of her choices.

"Might as well show us," Lucy said. "What's the worst that could happen?"

Allison made a strangled sound, and I tried not to think of the answer to Lucy's question.

I followed the little procession, staying as far from the racks of white gowns as I could, afraid I'd somehow manage to stain, rip, or otherwise disfigure a piece of clothing that cost more than I made in a month but would only be worn once. I stopped when the others stopped, and got my first look at my options.

Lucy studied them while I tried to think of something to say that wouldn't be offensive. She turned to Allison with a tight smile. "Why don't you leave us alone for a few minutes while we go through these?"

Allison's expression reeked of relief, and I fought down a hysterical giggle. When she'd gone, I let out the breath I'd been holding. Lucy shuffled through the dozen or so dresses on the rack, and I couldn't hold it in any longer.

"You might as well take out those pinks," I said. "The lavenders, the peaches, and my God, who would wear that shade of yellow? That brown is hideous—is that actually a color someone would wear for a wedding? And I look terrible in silver."

That left about three dresses. Lucy pulled them out and hung them against the rail so we could see them.

"That dark green's an okay color," I said, "but good lord, that bow is bigger than my butt, and the blue one would do a great job of showing the cleavage and hips I don't have. Besides, it's…" I snorted. "Four hundred dollars."

"Well," Lucy said through her teeth. "That leaves this lovely black one."

"Now that's a color I could live with. But what about that funky skirt, or whatever you call the bottom part of a dress. Is it supposed to look like that?"

Lucy stared at me, her expression flat, and I realized what I'd just done.

"I'm sorry, Luce. I'm sorry. It's your show. I'll try on whatever you want. Except maybe the pink ones."

She looked at me some more.

I shut up.

In the end she pulled out one of the lavenders, the gold (it *wasn't* yellow, she explained stiffly), and the last three.

"Shoes?" she asked.

"I don't have any."

"I know that," she said evenly. "What *size?*"

"Oh. Eight. Sometimes eight and a half."

She left, and I heard her talking to Allison in the front room. Tess sat in the corner, watching me like you would an unfamiliar dog.

Lucy returned without any shoes.

"Didn't have my size?" I asked.

She cocked her head. "Can you wear high heels?"

"Well…"

"That's what I thought. We'll figure that out later." She grabbed the lavender dress off the rack and shoved me toward a stall with a curtained doorway. "Just try this on."

I tried it on. I tried them all on. I tried on more styles that Allison brought us. Some that she'd had in storage that had gone out of fashion two years before. I even tried on one of the pink monsters. But when it came down to it, I might as well have been one of my cows trying on the dresses. They just weren't…fitting.

"I'm sorry, Luce," I said when I'd changed back into my clothes.

"Yeah." She led us back through the store and paused to check out the display of white gloves near the counter.

"Hey," I said. "Look at that."

A poster for the concert the night before was taped to the door, showing Tom Copper in front, with the rest of the group angled out behind him, like a fan. Genna stood directly to his left, a hand on his elbow. A lump formed in my throat.

"I was going to go to that," Allison said.

I looked at her with more interest, surprised someone working in a wedding boutique could have good musical taste. She was leaning on the counter, her elbows resting on the glass.

"You didn't go?" I asked.

"Nope. Husband got sick. It was too short notice to find someone else, and I didn't really want to go by myself. Guess I'm glad I didn't get there, the way it turned out."

"We were there," Lucy said.

Allison stood up. "Really? With the bomb threat and everything?"

"Yeah." I put a finger on Genna's picture. "She's the one who…" I glanced at Tess, who was listening all too carefully. "Who was on the news."

Allison wrinkled her nose. "Oh, wow. That's…that's too bad. She was nice."

"You *knew* her?"

"I used to go to their concerts when I was at Temple. Five, six years ago. I was kind of a groupie, actually. You know, they only did local shows, then, before they got bigger and started touring." Her face grew nostalgic. "I used to follow them to the bars where they'd hang out. Went out with Donny a couple times, actually. The guitarist? Loved that bull tattoo on his arm. He had another one, too, of a dragon, but you wouldn't see it unless—" She broke off, color creeping up her neck. "Anyway…"

"Which drummer was with them then?"

Her forehead wrinkled. "What? Parker. He was always…oh, that's right. They got a new one, didn't they? A year or so ago? I stopped hanging with them a year or two before that. I did hear they switched, though. Not sure why."

"How come you stopped hanging out?"

"Different reasons. I graduated, moved out of the city. But Tom Copper got married, too, and that changed things. The band sort of seemed to get over the whole groupie girl thing, became a little more tight with just a few. You know. You get older. Wiser."

She leaned back against the counter and gestured around the shop. "Life happens. People get married. Move on to different things. Better things, if you ask me. Things that last a lifetime." She smiled at Lucy. "Right?"

Lucy smiled back. No reason to tell the girl that Lucy had already had that better thing, and it hadn't lasted a lifetime. Brad, her first husband, had died two and a half years before. But now Lucy had Lenny, and was ready to add a new dimension to her life. And hope that this time it did last as long as one would hope.

And Lucy was still smiling. "Better things," she said, "can still include good rock and roll."

"Oh," Allison said. "Absolutely."

Maybe this chick wasn't so bad, after all.

She looked at me, seeming a little more comfortable now we'd had this chat. "So you didn't find anything back there?"

I shrugged. "I'm not made for this girly stuff. I'll find something somewhere."

She laughed and looked at Lucy, who rolled her eyes.

"Just wait till it's your wedding," Allison said to me. "Then you'll see how important it is what your bridesmaid wears."

"I'm not having a wedding," I said.

Lucy and Tess looked at me, probably wondering if Nick was aware of this.

I smiled. "I'll just elope."

Chapter Six

Lucy didn't talk much on the way home. She was probably worried about what I'd show up wearing next Saturday, and in her place, I would've been, too. I guess I should've been more concerned about her feelings, but it was hard for me to get worked up about a frou-frou dress when Jordan's fiancée—or whatever she was—was dead.

Then again, it was Lucy's *wedding*.

"I'll find something," I said. "I promise."

The way her jaw bunched wasn't exactly a show of confidence.

"You could wear that fancy white and black leather outfit you showed me," Tess said.

"Oh," I said. "I'm not sure that would be…appropriate."

Lucy snorted. "If you're talking about the one with the short shorts and halter top that you won at the HOG Club winter party, I have to agree."

"Yeah," I said. "Not real wedding-like."

Tess pouted. "But it's pretty."

"Well, then," Lucy said, "we'll let Stella wear it for *her* wedding. But oh, no, she's not *having* a wedding."

I glanced into the back seat, giving Tess the finger-across-the-throat cue. I hoped she got it.

When Lucy parked in the driveway, she stepped out of the car without saying another word. I took a deep breath and let it out. I truly didn't *mean* to be a pain in the ass.

Inside the house, Lucy went upstairs, shutting the door with excessive force, and I went into the kitchen, Tess skipping along behind.

"Guess I didn't deserve the pizza for lunch," I said. "Sorry."

She shrugged. "You got any frozen ones?"

I did, and we pulled it out, sprucing it up with some mushrooms and sweet peppers Lucy had put in the fridge. I hoped she wasn't planning on using them for supper, or I'd be in even deeper doo-doo.

We had just stuck it in the oven when Lucy stopped in the doorway. "I'm going out to work in the garden."

"You don't want lunch?"

"I'm not hungry."

"All right."

But she didn't hear me, having already left the kitchen. The outside door shut—again, quite firmly—and she marched past the window toward the vegetable plot.

While the pizza cooked Tess set the table and I checked the answering machine. Nothing from Jordan or any other Granger, and it was too soon for Nick to be home. The only messages were from Lenny, who had a question about food for Saturday, and Allison, from the bridal shop, saying she forgot to ask if we wanted to schedule another fitting time.

Somehow that message ended up getting erased.

After Tess and I inhaled all but one piece of the pizza we went out to the garden, where we found Lucy cutting some rhubarb into a bowl. Packets of seeds for zucchini and sweet corn lay on the ground, ready to be opened.

"I'm going out to work on fences," I said.

She looked up. "I saw a nice hole over on the west side. Looks like a snow plow hit it good."

"Yeah, I'll get that."

Lucy's face had relaxed, the lines in her forehead smoother than during the ride home from Harleysville.

"Sorry about the dresses," I said. "I really will find something nice. You don't have to worry."

The corners of her mouth twitched, like I'd said something funny. "I think I'll just leave it up to you."

"No requests?"

She did smile this time. "Like that would matter?"

I swallowed. It did matter. But I had pretty much vetoed everything we'd just looked at. "Have you tried praying about it?" I asked, trying to lighten the mood.

Lucy's eyes widened. "Every day."

I managed a little laugh. The problem was, she was probably serious.

After grabbing some fence-mending tools—wire cutters, a roll of heavy wire, and a bucket for scraps—I headed out across the pasture. The spring weather had dried off the grass, making for an easy walk. In fact, it hadn't rained in about two weeks, a strange occurrence for April. Lucy would be watering her garden every day if this kept up.

I'd mended one big hole on the north side—looked like some snowmobilers had gotten a bit aggressive—and was started on the second when two men came walking across the pasture. I straightened up, my wire cutter in my hand, until I recognized one of them. I dropped the tool into my bucket and stretched my shoulders.

"Ms. Crown," the bigger man said, his eyes looking straight into mine.

So it was *that* kind of a visit.

"Detective Willard," I said, hoping I was following his cue correctly.

He nodded briefly. "Ms. Lapp directed us this way after we talked with her. I hope it's all right."

I stared at him, marveling at his behavior. The last I'd seen Willard was over a huge pot of chili Lucy had cooked, having invited the entire Willard family over for Sunday dinner. Now he was acting like we'd never exchanged more than a howdy-do. I figured there must be a reason.

He gestured to the man beside him. A plump, smiling, gray-haired guy with a notebook. "This is Investigator Alexander from the Philadelphia police. He's working on the incident from last night."

Ah.

"Which incident?" I asked. "The bomb? Or Genna?"

"Both," Alexander said cheerfully. "I'm working on both."

I caught Willard's eye, but his expression was unreadable.

"Do you know how Genna died?" I asked. "Was she really trampled trying to get out?"

Alexander shook his head sadly. "We have yet to receive answers. The autopsy has been put off until later today or tomorrow, because of a backlog."

I thought back to the morning news. "The Mafia killings?"

"You are remarkably well-informed, Ms. Crown." He smiled some more.

"Okaaaay," I said. "Why are you here? I gave the cops a statement about the concert last night."

"But you didn't give *me* a statement," Alexander said. "And I'd find that ever so much more helpful. Is there a place we could sit?"

Was this guy for real?

"Grab a fencepost," I said. "They work great to lean on."

"Fine, fine." He stayed where he was and pulled a little device from his pocket. It looked like a phone.

"I like to record my interviews," he said, holding up the thing. A Dictaphone. "Do you have any objections?"

"I guess not."

"Wonderful. So, could you please recount your experiences last night at the concert?"

"Well, when the music cut off in the middle of the song, I grabbed my friend Lenny and followed him toward—"

"No, no," Alexander said. "Forgive me. Could you please start at the beginning?"

"The beginning? Of the concert?"

"Of your time there. From when you arrived at Club Independence."

"You mean starting outside?"

He showed me his incisors.

"Well, all right. It was freaking cold, and we did our best—"

"'We' being?"

I sighed. "Lucy Lapp, who you just met. Lenny Spruce, her fiancé. And Nick Hathaway, my boyfriend."

He scribbled in his notebook. "Thank you. Please continue."

"We waited outside for close on an hour before finally getting inside."

"And while you were outside did you see anything out of the ordinary?"

I thought back. Fred, the toothless beer-guzzler, was a bit unappetizing, but hardly unusual. The group of Harleys, the staff guy telling us we couldn't take cameras inside...

"Nope," I said.

"Thank you. Go on."

"We went through security, and Nick got to keep his phone even though it takes pictures."

Alexander stopped scribbling. "And did he take any?"

I shrugged. "Don't think so. I can ask him."

"He's not here?"

"He's on his way home to Virginia."

"You can give us his phone number?"

I recited it.

"Thank you. And you were saying?"

"I don't know. What was I saying?"

Willard cleared his throat. "You went through security."

"Right. Gave our tickets to the guy— Is he part of your investigation, too?"

"To whom are you referring?" Alexander asked.

"Robert Baronne. The missing Club Independence guy. He's the one who took our tickets."

Alexander nodded. "I would be very interested in anything you have to say about him."

"I don't really have anything to say. I was just asking."

"Okay. Continue."

"We gave Baronne our tickets— Oh, I guess I do have something to say about him. After the bomb scare, when we were at the parking lot, the owner of the club came running up to another guy—" I held up my hand before he could interrupt. "Don't know who he was. Anyway, he was asking if the other guy had seen 'Bobby.' When I saw the news this morning, I figured it was the same guy." I waited until he finished scribbling and looked up at me again.

"Anyway, after we got in the lobby—"

"We're back to before the concert?" Alexander asked.

"Yes. Jordan took us—"

"Jordan?" Alexander said.

I gritted my teeth. Telling this guy a story was worse than pounding your finger with a hammer. Repeatedly. "Jordan Granger. He's the band's sound man, and a good friend of mine. He took Nick and me backstage to meet the band."

"Not your friends Lucy and Lenny?"

"Didn't she tell you?"

He smiled. "I'm interested in *your* story."

I snuck another look at Willard. His eyes were focused on my tool bucket.

"So Nick and I went backstage, *without* Lucy and Lenny, where we met the Tom Copper Band."

"All of them?"

I felt a lightbulb go on above my head. Or perhaps I'd inadvertently shocked myself on the fence.

"Actually, not quite all of them. We met Tom Copper, Donny, LeRoy, and Genna. Don't know any of those last names. Met the old drummer, too. Parker Somebody. But we didn't meet the *new* drummer, or not exactly."

Alexander looked at me with interest. "How can you 'not exactly' meet someone?"

"Jordan took us on stage for a minute on our way back out. We were in the wings, where we couldn't be seen by the audience, and we heard the drummer say he was going to wring someone's neck."

Alexander and Willard both looked up at that.

"You're sure it was him?" Willard asked.

"We heard his voice from the other side of the curtain, then he came stomping past. We didn't see the other person. Jordan said there's another way out."

Alexander scribbled energetically in his notebook. "Anyone else there?"

"On the stage? Not that I know of. But we left right away."

"And did you see anyone else close by?"

"The owner of the club passed us on our way out the backstage door. Oh, and two girls on our way in. What were their names?" I clicked my tongue, looking out over my newly planted cornfield. "A rock star."

"One of the girls was a rock star?" Alexander asked.

"No, named for one. Marley. That's it. And the other girl— the smaller one—was Annie. She helps Jordan with sound stuff, I guess. Anyway, then Jordan left us and we went out to find Lenny and Lucy."

"Okay. Fantastic. Now, why don't you tell us about the concert."

I talked about finding Lenny and Lucy, the crowd's wild response to the band, and Nick leaving during the first break. Then how the panic had started, how I'd almost gotten pushed over the railing, and how we'd stopped to help Norm and Cindy negotiate the stairs and get rid of their wheelchair. How I'd fought down the stairs and outside into the fresh air, where I couldn't find my friends and got no help from the fresh-faced cop.

They liked the method I used—Loader—for finding Lenny and Lucy in the parking lot.

I described the ambulances, finding Nick, and repeated what I overheard Gary Mann say to the other guy about looking for Bobby. And how we'd found Lucy and Lenny again.

"Then Jordan found us," I said. "Bringing Marley and Annie, and Ricky got there quick after phoning Marley. None of them had seen Genna, and they were pretty worried."

Alexander watched my face. "You believed none of them had seen her?"

"Sure. The guys were both a bit panicked, and the girls really didn't seem to care."

"Hmmm." He wrote something down. "Now Jordan Granger. You know him well?"

"Real well. Like a brother."

"And he's the sound man for the band? Is that his only occupation?"

"When he's not touring with the band he's working at his brother's welding shop. Granger's Welding."

"And do you know anything about his relationships with members of the band?" Alexander asked.

"No." I didn't *know* anything. Everything I *thought* I knew was completely my own imagination.

"He's never mentioned any problems he's had? Anyone with whom he had disagreements? Tensions?"

"What? No. He's living a dream. All he's ever mentioned to me is how much fun he's having."

"He never said anything about a relationship with Genna, the female vocalist? Or her boyfriend, the drummer?"

"No. He's never said anything— Wait a minute. What are you trying to say here?" I'd been about three steps too slow. "Jordan would never hurt anyone. Especially not Genna."

Alexander raised his eyebrows. "No? Why 'especially not Genna'?"

Shit.

"Because he's a gentle guy. He's a *nice* guy. He's never said anything bad about *anybody* in the band. He's never said anything *at all* about anybody in the band, except that he loves being with them."

Alexander wrote something down. "What would you say if I told you Jordan and Genna had an argument before the concert?"

I stared at him. "Are you serious?"

"Oh, yes."

"What were they arguing about?"

He smiled. "That's not important. But did you know anything about it?"

"Of course not." But I remembered the tension. How Jordan barely looked at Genna backstage, and how she left the room so quickly after Jordan introduced Nick and me.

"You're not really looking at him as a suspect?" I asked. "Jordan wouldn't hurt anyone, and he would definitely not set a bomb."

Alexander remained mute. Willard wouldn't meet my eyes.

My heart thudded in my chest, and my skin went cold at the thought of Jordan being the center of their investigation. "I at least hope you're smart enough to be looking at other people? People like Ricky, who said he'd wring someone's neck?"

Alexander smiled at this.

Willard didn't.

Chapter Seven

After Willard and his sidekick left, my anger kept me so motivated I pounded around the fences for another hour and a half. The thought of Jordan masterminding a bomb scare and a murder—perhaps even the kidnapping of Bobby Baronne, if Alexander had his way—was so outrageous that twice I almost cut off my finger instead of a broken wire. Fortunately, I realized before it was too late that I'd better take a break. I made it back to the house without any missing body parts, and found Lucy sliding a loaf of bread into the oven.

"They interrogate you, too?" I asked.

Her brow furrowed. "Bunch of strange questions, asking about Jordan's demeanor and anything I know about him and Genna. I had no idea there was anything *to* him and Genna, other than knowing each other, and him looking for her last night. Was there?"

I slumped onto a kitchen chair and put my feet up on the one across from me. "Not that he told me. All I know is I felt the vibes when we saw her backstage. She did her best not to look at him, and he ignored her, except for telling us her name. Of course, after the bomb scare he was practically hysterical looking for her. But the biggest thing…" I stopped, trying to put my mind around it.

"What?"

"Jermaine told me Jordan had set himself up at the police station saying he was waiting for news on his *fiancée*."

"Fiancée? But wasn't that drummer guy her boyfriend?"

"Um-hmm." I leaned back and studied my fingers, thankful they were all there. "I didn't tell the annoying detective any of this, since it's all stuff I don't really know. I've never heard it from Jordan." I glanced at the answering machine. "I take it none of the Grangers has called? Or Nick?"

"Nope."

I checked the clock. Nick should've been home by now, but I supposed it could still be a while before he had any answers from his doctor.

I leaned back on my chair, trying not to overbalance as I reached for the phone. Lucy, rolling her eyes, walked over, grabbed the phone, and handed it to me.

I took it. "Thanks."

She went back to the counter and began cleaning out the breadmaker, where she'd let the dough rise before taking it out and putting it in a real bread pan.

I tried calling Jordan at home, but had no luck. Then I called all the Grangers, but none of them had heard from him, either. Jermaine told me Ma was about ready to take off down to the city herself if she didn't hear anything soon, and they were all trying to talk her out of it. I reminded him to let me know if he heard anything, and gave him a heads-up that the cops were looking at Jordan as a suspect. Needless to say, this didn't go over well. He gave me Jordan's cell phone number, and I called it without getting any response.

I pushed myself off the chair and hung up the phone, realizing I'd better get back out to the fences if I wanted to finish them that day. "I'm headed out. Can you come get me if somebody calls?"

"You bet."

I was more under control now, and fence mending went quickly enough that I was back in time to help Lucy with milking. She usually took the evenings, but it was a routine I enjoyed, and I wouldn't have felt right sitting in the house doing nothing while she was putting in the hours. By the time we were done, though, I was ready for my supper and my bed. Lucy's bread was warm and soft, and the roast chicken she'd cooked in the crock pot went down easy.

My stomach and I would be in mourning once next Saturday arrived.

By the time I'd taken a shower and put clean sheets on my bed, Nick still hadn't called. I said goodnight to Lucy, who'd sent Tess upstairs an hour earlier, and picked up the phone in my room. Instead of Nick, I got a computerized message telling me the cellular phone customer I'd dialed was not available, along with some numerical code. I hung up and tried again, hearing the same recorded message. Strange. Nick never turned off his phone. Maybe the battery had died in all his traveling and fatigue. Or he'd been told to turn it off at the doctor's office and had forgotten to turn it back on. Or it had fallen out of his pocket and gotten run over by a bus.

I hung up, not believing any of the excuses I had created, and snuggled under the covers, feeling colder and emptier than I had in some time.

Sunday dawned clear and chilly, and I pulled a flannel shirt on to head to the barn. The news over breakfast held nothing helpful about Genna, the bomb scare, or the disappearance of Bobby Baronne. At least they didn't announce that they were looking for Jordan to "help with their investigation."

Lucy came out to help with the clean-up after milking, since Zach didn't come on Sunday mornings, and by eight-o'clock we were watching our herd with anticipation. They'd been inside for several long winter months, and they were more than ready for the outside. Since I'd repaired the fences the day before and we'd readied the barnyard, it was time to set them free.

"Give me a minute to try Nick again?" I said.

Lucy smiled. "Sure."

But Nick still wasn't answering, and I set the phone down with care. I was tempted to call one of his sisters, or his mom, but really wanted to hear his voice, not theirs. I assumed that if he hadn't made it home they would've called me, since I'd gotten to know them at least a little bit during my once-a-month visits to Virginia. They wouldn't leave me hanging.

Like Nick was.

No one from the Granger clan had called, either, which made me feel even more out of the loop. I wished somebody would think to keep me informed about some aspect of my life.

Back in the parlor, Lucy had unclipped the herd and was waiting by the back door.

"No news?" she said.

I shook my head. "Ready?"

"Ready."

Each grabbing a handle, we slid the doors along their tracks, letting in the sun. Nala, the cow closest to the door, perked up her ears. Slowly, she shifted her body out of her stall and made her way to the door. In a sudden burst of understanding—well, instinct, probably—she burst from the barn, kicking her heels and swishing her tail like a calf.

Lucy giggled, and I could feel the laughter bubbling up in my chest, too. I let go with a chuckle.

One by one the closest cows realized what was happening and backed out of their stalls, crashing into each other and wrestling to be the first out the door. It was turning into a mini stampede, and Lucy and I edged out of harm's way.

Once they'd all exited, prancing and kicking, Lucy and I stood in the doorway surveying the scene. The cows ran back and forth, tossing their heads, holding their tails up. Some were racing to the fence at the far end of the pasture and back, working out the kinks in their winter legs. I glanced at Lucy and recognized the joy in her face.

"It's like they have a new lease on life," I said.

She smiled. "It is."

"Kind of like you. Getting married again and all."

Her smile grew. "Yeah. My second chance. Although I hope Lenny and I don't run over each other in the process." She pointed out a pair of cows fighting over a particular patch of grass in the pasture, like there weren't a few acres of the green stuff surrounding them.

"Think we'll get them back in for tonight's milking?" I asked.

She laughed. "Gonna be a chore."

"Eh. They'll be ready once they feel their udders filling up."

"I guess we'll see."

We were still standing there when we heard Lenny's bike thundering up the drive.

"Goodness," Lucy said. "What time is it?"

"Eight-thirty. He's early. The poker run doesn't even start till ten, and we only have to get down to Norristown."

"Even so, we'd better get ready."

Lucy's Sunday morning "getting ready" would be different from usual. Where she usually got herself and Tess in church clothes, today they'd be getting dudded up in jeans and leather for a HOG outing. We'd heard about it a couple of weeks before and had been looking forward to the ride.

We walked back through the barn and met Lenny in the driveway, where Lucy gave him a kiss. "Give us a few minutes, hon. We were just letting the cows out."

"They pretty happy?"

"Oh, yeah."

"Mornin', Stella," Lenny said.

"Same to you. Bart not coming?"

Lenny shook his head. "He thought about it, but it's a busy time of year at the store, and he didn't want both of us to be gone, especially since next Saturday's a wash."

"I hear you." Bart, Lenny's business partner at the Biker Barn, their Harley-Davidson dealership, would be serving as Lenny's best man at the wedding. I wondered if it had crossed Lenny's mind to be concerned about what Bart would be wearing.

"So are we gonna freeze today?" I asked. "Was it cold on the way over?"

"Nah. You'll be fine if you wear your chaps."

A half hour later I was wearing them, and Lenny had Lucy decked out in a pair from the Biker Barn. We didn't have any small enough for Tess, so she wore two pairs of jeans and her winter jacket, along with a good pair of gloves. Her helmet and its face shield would keep her head warm.

"You get your scooter fixed up okay for Tess?" Lenny asked.

I pulled my bike out of the garage. "I put blocks on the foot pegs for her. She should be able to reach those no problem." I pointed out the chunks of wood I'd secured where Tess' feet would rest. I'd also attached a seat Lenny had loaned me with a wider pad and a back rest. "She'll be good and comfy."

Lucy and Tess came out, and Lucy eyed my bike. "You're sure she'll be all right?"

"She'll be fine, sweetheart." Lenny put his arm around her. "Stella's been riding for years. And Tess don't hardly weigh a thing. Won't change the balance much at all."

"And you'll hang on tight, right, Punkin?" I said.

Tess grinned and nodded.

"We ready, then?" Lenny asked.

I hesitated and looked toward the house, wondering if I should give Nick's phone another try.

"You want to call him one more time?" Lucy asked, reading my mind.

I pulled on my riding gloves. "No. He'll call when he's ready."

"Okay, then," Lenny said. "Let's head out." He swung a leg over his Wide Glide and turned the key in the ignition, ready to push the Start button.

I sat, too, and Lucy gave Tess a hand getting settled behind me.

"You're sure you're okay?" she asked. "You hang on tight to Stella."

Tess groaned. "Oh, *mooooom*."

The morning was clear and beautiful as we headed down 363 toward Norristown. We met other groups of bikes on the way, probably headed toward the same event. When we arrived at Montgomery County Harley-Davidson the parking lot was crowded with bikes and leather-clad riders waving and calling to friends. We dismounted and waited in line a few minutes to register for the ride.

"See that guy?" Lenny asked Tess. He pointed at a photo of a smiling man on a Road King. The photo sat front and center on the registration table. "He got hurt at his job, and can't work any more. The money from this ride is going to help his family pay the bills."

Tess frowned. "Does he have kids?"

"Three, I think. Around your age. Little younger, maybe."

Her lips pinched together as she took in the information, and Lucy patted her shoulder.

"That there's Mike," the lady at the table said, gesturing toward the picture. "We sure appreciate you coming out for him today, and so does he."

"Glad to help, ma'am," Lenny said.

He forked over our fifteen-dollar-a-person charge (with a little extra tucked in, if I saw right) and we received our poker sheets. During the ride we'd travel to four more spots they'd outlined on a map, all with tables manned by members of the Montgomery County chapter. At each spot we'd pick a card from a deck and write it on our sheet, and at the end of the day, whoever rode in with the best "hand" would win a prize.

"Go on over to that table," the lady said, "and pick your first card."

We followed her directions to a card table where a man in a chapter T-shirt sat with a deck of cards spread out before him.

"Choose a card, any card," he bellowed.

Lenny went first, emitting a growl at his four of hearts. Lucy picked a jack of spades, which Lenny threatened to steal. She smiled and tossed it back onto the table, where the man shuffled it back in with the rest of the deck.

"Go ahead, partner," I said to Tess.

She reached out tentatively, her lips twisted to the side in concentration. When she finally made her pick, she held out an ace of diamonds. "Is that good?"

Laughing, we assured her it was. I took my turn, pulling out an unremarkable eight of spades.

The guy at the table initialed our sheets and sent us on our way. I tucked my paper into my jacket pocket and helped Tess put hers away in her jeans.

"Here we go," Lenny said.

The trip was well-marked and pleasant, and with our multiple layers we all were able to stay warm. At first Tess kept such a tight grip on my jacket I was afraid we wouldn't be able to unclench her fingers once we got to the final stop, but by the time we pulled into Valley Forge Beef and Ale a couple hours later she was much more relaxed, and enjoying herself.

We meandered over to the final card table, stretching and trying to slap some life back into our rear ends.

"Ready for your cards?" the lady at the table asked. She waved us over.

"Not that it makes much difference," Lenny muttered.

"Oh, poor baby," the lady said, looking at his sheet. "Didn't get nothing, did you?"

And he didn't this time, either, pulling a ten of clubs.

Lucy ended up with a pair of jacks, which at least was something, but Tess was the one to watch.

"Ooo, two aces and two nines," the lady said. "Come on, darlin', see what you can do."

Tess' fingers hovered over the cards, until she plucked one from the bottom of the pile.

"Ah, darn it," the lady said. "A queen don't help much, does it? But you've still got two pair, aces high. Wouldn't surprise me if you got a prize."

Tess grinned as the lady initialed her sheet.

I got another eight, but seeing how the pair was joined by three completely different cards, I didn't think I'd be receiving much of anything.

"Lenny Spruce!" A little old man trotted over, his hand outstretched.

Lenny took the hand and gave the man a hug with his other arm, dwarfing him. "Dennis, my man, what's happening?"

"Didn't get shit for my poker hand, but we got a nice ride in. Sheila's around here somewhere. You folks gonna get something to eat?"

"That's the plan. Dennis, this here's my fiancée, Lucy Lapp. We're tying the knot this Saturday."

"My pleasure, my pleasure," Dennis said, shaking her hand. "You are either a very lucky woman or a very brave one. Maybe both. I can tell just by looking at you that Lenny here's getting the better part of the deal."

Lucy laughed, obviously not quite sure how to take the comments.

"And this?" Dennis turned to Tess and gently took her hand.

"Lucy's daughter, Tess. She just turned nine. And you've probably seen Stella around."

"Sure." He gripped my hand and smiled. "Oh, here she is. Sheila honey! Look who I found." After she hugged Lenny Dennis gave the introductions, somehow remembering everyone's name. "They're gonna join us for lunch. Right, Len?"

Lenny laughed and looked at Lucy, who nodded her okay.

"Then let's go eat," Dennis said. "I'm about starved."

We'd gotten seated with salads in front of us, Dennis gabbing all the while, when he said, "You folks hear about the Tom Copper concert the other night in Philly?"

"Hear about it?" Lenny said. "We were there."

"No kiddin'. So were we, weren't we, honey?"

Sheila smiled, but I had yet to hear her say anything. I guess Dennis talked enough for both of them.

"'Bout lost Sheila here when the grand exodus happened, but I managed to keep a hold of her belt loop. Good thing she was wearing jeans or I'd'a lost her. What do you guys hear about the bomb and the dead body and all?"

Lucy sucked in her breath and Dennis slapped a hand over his mouth. "Sorry, ma'am, forgot about the little one."

"I'm not little," Tess said.

"Of course you're not," Dennis said. "But moms protect their kids and don't like bigmouths like me saying stupid things. I'm right sorry about blurtin' that out."

How could Lucy be mad at him after that?

"Anyhoo," Dennis said, "you folks hear anything?"

"Just that the lady in question was part of the band," Lenny said. I guess Lucy hadn't had time to fill him in on Jordan's involvement, which was fine with me. If Dennis got a hold of that, the entire suburban area would know it by nightfall. "Don't know nothing about the bomb."

"Yeah, us either," Dennis said.

"Do you know much about the band?" I asked. "Like why they switched drummers last year?"

Dennis looked at his wife. "Didn't we read something about that not too long ago? In a magazine or something?"

"The paper," Sheila said. I restrained myself from shouting, "She talks!"

"That's right," Dennis said. "There was an article in the *Inquirer* last year when they came out with their new album. Last one with the old drummer. *Blue Copper?* Forget what the article said, though. You remember, honey?"

Sheila shook her head.

We leaned back in our seats as our waitress put our main courses in front of us, the smell alone enough to shut up even Dennis as he tucked into his burger. But not for long.

"All I remember is," Dennis said around a mouthful, "it was his choice. The old drummer, I mean. He left 'cause he wanted to, not 'cause they made him. Burnout, maybe? Not sure how the new guy got in, though."

"What about the office manager who's missing?" I asked. "Know anything about that?"

He shook his head. "Probably just took off with the money. Can't trust anybody these days. Might be he even has ties with the Mafia. You never know anymore."

And the Mafia did have a big firefight that was putting off Genna's autopsy. I hadn't heard that Baronne was one of the casualties, but that didn't mean he wasn't involved. I wondered if Detective Alexander has paused for even a moment in his quest to nab Jordan to consider that possibility.

"Stella and I let the cows out this morning," Lucy said. Her pointed look at the rest of us made it clear it was time to move on to other subjects. We did.

By the time we were done with dessert, which Dennis insisted on buying for us, it was mid-afternoon. We were standing outside, the guys picking their teeth with toothpicks, when I saw another familiar face.

"Jermaine!" I made my way through the parking lot to where he was standing by his Fat Boy. "Wasn't expecting to see you out today."

"What? Because of Jordan?" He rolled his shoulders, loosening them. "I spent all day yesterday and half of last night trying to get in touch with him, not to mention staying up with him all night Friday. I'm sorry for him and all, but he's gotta make the next move. I can't put my life on hold forever." He peeled off his riding gloves and tucked them into a saddlebag. "If I hadn't gotten called in to work security that night, I wouldn't know any more than anybody else. And I don't know much, as it is."

Join the club.

"What's the story on your getting brought in to work the concert, anyway?"

He scratched his face, obviously not shaved in the past day or so. "The head of security called in sick at the last minute. Must've been pretty bad if he'd do that. One of the other guys had to step up to that job, so they needed another body. Jordan heard somebody talking about it and gave them my name. Since I have some experience and passed their little test, I got the job. Shoulda been an easy gig, since they have such a good security team."

"I guess you haven't heard any more about the bomb?"

"Not a word. The cops came around to ask me about stuff, but didn't tell me anything in return."

"Sounds familiar. So how's Ma?"

"Ready to pop. Vernice is over at her place now with Lavina, trying to get her mind off things."

If anybody could distract Ma, it would be Jermaine's cute little girl, currently the youngest Granger grandchild.

"Don't suppose you know anything more about the office manager that disappeared, do you?"

He shook his head. "Like I told you, the only time I talked with him was to sign my contract for the night. After that, I never saw him again. And nobody's asked me about him. 'Cept you."

Three guys from our HOG club came up, greeting me. "You about ready for some chow, Granger? We're going in."

He looked at me, and I waved. "I gotta get back to my gang, anyway. See you later."

He left and I found my three at the card table, where Tess' poker hand was temporarily listed on the board in second place, after a flush.

Tess skipped toward me. "The lady says if I stay in second I'll get a prize!"

"Cool beans. When will you know?"

"Final rider has to be in in an hour," Lucy said. "They said they'll call if we're not here anymore."

"You know," the lady at the table said, winking at Tess, "I can't imagine there will be anybody else beating you out. And even if they do you should get the prize for being the youngest rider. Why don't you come on over here and pick a prize from the table?"

Tess looked to Lucy for approval, which of course she gave. We followed her over to the selection.

She took a few minutes looking through the stash, which included a couple of T-shirts, a mug that read *When I die, I'm riding my HOG to heaven*, a stuffed pig with a leather jacket, and a silver cigarette lighter. The prize that caught Tess' eye, though, was a leather skull cap with *Harley-Davidson* embroidered on the front.

"You're sure, honey?" Lucy asked, apparently not quite sure herself.

"Can I have it? Pleeeease?"

Lucy studied her for a moment. "All right. If that's what you want. Need some help putting it on?"

So we rode home, Tess pleased as punch to have her new skull cap flattening her hair under her helmet, and the rest of us weary but pleased to have had such a nice ride. It had been a lovely day.

We pulled into the driveway and rode around the white Chevy truck sitting in front of the house. We parked and turned off the bikes.

"Who's that?" Lucy asked.

I watched the man sit up in the front seat of the truck, where he'd apparently been taking a nap.

I took a deep breath and let it out. "Thank God. It's Jordan."

Chapter Eight

Lenny took off in a roar, having promised Bart he'd check in at the shop before heading home, and Lucy herded Tess into the house, where she'd get her busy with something before figuring out our after-milking supper. I walked up to Jordan's truck, where he leaned against the front bumper. Queenie snuffled around my feet, and I reached down to pet her.

"Your family's worried sick about you," I said.

Jordan made a face. "I know."

He looked like hell, his hair greasy, his eyes sunken above dark circles. His skin was pale almost to the color of his truck, and I wondered when he'd last eaten.

I sat beside him, crossing my ankles on the gravel. "Where have you been?"

He leaned forward, his hands pressed against the steel under him. "Here and there."

I waited, but nothing else was forthcoming. "I heard you hung out at the police station for a while on Friday night."

"Yeah."

"Saying Genna was your fiancée."

He kicked at a stone. "I guess."

"Is it true?"

His eyes flicked up toward me, but didn't stay. "Unofficially. But don't tell Ma."

"She already knows."

He lurched off the bumper and took a few steps away, running his hands over his face and through his hair. Lowering his arms, he turned toward me. "What's she doing?"

"What you'd expect. Trying to get in touch with you. Threatening to head off to Philly to find you herself. You know."

"Yeah. I know." He came back to the truck and leaned over it, resting his elbows on the hood. "God, I feel awful."

"Come on. Let's get you inside. You need something to eat."

"I'm not hungry."

"Maybe not. But you're gonna keel over if you don't put something in your stomach."

He dropped his face onto his arms, then pushed himself up. "Okay. But you're not going to make me call Ma, are you?"

I studied him. "Let's just get you inside and fed. We'll see what happens next. Deal?"

He nodded, and I got up to turn toward the sidewalk. "Stella?" His voice was quiet.

"Yeah?"

"The band's having a memorial service tomorrow. For Genna. Will you go with me?"

I looked at him. "You're sure?"

"Please. I need you."

He had seven brothers, six of which were in the area. Five sisters-in-law. And Ma. Ma, I could understand not wanting to take to the memorial service for the woman he loved. She was his mother, after all, and he'd want to be treated like an adult, not a protected child. But why not the others?

"I take it no one else in your family knows the truth about you and Genna?"

"Not from me. Well, except for Jermaine."

"And in the band?"

He laughed, but it was a sad sound. "Everyone in the band knows about me and Genna, in some way. At least they think they do. But everyone also thinks she's still...she *was* Ricky's girlfriend."

I winced. "What did she ever see in him, anyway?" But I knew. That bad boy, good body, rock-and-roll star thing was what she saw. It took her a while to see the good boy, ordinarily handsome, blue-collar guy standing in front of me.

"Don't ask me that," Jordan said.

We walked side by side up the walk, Queenie trotting along behind.

"So where have you been?" I asked again. "Other than the police station?"

He blew his bangs off his forehead. "Outside the club, in my truck, stopped off at my place for a while."

"Didn't think to check your answering machine? Or your cell?"

"Didn't want to. I knew what would be on them."

His family, wanting to make sure he was okay. Maybe Ricky. But not the only person he truly *wanted* to hear from.

I stopped, my hand on the door handle. "Do they know yet how it happened?"

He breathed through his nose. "No. Can you believe they're doing some gangsters first? The freaking Mafia?"

"I heard." I pushed open the door and led him inside.

Lucy came out from the kitchen. "Hey, Jordan."

He swallowed. "Hey, Lucy. Just so you know, the band's still planning to play your wedding on Saturday. They'll honor the contract. And I'll do the sound at the church."

"I'm not worried about that, I'm worried about you." But I saw the relief in her eyes.

"He needs food," I said.

"Yes," she said, "he does."

I sat him in one of the kitchen chairs, and Lucy put a glass of orange juice in front of him.

"Drink," she said.

He took a sip.

"Now finish that while I make you a sandwich."

He took another swallow. "Yes, ma'am."

I leaned against the counter and watched Lucy layer turkey, cheese, and lettuce on some of her oatmeal bread. It looked good, but I was still stuffed from our late lunch.

It took Jordan a minute to get going on the sandwich, but once he started I'd lay bets he set a record in speed eating.

"Another one?" Lucy asked.

"Better not," he said.

I glanced at a Tupperware container on the counter. "How about some of your brownies, Luce?"

She grabbed the box and tossed it beside Jordan. "All yours."

He didn't say no. Along with the glass of milk Lucy poured him, he finished off the entire batch.

"You know the cops are interested in you," I said when he'd finished.

Jordan jerked his chin up. "In *me?* What for?"

"For everything. The bomb, Genna…"

"Genna?" His face went back to its pre-meal color, and I was afraid I'd shared the news too quickly.

"They say someone heard you arguing before the concert. They're making it seem like a big deal."

He looked across the room, toward the feed store calendar hanging above the phone.

"Jordan? Is it true?"

"We…talked. Maybe it got a little loud. But I didn't think anyone heard us."

"What were you talking about?"

He snapped his head toward me, and Lucy glared at me from across the kitchen.

"I'm not trying to be nosy, Jordan," I said. "Really. But could someone have heard something important?"

He picked up his glass, drained the last few drops of milk, and set it back down. "It was important to me. To us. But not anyone else's business." He stood up and pushed his chair in. "Thank you for the food, Lucy. I do feel better."

"You're welcome." She put a hand on his arm, then took his plate and glass to the counter.

I got up. "I'll walk you out."

"Whatever."

Queenie met us on the sidewalk, and Jordan absently let his hand fall onto her head. She licked his fingers, and he jumped, as if surprised to remember where he was.

"You going home?" I asked him.

He sighed. "I guess."

"You'll let your family know you're okay?"

"I'll let them know I'm back. I'm not sure I'm okay."

I watched his hunched shoulders as he turned toward his truck. "Want me to drive to the memorial service tomorrow?" I asked.

He stopped. "Sure."

"What time should I pick you up?"

He stared at the barn so long I thought he'd forgotten what I'd asked. "Eleven-ish?" he finally said.

"I'll be there. At your house. Oh, and Jordan?"

"Yeah?"

"Call a lawyer. The cops are going to find you, and they're not going to be sympathetic."

He bit his lips together. "I didn't *do* anything."

"I know that."

He closed his eyes and tipped his head back, blowing out a gush of air. "Fine. Any suggestions?"

"Actually, yes. Hang on."

I trotted to my office and scribbled the number of David Crockett, a lawyer I'd met at a HOG event last summer. He'd already helped Lenny out of a jam, and I was sure he'd be able to help now.

I jogged back outside and handed the paper to Jordan. "Don't talk to the cops without him."

He took the paper, and without another word got into his truck and drove away.

Chapter Nine

The cows were remarkably willing to re-enter the barn for milking. I guess they really did feel the call to empty their tight udders. But they were eager to get back outside when they were done, and scurried away (if grown cows can scurry) as soon as their collars were unclipped.

"You know evenings are my job," Lucy said, scraping some sodden newspaper onto the manure conveyor.

I tossed some clean bedding into a nearby stall. "Yeah, I know. But what else am I going to do?"

She paused, leaning on her pitchfork. "Anything you need to figure out before, say, Saturday?"

Oh.

"Clothing stores aren't open this time of night," I said. "Especially on Sundays."

She gave me a level look.

I feigned surprise. "They are? I guess I wouldn't know."

"No." She stuck her pitchfork into another lump of paper. "I guess you wouldn't."

I spread out my remaining bedding and went to get some more. When I came back I said, "I'll figure something out, Luce. Really."

She didn't answer. I wasn't sure if that was a good thing or not.

Once we made it inside, washed up, and ate, I was feeling the effects of Friday night's lost sleep. I said goodnight to Lucy and

Tess and went upstairs. Nick still hadn't called, and I wasn't sure what to do about that. I stared at the phone, willing it to ring.

But the next sound I heard was my alarm clock, telling me it was time to get up and start another day.

Jordan still wasn't on the news, which was a good thing, but the bomb and Genna's murder had practically disappeared, which wasn't. They were mentioned in passing, when the call went out that Robert "Bobby" Baronne was still missing, but only because they were associated with the time frame of when he disappeared. The dead Mafia guys, being more newsworthy, apparently, got at least two minutes of air time.

A few of the cows lay in their stalls in the barn, but this morning I needed Queenie to help me round up the rest of the herd from the pasture. I was still slapping the flanks of a last lazy few when Zach arrived, dropped off by his dad. He didn't usually work weekday mornings, but his school was closed for a teacher development day, or something.

"You wanna get them clipped in?" I said.

He started on one aisle while I did another. We worked in silence until we met at the end of the row.

"Jordan's home," he said.

"Oh?"

He squinted at me. "I thought you knew. At least, he said so."

"Right. I just didn't know that you knew I knew."

He nodded slowly, clearly thinking I was being a weird adult. "I'll get the buckets."

"Great. You do that."

He didn't talk to me again for a while.

I spread out the hay and distributed the grain while Zach milked. When I finished I went and stood beside him while he wiped off Lady's udder. Seemed I was always looming over him while he was doing this.

"So did you actually see Jordan last night?" I asked.

He glanced up. "Huh-uh. Jermaine called to say Jordan was back, and my dad and mom drove over to his place."

"What did they say? How was he?"

He looked at me again. "You saw him."

"I know. I just wondered what they said."

He sat back on his haunches, his elbows resting on his knees. "They said he looked terrible, like he hadn't slept since Friday. And that he told them all to just leave him alone."

I was afraid of that. "Anything else?"

He made a last swipe at Lady's teats and stood up. "Not that they're telling me."

So nothing about the police interrogating him or anything.

We finished up and headed outside, where Zach helped me check the silos that had been emptied over the winter. We'd soon be filling them again, and they needed to be ready. We worked for about an hour until the milk truck came, and I went over to make sure the driver had everything he needed.

Lucy and Tess were in their vegetable patch, Lucy planting tomatoes and Tess putting cages around them. Lucy was determined to have the crops entirely in before the weekend, so she could go on her honeymoon free of guilt. Knowing her, she'd still feel guilty about leaving me on my own, but at least she'd know the garden was in good shape.

A little while later Zach and I had seen off the milk truck and were sitting in the side yard drinking lemonade and taking turns wrestling with Queenie when a police cruiser pulled into the drive. I watched it come with growing tension, until it stopped and Detective Willard got out.

"Break time?" he said.

"Yeah. Want some?"

He looked at the glass I held up. "What is it?"

"Lemonade."

His eyes lit up. "Lucy's homemade?"

"You called it."

"I'd love some."

Zach drained his cup. "I'll get it. I need a refill, anyway."

"Here," I said. "Fill me up, too."

He grabbed my glass and went inside.

Willard stuck his hands in his pockets and surveyed the farm.

"What's with the cop car?" I asked. "And the uniform?"

He looked down at his clothes. "I'm heading to do security for a big library function. Special fund-raiser tea thing, with some cash involved."

"Why are you, Mr. Fancy Detective, pulling guard duty?"

He smiled. "I do my share of grunt work. Keeps the officers on my side." He sank to the ground beside me and rested his elbows on his knees.

"Glad you didn't bring your little buddy Alexander today," I said.

Willard grimaced. "He's no buddy. But as a favor to the Philadelphia police I did tour guide duty." He looked sideways at me. "And I'm here today to ask something else."

I glanced back to make sure Zach was still inside. "What?"

"Do you have any idea if Jordan knows Robert Baronne?"

"The guy who's missing?"

He nodded.

"I guess he probably does. I mean, working at the club and all, he'd at least know who he was. Why? Does Alexander think Jordan had time to kidnap Baronne at the same time he was murdering Genna and trying to blow up the club?" I couldn't keep the sarcasm from my voice.

Willard held a hand up. "He's just covering all the angles."

"Yeah, yeah, whatever. So why are you asking?"

He was quiet for a moment, but he looked like he wanted to tell me. I waited him out.

"Seems like Jordan's been talking on the phone to Mr. Baronne," Willard said. "A few times last week, including the morning of the concert."

"So what? Baronne worked at the club. Jordan is the band's sound man. Wouldn't it be a natural thing for them to be talking logistics?"

Willard plucked a long grass strand and put it between his lips, talking out of the side of his mouth. "It would."

"And I'm sure Baronne was talking to lots of other people, too."

"He was."

"So there's something else?"

He raised his eyebrows, not looking at me.

"What?" I said.

He took the grass out of his mouth. "Jordan say anything to you about arguing with Baronne before the concert?"

"Oh, good lord."

The screen door slapped shut, and we stopped talking while Zach came out and handed us each full cups. I took mine and downed half of it.

"I'll be out helping Lucy till you're ready for me again," Zach said.

I nodded. "Thanks, buddy."

Willard held up his cup in a salute. "Thanks for the drink."

Zach loped to the garden, sipping as he went.

"Nice boy," Willard said.

I ignored him. "So not only was Jordan fighting with Genna before the show, he was also fighting with Baronne? Anybody he wasn't fighting with, according to your sources?"

"These things are coming to us—"

"And Alexander's not looking for them? Give me a break."

Willard's mouth straightened into a hard line, and his eyes grew thoughtful.

"What?" I said. "There's something else, isn't there?"

He sighed, dropping his head.

"Come *on*."

He raised his face and looked at me straight on. "You keep reminding me that Jordan is the Tom Copper Band's sound man."

I lifted a shoulder. "He is. That's why he was there."

"Well, you see, that's the problem."

I stared at him. "Why would that be a problem? It's a legiti-mate occupation."

"I know that. But the thing is… You know the bomb? The one the building was evacuated for?"

"Of course."

"It was rigged up as part of the sound system."

Chapter Ten

The memorial service was not at a church. Instead, Jordan and I pulled into the packed driveway of Tom Copper's beautiful stone house in New Hope, a haven amid the tourists and antique shops and traffic. We hadn't talked much on the way down, me a bit freaked out by Willard's revelation, Jordan in his own world. I wanted to ask Jordan about the sound system, if he'd noticed anything unusual, why there'd been that delay before the second set, how those cables Annie had taped down had come unsecured. But he wasn't really with me in spirit, and I figured it could wait until our ride home.

I sat in the truck, awestruck at Tom Copper's green yard, which lay fenced in by stone and framed by tall oaks and blooming fruit trees. This all fronted the house like a movie set from *Gone with the Wind*, although I guess that would've been a different sort of house. A glimpse of the back yard promised a lot of space, too; several acres, at least. Beside the house, about twenty yards away, stood a small old barn, with two horses in a fenced-in paddock eating something out of people's hands.

"I guess Tom has done well for himself," I said.

We got out of the truck and started up the flagstone walk.

"The band used to be just a local college group," Jordan said. "But their fan base grew like crazy when they began touring out of town. Makes the home crowd think you're a more valuable commodity when other people are listening, too." He smiled crookedly. "You know that old saying, 'You don't know what you've got till it's gone.'" He swallowed, obviously thinking of something other than the band. "Now whenever the band plays locally it's to a sold-out crowd."

We walked around the house, making our way to the back yard, which was just as big as I'd guessed. There must've been over a hundred people spread out on the lawn, blankets under them. Several circles of occupied chairs also dotted the space. A long buffet table sat under a tent, filled with an assortment of goodies from quiche to cherry tarts to melting Brie. The music of the Tom Copper Band spilled from two large speakers at either end of the enclosure, Genna's voice in the mix. Several large coolers held beer, water, and soda packed in ice, with open wine bottles on a small table beside them. People in the yard balanced plates on their laps, their soda cans and beer bottles on the ground beside them.

"Hungry?" I asked Jordan.

He didn't answer.

A group of people to our right burst out in laughter while one man jumped up, his pant leg wet with whatever drink had spilled.

"You think they even remember why they're here?" Jordan asked, his voice quiet.

"Makes you wonder." I looked around, trying to find someone who looked appropriately sad. "Is there anybody you want to talk to?"

"Not yet."

We stood there a little longer while he studied the people, until I realized one group was staring at us. I stared back until I saw a few familiar faces. Ricky was at the center of the now-silent cluster, being comforted, I was sure, by the attentive young women surrounding him. I recognized Marley, the dark-haired girl from the concert, sitting at his left elbow, gazing into his face. Annie, the smaller, blonder one, sat next to her friend. She looked from Ricky to Jordan, her face unreadable. Ricky's expression, however, was plain. He pushed his way up from the blanket and stalked over to Jordan.

"You're not here to cause problems, I hope," Ricky said. Jordan sighed, not looking at him. "You know I'm not."

"Because Genna was *my* girlfriend, you know. Not yours." Jordan looked at Ricky, and for a moment I thought he was going to tell the bastard his little secret about being engaged to his "girlfriend."

"I'm sorry for your loss," Jordan said. "I'm so glad to see you have plenty of other girls to ease your pain."

Ricky's mouth twitched. "Yeah, well, just don't try to make this into your show. Because it's not."

"Wouldn't dream of it," Jordan said.

One of the girls from Ricky's posse came up and put her hand through his elbow. She looked me up and down, conveying the impression that she wasn't sure what on earth I was doing there. "You okay, Ricky?" she asked.

He broke eye contact with Jordan and looked down at her. "Sure, yeah, I'm okay. Just chatting with a friend." He turned back to Jordan. "I'll see you later. If you decide to stick around."

Jordan regarded him stonily as he situated himself back among his groupies. Ricky said something we couldn't hear, and the girls had a round of tittering, stealing glances at Jordan and me. I wanted to slap some sense into them, but realized it wouldn't teach them anything. Annie, at least, looked like she had the sense to be embarrassed by the little scene.

The group beside us, the guy with the wet pants sitting down again, had stopped their laughing. Now they were in the midst of a loud rendition of "Kum-By-Ya."

"Come on," Jordan said. "Let's see if we can find anyone who actually cared about Genna."

We'd only taken a few steps when a young woman flew up and threw her arms around Jordan. I grabbed his arm to keep him from falling backward, and held on until he got stabilized. The girl sobbed into his shoulder loud enough the group beside us cut off their song mid-verse.

"Come on, San, honey," Jordan said. He gently picked her up, swinging her legs into his arms, and carried her back toward the house, where a few seats sat vacant on the patio. Once away from prying eyes he eased onto a wrought-iron loveseat, cuddling the girl on his lap. He allowed her to cry herself out, his own eyes remaining dry. I wasn't sure if he was all done crying, or if his grief was still too raw for tears.

I took a seat close by, not sure exactly where I should be looking or what I should be doing. My sole reason for coming was to support Jordan, but it was kind of hard to do that with a woman on his lap.

The girl, from what I could see, was small, her black hair pulled up in a messy bunch. There was no way to be sure how old she was from that angle, but I guessed her to be in her early twenties. If she was merely another groupie, she'd taken this a lot harder than the other female fans.

Finally she quieted, and I'd almost decided she'd gone to sleep when she hiccupped and scooted off Jordan's lap onto the other end of the loveseat. Jordan kept his arm around her, and she leaned the top of her head on his chin.

She suddenly noticed I was there, and jerked upright.

"That's Stella," Jordan said. "A friend of mine from home. She's cool with everything."

The girl looked at me with wide eyes, obviously unsure about my presence.

"This is San Powell," Jordan said to me. "Genna's sister."

"Oh," I said. "I'm so sorry for…for what's happened."

She shrank even further under Jordan's arm. "Can I…can I just talk to Jordan?"

Jordan winced, but I stood and patted him on the shoulder. "Of course. I'll be around when you need me, Jordan."

His eyes told me thank you, and I walked quietly away. San obviously needed a loving hand right now, and not some stranger taking the attention of the person she wanted.

At a loss among the crowd, I spotted the buffet table and realized I was hungry. It was noon, after all, and I hadn't eaten anything since a half a bagel after milking.

I loaded my plate with cheese, French bread, and little spinach quiches, then stopped to study a small arrangement of photos on an adjoining table. The photos showed the range of Genna's lifetime: as a toddler in a wading pool, as a teen-ager—with another girl I assumed was San—and with Ricky in front of the Art Institute of Philadelphia. I was leaning over to check out a photo of her on stage somewhere when I felt someone next to me.

"Finding what you need?" Tom Copper asked.

I stared at him for a moment, words escaping me. Even in this situation his celebrity was a bit tongue-tying.

"You're here with Jordan, right?" he asked. "Didn't he introduce us one time?"

"Friday night," I finally said. "Before the concert. Backstage."

He slapped his thigh. "That's right. Can't forget that tattoo."

I reached up to touch the steer head on my neck. "Yeah. It's a memory trigger."

He grinned. "Why don't you come join us? We're sitting over there." He gestured toward a small group at a lone round table under the far corner of the tent. I recognized LeRoy, the bassist, his big smile non-existent today as he leaned back in his chair, his hand loosely around a beer bottle. A woman I didn't know sat beside Donny, the guitarist. Her eyes were red and swollen, I guessed from crying.

"If you're sure," I said.

He picked up a red pepper cream cheese cracker thing and gestured me along with him. The group looked up at us.

"You guys remember…Stella, right?"

I nodded, dumbfounded. *Tom Copper* had remembered my name.

"Jordan brought her backstage Friday night," Copper said.

Recognition lit both guys' eyes.

"And this is my wife, Tonya." Copper put his hand on the woman's shoulder. "She and Genna go way back."

"We have pictures of us playing in a wading pool, diapers hanging down. There's one on the display over there." Tonya smiled crookedly, her eyes tearing up. She swiped at them with a tissue she had crumpled in her hand. "Sorry. I think I'm okay, then it hits me again."

"Please, don't worry." I hesitated by the table, not sure I should really intrude on these people's grief.

Tom pulled out a chair, the one next to LeRoy. "Have a seat."

I sat.

"So you're friends with Jordan?" Tonya asked. "He brought you to the concert where you met these guys?"

"Known him ever since I was little," I said. "Although not since the diaper stage. He got us the tickets for Friday. He also connected the band with my friends who are getting married this weekend."

"That couple up in Sellersville?"

"Right."

She dabbed at her eyes again. "Sorry. Here I go again."

Donny reached like he was going to put a hand on her shoulder, but Tom beat him to it, laying his arm on the back of her chair and rubbing her neck. "It's okay, hon. Nobody expects you to be any different."

"Hey," LeRoy said. "Isn't that Parker?"

We looked and saw the band's old drummer coming from the house. He passed by Jordan and San, glancing at them, then stopped at the top of the patio steps to search the yard. LeRoy waved until he caught Parker's eye, and their former drummer picked his way through the crowd toward us.

"I was curious," I said. "How come you switched drummers, especially since Parker's still friends with you guys?"

"He got tired," Tom said.

"Of what?"

"Everything, I guess. Being a drummer is a physically demanding job. All that equipment to haul around, and he's not getting any younger. Are you, Park?"

Parker pulled a chair into the circle from outside the tent and plopped into it. "Am I what?"

"Tom here's saying you're too old to play with us anymore," LeRoy said.

"Hey, now," Tom said. "Let's keep it in context."

Parker laughed. "The thing is, it's true. These old bones aren't up to all the touring crap for even one more day."

"Oh, come on," Donny said. "You ain't any older than the rest of us."

"I don't see you hauling a dozen pieces of equipment around. You just have one sorry-ass guitar."

"It can get heavy," Donny said.

I put my hands up. "Sorry I asked."

Tom jerked his thumb toward me. "Remember Stella, Park? Jordan introduced her the other night."

Parker looked at me. "Sure. Sure, I remember. And you're wondering why I quit?"

"Yeah, I guess."

"That really is the reason. My body can't take it. Plus, everybody in the business—well, besides these guys—treats us drummers like shit. Like we're a lesser species."

"Most drummers are," LeRoy said.

Tom laughed. "It's true. I remember this one drummer I played with before Park here. We could practice a song a dozen times and I still had to jump on him to tell him where to end the freaking piece. Had no touch whatsoever." He nodded to Parker. "This guy has what it takes. Intuition, brains. He can play the drums like you'd play any other instrument, with dynamics and a good feel for the music. He can control the way a band plays."

"Aw," Parker said. "You're making me feel all gushy inside."

Tom smiled. "I mean it, though."

"What about the guy you have now?" I asked.

They looked at each other.

"Ricky's a good drummer," Tom finally said.

"Not as good as Parker," LeRoy said.

Tom made a face. "Yeah. He's not too smart."

"And he ain't Parker, personality-wise, either," Donny said. "I mean, look at him."

We looked. Ricky was still in the midst of the groupie girls, although now he was standing up, swaying with a girl to one of the band's ballads being played over the stereo.

"You'd think this was a regular party," Donny said. He took a swig of beer and slammed it on the table.

Tonya made a growling sound. "He's an ass. I *told* Genna…" She stopped, the tissue once again finding its way to her eyes.

"We know, sweetheart, we know." Tom patted her back.

LeRoy cleared his throat. "Genna was a big girl, Tonya. And I think she was on her way to making some better choices."

The guys looked at me. I opened my mouth, then shut it again. I wasn't about to gossip with these guys about Jordan when I really didn't know anything. Anything official, anyway.

"I'm real sorry about Genna," Parker said to Tonya. "I wanted to get here today to make sure you knew that."

She nodded, sniffling.

We sat awkwardly, Tonya grabbing a napkin from the table and switching it with her sodden tissue.

"Touring's also hard on you emotionally," Parker said into the conversation gap. "I needed a chance to stay home. Do something steady."

"You guys tour a lot?" I asked. I knew they'd done some, but had no idea of their schedule.

"Oh, yeah," LeRoy said. "We spend a good chunk of time on the road. Starts to get to you after a while."

"It's amazing we're all still friends, actually," Donny said.

Tom grunted. "You mean just 'cause you can't sleep without that damn whistle your nose does?"

"It's no worse than the way LeRoy gnaws on those sunflower seeds all the time," Donny said. "It's hell cleaning up the van."

"What?" LeRoy said. "Tom's the one who has to get up at the break of dawn to do that horseshit yoga."

Parker smiled at me. "See? I don't have to worry about any of that anymore."

"Plus," Tom said, "we're moving on with our lives. I've got Tonya now, and maybe one of these guys will get lucky enough one of these days to find a woman who will have them."

"Hey, now!" LeRoy said. "There's all those beautiful groupie girls all the time."

They laughed.

"Yeah, right," Donny said. He rolled his eyes in an exaggerated circle, but the tightness around his mouth didn't match the attempt at humor.

I remembered Allison, the wedding shop girl, talking about being one of the groupie girls. "You guys aren't into them anymore, huh?"

LeRoy wrinkled his nose. "Nah. You start to realize that no matter how much those girls fawn over you, how much they adore you, they're going to do the same thing the next week with the next band, no matter who they are."

"There's two types of girls," Tom said. "The kind that get turned on by the whole rock star thing—you know, want to say they slept with you, or whatever—and the ones who get turned on by the music. You learn real quick that the first kind will just burn you out. The second kind, the ones who appreciate your work, just want to talk about music. They're cool. In fact, that's how Tonya and I met."

"Yeah," LeRoy said. "All you guys ever do is talk about music. None of that nooky stuff."

Tonya even smiled at that. I couldn't help but notice that Donny didn't. Instead, he gripped his beer bottle with whitened knuckles and ran a finger around the rim.

"What about those girls I saw backstage?" I asked. "Marley? And Annie?"

"Oh, them," Tom said. "Annie helps out with sound and stuff."

My mind flashed to Willard, and his pronouncement that the bomb was rigged to the sound system. Could that little groupie have done it?

"Marley likes the music, too," Tom said.

Tonya snorted. "I don't think that's all she likes."

I didn't think so, either, after seeing her at Ricky's side today.

"I'm going to get another water," Tonya said. "Anybody else want anything?"

Donny glanced at Tom, then stood up and stretched. "I'll come with you. I need something to eat."

They left, Tom watching as they approached the buffet table.

"She doesn't like Marley?" I asked.

Tom turned back toward me. "Marley's been hanging around for a while. And she'll probably be filling in for Genna until we find somebody permanent."

"She's that good?"

LeRoy gave a short laugh.

"No," Tom said. "She's not. But she knows all the songs, and she's available. We'll make do with her for the next couple gigs. She won't be Genna, but…" His face crumpled, but he got it under control.

I stood, feeling my time with them was up. "I think I'll go find Jordan, see how he's doing."

Tom nodded, and swiped a finger under his nose. "Yeah. Poor guy."

I wondered what his version of "Jordan and Genna" was. And what exactly the deal was with Donny and his feelings about Tonya. His heart wasn't exactly on his sleeve, but it was pretty darn close.

I nodded to LeRoy and Parker and made my way back up the yard, toward the patio. Jordan was gone, but San still sat on the loveseat, her knees pulled up to her chest. Her eyes were dry now, but I imagined it wouldn't take much to set her off again.

"You looking for Jordy?" she asked.

Jordy? "Yeah."

"He went inside for a minute. He'll be back."

I sat on the chair, hoping I wasn't intruding on her space.

"So what kind of name is San?" I asked.

She hiccupped. A laugh, I guess. "My name's actually Janet, but Genna couldn't say that when I was born. She called me San. It stuck." She sniffed, and I could see her jaw working.

Great. I'd brought up another memory about Genna. Way to go.

"So you just met Genna the other night?" San asked, her hiccups gone. She rested her head sideways on her knees, making her look even younger than before.

"Friday. Jordan took a friend and me backstage at the concert. I didn't talk to her, though, except to say hi."

She sighed and looked out over the yard. "I didn't talk to her that night, either. I wasn't even at the concert."

"Seen enough of them?"

"No." She pinched her lips together. "I was mad at her. Told her if she was going to throw away her life with that...that asshole over there—" she jutted her chin toward Ricky's gaggle of groupie girls "—I wasn't going to support it. Skipping the concert was my first act of tough love." Her voice caught, and she put her face on her knees.

I figured I should probably do something, like pat her shoulder, but I've never been good with crying women. I don't cry enough myself to know what would really help. Instead, I searched vainly for Jordan, who San had promised would soon return.

When he was nowhere to be found, I plunged back into conversation, hoping it would help. "Did you get to know Jordan through Genna?"

She sniffled again and rubbed her wet cheeks on her jeans. "Yeah. He's the main reason I was so pissed at her for staying with Ricky. Why she would choose Ricky over Jordan..." She shook her head.

"Maybe she didn't like Jordan that way," I said.

She made a muffled laugh. "She did."

"How do you know?"

She dropped her feet to the ground with a slap. "Because I made the mistake of mentioning I was going to ask him out. She about took my head off, saying she saw him first."

"I thought she was dating Ricky."

"Tell me about it. But I saw the look in her eye, and I wasn't about to get in my big sister's way. If she wanted him, that would mean she'd get rid of Ricky, and I would've given up Orlando Bloom for that."

"Orlando Bloom?"

"Or Nick Lachey. Any of those guys. Whatever could've gotten her away from Mr. Butthead." She paused, looking out over the back yard. "I was hoping my taking a stand on Friday night would help her see straight. I guess I was too late." Her eyes filled again, and she crossed her arms tightly over her stomach.

"Too late for her and Jordan?" San apparently didn't know about Jordan and Genna's unofficial engagement. I wondered if it existed outside of Jordan's mind.

"Too late to save her." Her eyes sparked. "The cops tell me they don't know yet what killed Genna. The autopsy's been put off. But I have my suspicions." She glared again toward Ricky and his girls.

"You think Ricky killed her?" Ricky's words from backstage flitted through my mind. *I'm gonna wring your fucking neck.*

Was he talking to Genna when he said it?

San opened her mouth to respond, but shut it when the back door slapped shut. Jordan loped across the bricks, accompanied by Gary Mann, whom I'd last seen on the news, speaking about being heartsick. Mann looked gray; not just his hair, which was shot through with silver, but his skin, too. He obviously hadn't spent the weekend sleeping, relaxing, or even eating.

Jordan stopped beside San and me. "This is Genna's sister, San. San, this is Gary Mann, the owner of Club Independence."

Mann took one of San's hands in both of his. "I can't tell you how sorry I am. I really thought I had everything under control."

She nodded and cleared her throat. "Thank you."

"Our security team is the best. I don't know how this happened. Your sister's death, the bomb…" His voice trailed off, and he blinked slowly.

Jordan gazed at San, and I was startled by the despair and hopelessness in his eyes. Mann still held San's hand, and I could see she wasn't quite sure how to respond. The three of them stood in some kind of weird stalemate; the sister, the unofficial lover, and the man who felt responsible. Enough time passed I felt something should be done.

"You mentioned your security staff," I said.

When Mann looked at me, San pulled her hand from his and scooted a bit closer to Jordan.

"My crew is the best," Mann said. "I hire only fully trained employees."

"Right, I've heard that. But you had to hire a temporary person on Friday night because your head of security called in sick. That seems pretty unusual."

He studied me for a few beats, his face still, before turning back to San. "I had it under control."

She stared at him with an unreadable expression before turning and marching up to the house and disappearing inside.

"I had it under control," Mann said again, then turned and walked zombie-like down the patio steps to the lawn.

"What was that about?" I said.

Jordan looked at me. "Jermaine getting hired last minute. You're the one who brought it up."

"I know, but what about that reaction. Why did it freak him out so bad?"

Jordan shrugged. "Because he feels responsible, I guess."

"Huh-uh. It's more than that. Something about the security guy calling in sick doesn't feel right."

Jordan sank onto the iron loveseat. "Nothing feels right."

"And what about that Baronne guy?" I said. "Do you really think he was kidnapped?"

Jordan looked at me blankly.

"Mann's office manager? The one who's missing along with the concert money?"

He blinked. "I forgot about him."

"Yeah. I don't blame you."

His forehead crinkled. "From what I've heard, Baronne's been with Mr. Mann for years. Since they were in college, I think."

"So Baronne's disappearance would hit him hard no matter why he's gone. Whether he took off or was kidnapped."

"Yeah." His attention caught on something in the yard, and I turned to see Gary Mann talking with Ricky, his arm around his shoulders. Ricky was putting on quite a show of the grieving loved one, resting his forehead in his hands, his shoulders slumped. The girls around him had varying expressions of concern pasted on their faces.

"I'm ready to go," Jordan said.

Chapter Eleven

Jordan assured me he'd be okay when I dropped him off at his apartment. I wasn't sure I believed him, but didn't feel I could force him to come home with me or let me sleep on his sofa. I also didn't feel like battering him with questions about Baronne or the bomb. I knew he hadn't set the thing. Why interrogate him like he had?

I stayed in front of his house, motor running, making sure he got inside before heading home. I hurt for the guy, but couldn't exactly stay on the curbside all night waiting for him to come running out.

When I pulled into my drive I stomped on the brakes. Nick's Ranger sat at the side of the house. What the hell?

I pulled my truck around his, not seeing him anywhere, and parked in the garage. I sat for a moment, my stomach churning, as I tried to reconcile his unresponsive cell phone with his return to PA. Sliding out of the truck I took a deep breath, somehow knowing his appearance here couldn't be good.

When I got to the house, Nick was sitting on the side steps petting Queenie, who sat with her head on his knees. I stopped in front of him and looked down into his face. He met my eyes with his. They weren't as bloodshot as they'd been over the weekend, but the skin around them looked bruised, and his color was bad.

"Remember last summer how we went out in the corn field and talked?" he asked.

"Yeah." It hadn't been a pleasant conversation.

He smiled briefly. "What do you say we go out there again?"

"There's no corn to hide behind. It's only a couple inches tall."

"We don't need to hide. Just walk."

I studied his face. "You don't want to take the truck?"

"Nah. It's too nice of a day."

"All right."

He held out his hand, and I pulled him to his feet. His arms went around me and we stood there for a few moments, Queenie snuffling at our knees, until he let go, easing a hand down to grab one of mine.

Without speaking we walked through the corn rows, watching our feet so we didn't crush the fresh plants. Queenie trotted alongside us, nosing at the mounds of dirt and chasing birds. I tried to ignore the developments I could see pushing up to my property lines, but the crop—even at its full height—wouldn't be able to hide the swarm of copycat condos. My stomach began to hurt.

In the middle of the field Nick stopped, turning his face toward the sun. "I gave you a hard time last summer, didn't I?"

"You mean out here?"

He nodded. "Saying you were going to end up old and alone if you didn't make some hard choices."

I pulled away from him and tucked both hands in my pockets. "Yeah. You basically told me I had to choose between my farm and my chance at having a family."

He winced. "That was a bit harsh, wasn't it?"

"Gee, you think?"

We were silent.

"You haven't had your phone on the last couple days," I said. "I tried to call."

He didn't reply, and I looked at him. His face was still as his eyes roamed the fields. I didn't think he was seeing the townhomes in the next plot.

"I needed some time to think," he said.

My heart plummeted. Was he breaking up with me? After our painful beginning? Our monthly visits? The way we'd come to understand each other? I clenched my jaw and looked at the ground.

"You've made some sacrifices to be with me," Nick said. "Leaving your farm to come to Virginia for weekendss, having a long distance relationship."

"You've done the same," I said.

"I know."

I could feel him looking at me, but kept studying the mound of dirt at my feet.

"It didn't seem like you even minded," he said.

"I didn't."

"I didn't, either."

I hated the way we were using the past tense. Whatever Nick was going to tell me wasn't going to be good.

He was quiet for a minute before saying, "I'm not sure how much more I can ask of you."

I squinted up at him. Were these monthly visits not enough? Did he want me to leave the farm even more? Oh God, he wasn't about to propose, was he?

"Nick, what's going on?"

He sighed loudly and closed his eyes. "Things have changed."

"How? You suddenly need more?" My breath caught. "You found someone else in Virginia who will be there all the time?"

His eyes popped open. "No. No, I didn't find someone else." He reached a hand toward me, but let it drop back to his side. "Remember this weekend, how I was feeling? How I was so tired?"

"Of course."

He squatted down and picked up a clod of dirt, crumbling it in his fingers. "I went to the doctor when I got home on Saturday. Mom called in a favor to get him to his office on the weekend." He stopped.

"And?"

"The doc sent me straight over to the emergency room for some tests. An MRI, a CT scan." He stood, brushing loose dirt from his hands.

"And what did they say?"

He glanced at me briefly, then turned toward me straight on, grabbing both my hands. "Stella, I have MS."

I stared at him. *"What?"*

"Multiple sclerosis."

I went cold, my head swimming.

"Stella?"

I pulled my hands from his and bent over, hoping I wasn't going to throw up into the corn row. When the nausea passed I stood up. "What does this mean?"

He took a deep breath and let it out. "Any number of things. I could have just this one episode. I could have periodic ones."

"But…are you going to die?"

He smiled gently. "Someday. Not any time soon." He paused, brushing his fingers through my hair. "But it could affect my lifestyle. There's no way to know."

"Affect you how?"

He swallowed. "Different ways. I'll have to take medication. Watch for symptoms of an upcoming exacerbation. I'll get tired easily, and my immune system will be compromised from the drugs."

"What about driving? You drove up here."

"Shouldn't affect my driving, except if I have double vision or something, which kind of happened this weekend when I was here."

"How about kids?" I asked. "Can you have them?"

"Sure."

"They won't get it?"

"Not from me. It doesn't work that way."

I pressed my thumb and forefinger against my eyes. What ever happened to happily ever after?

"So I wanted to give you a chance to re-think our relationship," Nick said. "If you want an out."

I stared at him. An out? "Nick, are you nuts? I love you. I can't just stop."

He stepped forward and put his hands on the sides of my face. "I love you, too. You know that. That's why I want you to think about this. This is going to affect you, almost as much as me. It will determine how often I can visit. How active I can be. Who knows where it could lead in the future? Do you really want to be tied down to someone..." He shrugged. "What if I can't keep up with you?"

I pushed him away. "Stop it. Just...stop." I turned away, my head reeling.

"Stella..."

I silenced him with a wave. I couldn't hear any more.

"Okay," he said after a while. "I think I'll go back to the house. Why don't you stay out here for a while? Think about what I said. I'll be there when you get back."

I wanted to reply, but my mouth was dry, and I ended up just shaking my head. When I finally turned around, he was already halfway home.

Chapter Twelve

The phone rang during my late supper with Lucy and Tess, and I jumped up to snag it before the loud jangling could wake Nick. When I'd returned from the corn field I'd found him sound asleep on the sofa in the front room, Tess' cat Smoky curled up at his feet. Lucy said Nick had gone in for a nap, and now, three and a half hours later, he was still out cold. Lucy had looked many questions at me during milking, but I ignored them, not anywhere near ready to talk about Nick's revelations.

"Stella?" a voice said on the phone.

"Hey, Jermaine. What is it?"

"You talked to Jordan?"

I pulled my chair over toward the phone with my foot and slumped onto it. "Earlier this afternoon. Why?"

"He's barricaded himself in his house. Won't talk to any of us. Not even Ma."

"Have the police been to see him?"

"Don't know. When he wouldn't let me in I left. I'm sorry for the guy, but I've about had enough."

I sighed and rubbed my forehead. "I don't know what to tell you, man, except maybe leave him alone for tonight."

He hesitated. "You don't think he'll…"

"Hurt himself?" I considered it. "No. I don't. But I'll call him to check in. See if he'll talk with me."

"I'd appreciate it."

"Want me to call you back?"

"Only if there's something I need to know. I'll assume he's okay unless I hear from you."

Great.

I hung up and dialed Jordan's number. I got the answering machine and started talking.

"Jordan. Stella here. Pick up, would you? Jermaine just called, worried about you. I won't make you talk to him. Just please come on or I'm going to have to go out again tonight to come to your place and check up on you, and you really don't want me to do that. Or I could call your mom—"

"I'm here. Stop talking. Please." Jordan's voice sounded tired and defeated.

"I'll stop if you tell me you're going to be okay tonight. Or at least that you'll be all right till morning."

"I'll survive."

"Good. Now, is there anything I can do for you right now?"

He cleared his throat. "No."

"Nothing?"

"No."

"All right. But you can call me if you need to. You hear?"

"Yeah. I hear."

"Good night, Jordan."

"Stella?"

"Yeah."

"Thanks."

I hung up and left the kitchen, avoiding Lucy's eyes, and walked into the front room, where Nick lay on the sofa, his face relaxed and pale in sleep. I studied his features in the light that leaked in from the living room. His looks hadn't changed, but a vulnerability had seeped into him. Or perhaps in my perception of him.

An afghan crocheted by my mother twenty years before lay folded on the back of the couch, made with a combination of brown, green, and yellow, with orange highlights. I picked it up and sat on the rocking chair across from Nick, holding the afghan on my lap. Poking my fingers through the holes in the pattern, I dug into the soft yarn. Memories from long ago days assaulted me—lying on the couch, Mom feeding me toast and chicken noodle soup, my throat sore from strep or some other virus. Cuddled with my mom under the blanket, watching *E. T.*, handing her tissues while she cried at the sad parts. The comfort of being taken care of, of being loved, of security.

I leaned my head against the high back of the rocking chair and watched Nick sleep. His breathing was quiet—so quiet I had to really concentrate to hear him.

MS?

My God, could nothing be easy? Ever?

I thought of what Nick had implied out in the corn field. Wondering if I wanted to call it quits. Had I proved so unreadable that he assumed the worst of me? That I could turn off my love at will?

I fought down a rush of anger. At him. At myself. At the disease.

But just as quickly a wave of sadness came over me, and I doubled over in the chair, burying my face in the afghan. The possibilities the illness presented were too many to consider thoughtfully: I'd spend years nursing Nick when I'd thought we'd be equal companions; Nick would leave me, unable to believe I could still love him; I'd have to move to Virginia, following Nick to where he'd be most comfortable.

Or that Nick—the love of my life—would die, leaving me alone. Again.

Eventually the tide of emotion passed, and I raised my head to look at Nick, sleeping so soundly, his right arm dangling over the sofa's edge, his fingers brushing the floor.

I lifted the afghan off my lap and unfurled it, gently laying it over him, pulling it up to his chin and tucking it around his feet. And wondered how many more times I'd do it in the years to come.

◇◇◇

I woke up early and stretched out a hand to turn off my alarm. I wondered how Nick had slept, and if he'd managed to stay comfortable on the couch. I pulled on some clothes and tiptoed downstairs.

A peek into the front room showed me that Nick hadn't moved, and I left him to sleep. I watched the news while I ate my Wheaties, but there was nothing new about Genna or Bobby Baronne.

Queenie joined me for milking, but I couldn't bring myself to tell her about Nick. I couldn't even tell the cows.

By the time I was done in the barn Nick was awake, sipping some hot tea Lucy had brewed after getting Tess on the bus. I could feel his eyes on me as I stood in the doorway, and I raised mine to meet his.

"Long sleep," I said.

He looked down at his mug. "Yeah."

Lucy eyed me from across the room.

"Got another cup of that?" I asked.

"Sure," she said. "It's peppermint."

She poured me a cup and I drank it without sweetener, enjoying the tartness of the brew.

"You staying for lunch?" Lucy asked Nick. "I'm making creamed eggs to put over fresh bread."

He smiled. "Sounds good, but I need to head home."

I clenched my jaw and stared into my tea.

"Want anything to eat now?" she asked him.

"No. Thank you. I'm not really hungry."

The tension in the room was unmistakable, and Lucy soon left.

I pushed my mug away. "You all right to drive?"

"Yeah. My vision's cleared up just fine."

"You're not too tired?"

He gave a soft laugh. "After that sleep? I better not be."

My head throbbed, and I closed my eyes, taking a breath. "So what now?"

"I head home. Have some more tests. See some more doctors."

"What kind?"

"Ophthalmologist. Neurologist. Internal medicine."

I shook my head. "And what will they do?"

"Tell me how advanced it is. How to hold it off. Start me on medication."

Were we really having this conversation?

He stood and pushed his chair in, then stepped behind me. Putting his hands on my shoulders he rubbed them, working the knots in my neck with his thumbs. I couldn't relax like usual with his massage and shrugged him off, scooting out of my chair.

"I'll call you when I know more," he said.

"That's what you said last time."

He sucked in a breath. "I know. I'm sorry." He stepped toward the kitchen door. "See me out?"

I followed him to his truck, where I allowed him to take me in his arms, Queenie brushing around our legs. I rested my head on his shoulder for a moment before stepping back, his hands sliding to my elbows.

I looked him in the eye. "Drive carefully."

He dropped his hands, his expression pained. "I always do." He didn't move. "You'll think about what I said? Out in the field?"

About ending our relationship? Leaving him in times of trouble? Being a flighty, fair weather lover? "I'll think about it."

There was nothing left to say.

He got in his truck and drove away as I stood at the end of the walk, my arms crossed against my stomach. It wasn't until I couldn't see his truck anymore that I realized there *was* something else to say, but I'd forgotten. I'd forgotten to tell him I loved him.

"Everything okay?" Lucy stood on the house steps, her face full of concern.

My throat tightened, any words I might have said caught before reaching my mouth. I ended up shaking my head, looking at the sky, and walking out to the tractor barn, where my truck was parked. Not wanting to go back in the house, I grabbed the extra set of keys I kept in my toolbox and got into the truck. Lucy was still standing on the steps when I drove past.

I soon found myself parked at Ma Granger's house, not quite sure how I'd gotten there. I got out and went up the walk, not surprised at all when the door opened before I even reached it.

"You have news about my boy?" Ma asked.

Assuming she meant Jordan, I said, "I talked to him last night."

"And?"

"I don't know what to tell you. He's miserable. But he'll be okay."

Eventually.

"Well, come on in. I want to talk to you."

I supposed I wanted to talk to her, too. Why else would I be there?

The answer hit me when I walked in the door and saw her quilt rack set up in the parlor.

"Ma?"

She turned from where she was clearing a pile of fabric from the seat of an easy chair. "Yes?"

"Think you could make me something to wear for Lucy's wedding?"

She looked at me. "For this Saturday."

"Well. Yes."

She looked at me some more.

"Please?" I said.

Big sigh. "All right. Stay there."

She went into another room and came back with a measuring tape, a pencil, and a pad of paper.

"Stand still," she said.

While she measured more parts of my body than seemed necessary, she quizzed me.

"So, what do you know about this Genna girl Jordan's so broken up about?"

I shrugged.

"Hold still," Ma said.

"I don't really know much about her," I said. "I only met her Friday night, and that was real brief."

"What was she to Jordan?"

"Ma, I don't really—"

"Did Jordan tell you they were engaged?"

Right. She knew about that. "Just unofficially. And he didn't tell me until Sunday night. The first I heard of that was from Jermaine. Ouch!"

"Sorry." But she wasn't. I could tell.

She let the tape go from around my upper arm and swatted my legs apart so she could measure my thigh.

"Ma, if you're making a dress, why do you need—"

"Did I ask for your input?" she said.

She scribbled on her tablet, then pushed my hips so I'd slide my feet back together. While she was measuring my hip width she said, "So now Jordan's got himself shut in his house. Won't talk to me, his brothers, his sisters-in-law… Seems the only person he'll answer the phone for is you."

"That's only cause I threatened him, Ma."

"Well, so did I. Didn't work for me."

She was quiet for a moment while she scratched more numbers onto her tablet. "Arms up," she said.

I lifted them while she measured my chest. Not a number I really needed to know.

"So how's that good-looking boyfriend of yours?" she asked as she squeezed my boobs with the tape.

"Fine," I said. Reflex.

She let the tape drop and stood in front of me, squinting up into my face. "That didn't sound right."

"Oh, well."

She raised her eyebrows, surprised at my rudeness. I was, too.

"Sorry, Ma. He just left this morning and I'm feeling a bit touchy."

Her expression softened. "He's a nice boy."

"Yes, he is." I swallowed, wishing she would stop talking about him.

She shook her head, hands on her hips. "You and Jordan. My goodness. You'd think I was asking you to betray the Lord himself the way you two keep these things so close to your chests."

"You know me, Ma."

"Yes, I do. And that's why I want you to be Jordan's special keeper."

"What?"

"You've already started. Checking up on him and all. Our family has tried and he's not having any of it. So I want you to act like the sister you've become. When you leave this house I want you to go make sure my boy's okay."

I looked at her, determination sparking in her eyes. How could I say no?

"I'll go," I said. "But this dress...Please, no bows or lace or—"

"Remember?" she said. "I know you. You just said so. You'll have to trust me."

I looked down at her and felt an overwhelming surge of affection. "I do trust you, Ma. More than anyone I know."

She looked at me a little longer, like she knew there were things I wasn't telling her. But I wasn't ready to share about Nick.

"Okay, then."

She measured a few more parts of me and stepped back. "I talked to the police yesterday." She held up a hand. "But not till I spoke to that lawyer of yours. The one you told Jordan to call."

"He helped you out?"

She nodded. "The police really think Jordan...did something to her. Don't they?"

I looked at the floor, then at a pair of ceramic praying hands that sat on top of a bookshelf. "Yes, Ma. I think they do. But they're wrong." I turned toward the kitchen, where I'd find a phone to call Jordan's house and see if he was there.

"Stella?" Ma said.

I turned to her.

"Jordan really loved this girl, didn't he?" Her face sagged with the weight of the cops' suspicions.

"Yes, Ma," I said. "He loved her. He never would've hurt her."

I believed it from the bottom of my heart.

I hoped my heart was right.

Chapter Thirteen

Jordan's cell phone was turned off, as usual, and he either wasn't answering his home phone or he was gone. Granger's Welding was on the way to his place, so I stopped in, just in case he'd shown up for work.

"Haven't seen him," Jermaine said, then looked at me accusingly. "You said you'd call if he wasn't all right."

"I know. And when I talked with him last night he was. But I spoke to your mom this morning…"

Jethro, Zach's dad and the oldest brother of the Granger clan, nodded. "We know what that means. You've been put on the case."

"That's right. So I'm trying to find him. Thought I'd check here first."

"Before his house?" Jermaine sounded surprised. "I thought he was holed up there."

"I tried calling, but he didn't answer."

"And where'd you call *from?*"

Oh. "Does he have Caller ID?" I asked.

They both nodded.

No wonder he wasn't answering. His mother's phone number had shown up on his screen.

"I guess I'll check there, then."

They went back to work and I headed up the road.

But Jordan wasn't home. I knocked, rang the doorbell, looked in the windows, and made such a spectacle of myself I was afraid the neighbors would call the police. No response from inside, and I couldn't see any lights or movement.

I gave up and drove home, where I could maybe get some inspiration on where to check next.

Lucy was in the garden, setting up the sprinkler amongst the seedlings. She saw me and waved. An idea struck me, and I walked over.

"You have a contact number for the Tom Copper Band?"

"Sure." She pushed some errant bangs out of her eyes. "Inside."

"Can I get it?"

She dusted her hands off on her pants. "It's in the midst of all my wedding stuff. Better let me find it."

"That would be best." Lucy's "wedding stuff" comprised about two boxes' worth of scribbled notes, sample invitations, business cards, fabric swaths, *Bride* magazines, and much more crap than I ever wanted to know about. I meant it when I'd said I'd elope.

We walked toward the house. "Can I ask why you need the information?" Lucy asked.

"Jordan's missing. I thought maybe the band has seen him."

"Can't hurt to check." She was quiet for a few seconds. "Everything okay with you and Nick?"

We'd reached the house, so I opened the door and walked in. Lucy, realizing I wasn't answering, went to find what I needed.

She soon came back with a phone number scribbled on a piece of paper. "I've actually not called the number, since Jordan did all of the arranging. I'm not sure exactly who it'll reach."

I looked at it. An unfamiliar exchange. Not Philadelphia.

"I'll try it. Thanks."

She looked at me a moment longer, then went back outside. I walked to the kitchen and picked up the phone. Someone answered on the third ring saying, "Tom Copper Band."

"Stella Crown here," I said. "May I ask who I'm talking to?"

"Stella? We met the other day. This is Tonya Copper."

So not a PR firm. And the unfamiliar exchange must've been for New Hope. "Sure. Hi. Hey, I'm looking for Jordan. Any chance you've seen him?"

"No, he hasn't been around."

"Could you do me a favor and call the other guys, see if they've been in touch with him? Or give me their numbers so I can call?"

"I can call them." She stopped, but from the tone of the silence it didn't seem like she was done.

"What?" I said.

"Nothing. I'll get back to you if you tell me where to call."

I rattled off my number and hung up. Ma had been explicit in her instructions to baby-sit her third-born, but I was at a loss to know where else to look for Jordan. I headed outside to do some of the farm work I'd been neglecting. The parlor was a mess from having the herd as winter residents, so I set to work with some spring cleaning. I was deep into it when the phone rang. Tossing my pitchfork aside, I jogged to the office and snatched up the receiver before the call rolled over to voice mail.

"Stella? Tonya Copper."

I wiped a bead of sweat from my forehead. "You find him?"

"No. He'll probably be at rehearsal tonight, but I'm assuming you want to talk with him before that."

"If I can."

"Well…" She hesitated, and I remembered our earlier conversation, when she seemed to be holding something back. I hoped she'd let it out this time.

"I could be wrong," she finally said, "but I have a pretty good idea where you might find him."

"Great," I said. "Tell me."

She did.

◇◇◇

Philadelphia's Fairmount Park is the largest urban park in the U.S., encompassing over nine thousand acres of land. The area where I parked was springtime beautiful; a long, grassy swath along the Schuylkill River with flowering trees and sunny skies. Runners were taking advantage of the weather along with cyclists, roller bladers, dog walkers, fishermen, and adults pushing strollers. Besides the exercising foot traffic, Fairmount Park is home to the Philadelphia Zoo, as well as Boathouse Row, a central rowing spot, and from where I parked my truck I could catch glimpses of the Art Institute.

I could also see the backed-up mess on the Schuylkill Expressway. Thank God Tonya had given me good directions for coming down on Kelly Drive.

Jordan sat where Tonya had expected, and a stab of sadness shot through me when I recognized his hunched shoulders. I weaved through the joggers and made my way down the gentle slope to him, where he tossed bread to a cluster of apparently starving geese.

I sat next to him on the bench, and he glanced over at me, surprise lighting his eyes. He turned back to the adoring flock surrounding him and resumed tearing off chunks of stale whole wheat slices. I let out a big breath and straightened my legs, enjoying the warmth of the sun. Closing my eyes and resting my hands on the bench, I waited to see just how long Jordan would stonewall me.

It was a long wait.

"What are you doing here?" he finally said.

I opened my eyes to see he'd used up the entire loaf of bread, and his feathered friends were waddling off to find more fertile grounds.

"You gonna tell me to scram, like you did your family?" I asked.

He gazed out at the river, his elbows resting on his knees. "Nah. You wouldn't listen, anyway."

I smiled. Ma wasn't the only Granger who knew me.

"Ma send you?" he asked.

"Ordered me to find you. Make sure you were okay."

He scrunched the bread bag up and hid it in his hand, checking to make sure none of it was visible. Then he opened his fingers and the bag expanded, crinkling and shining in the sun.

"So am I okay?"

I looked at him. "I don't know."

He didn't say anything else, and I watched the scullers glide by—singles and multiple rowers. I'd never done organized sports, and wondered how it would feel to be part of such a smooth and flowing team.

"How'd you find me?" he asked, after a while.

"Tonya Copper. I called her to see if anyone in the band had talked to you, and she figured you were probably here. Said you and Genna came here a few times."

He looked at the ground between his feet, reached down to pick up a pebble, and tossed it into the water. "I don't know how she knew that."

"Genna told her."

Jordan's head jerked up. "Really?"

"Apparently Genna was feeling...conflicted."

He let out a short laugh. "Conflicted."

"She needed someone to talk to. The times the two of you came here were special to her. And confusing."

His mouth twitched, and he looked away from me, toward two moms with strollers.

"The band seems like a pretty close-knit group," I said, when it was obvious he wasn't going to offer anything else.

He nodded. "They are. The three original guys who are left, anyway. After all, they've been together, what? Fifteen years, maybe. Since high school."

"Really?"

"Yup. All Philly kids. Public school. Somehow they recognized each other as musicians and got together. Been together ever since."

"What about Parker?"

"He was with them from the beginning, too. But of course he left the band last year."

I sat forward, leaning on my hands. "What's the deal with the switch of drummers? From your perspective?"

He shrugged. "Parker was ready to try something new. He was tired of being a drummer. The only way to get ahead in the music business is to be the one writing the songs, and drummers don't usually get that chance."

"How come?"

"Don't know. Just the way it is. And with the Tom Copper Band…"

"What?"

"Everyone knows Tom's the songwriter."

"Yeah?"

"I mean, the others have written a couple here and there, but the big hits, the ones everyone knows, those are Tom's."

I stared out at the water while a goose landed in the river, splashing as it hit. The band—*Tom*—hadn't mentioned the songwriting bit the other day when I'd been asking them about Parker's change of career.

"Anything else?" I asked.

"You mean about Parker leaving?"

"Yeah."

He got up, walked to a trash can to dump his bread bag, and came back, standing with his back to me, looking at the river. "There was tension in the band about some accident they'd had. I don't know a whole lot about it, but I think it played into Parker quitting."

"Why?"

He squatted down, found a flat rock, and skipped it out on the water. "Parker was the driver, I guess. Fell asleep at the wheel one night on tour. Miraculously everyone was okay except Tom, who got thrown through the windshield and ended up with a damaged leg. Actually had a ballpoint pen jammed into his thigh."

"Ouch."

"Yeah. He was on crutches the next several months and ended up addicted to painkillers. Had to go through rehab to get clean before they could resume touring at a regular clip."

"Wow. I can see why there would be some issues."

He spun another rock across the water. "They're pretty much over it now. Parker comes by once in a while, and everybody seems to be okay with it."

I remembered the atmosphere backstage before the concert, with the good-natured ribbing. At least I'd assumed it was good-natured.

"How about the others?" I asked. "LeRoy and Donny? They get along with Tom okay?"

"Everyone does. He's a great guy."

"No clashes?"

He jostled a couple of rocks in his hands. "Not that I've seen. LeRoy's a devout Christian and church-goer, which makes for some interesting conversation and schedule-juggling, but they're all sensitive to it. It's rare to have someone religious in a rock band, but it works."

"And Donny?"

"Donny just sort of goes with the flow. Real laid back."

But I'd seen fire in his eyes on Monday at Tom's place when Ricky was putting on his show of grief. And his expression when he'd reached to comfort Tonya, only to be beaten out by Tom. Her husband.

"What's the history with Donny and Tonya?"

Jordan shrugged. "Didn't know there was any." His face held no sign that he was lying. "Why?"

"Just curious. What about with Ricky? Donny get along with him?"

He glanced at me, his face closing. "They all tolerate Ricky."

I shook my head. "But why? They could get another drummer. They're the *Tom Copper Band.*"

Jordan lobbed a few last rocks into the river and looked at his watch. "I should probably get to rehearsal. You feel good enough about my well-being you can give Ma a report?"

I stood up. "How 'bout I give you a lift to practice?"

He sighed, resignation flooding his face. "You won't just leave me alone?"

I smiled.

"I was afraid of that," he said.

Chapter Fourteen

"I don't really have to be here," Jordan said. "But I often pop in on rehearsals because they have questions, and…" His voice trailed off, but I finished the sentence in my head: …it was where he got to be with Genna.

"We rehearse at Club Independence sometimes," he continued, with a tour guide's forced energy, "but Mann's often got a gig going, so we end up here. This week nobody wanted to go back to the Club, so we were lucky to get a time slot here at such short notice."

The warehouse-turned-practice-space we stepped into had signs pointing to a theater on the upper level, but the current show ran Wednesday through Sunday, so the band's music wouldn't disturb any patrons of the quieter arts. And the music I heard coming from the inner room would disturb just about anybody.

Jordan winced at the discordant clashing, and we hesitated at the door.

"Sure you want to go in?" I asked.

His jaw tightened, and he slowly walked into the room.

"Okay," Tom Copper was saying quietly. "We need to try that again."

Ricky, who sat behind his drum set in a white sleeveless undershirt, rolled his eyes. "Come on, Copper. How many times we gonna do this?"

Tom turned slowly toward the drummer. "Until we get it right. *All* of us."

Jordan sucked in a quick breath, and I followed his eyes. Marley, the dark-haired groupie girl from Ricky's inner circle, stood at a microphone, her eyes red from what I assumed had been crying. I remembered Tom saying she would probably fill in for Genna until they found someone else, and it looked like that's what they were testing today. I also remembered Tonya Copper's reaction to the idea of Marley as the female singer. It was anything but positive. I'd think an audience's reaction wouldn't be much better, the way it had sounded.

Donny and LeRoy noticed us in the doorway, but acknowledged us only by jerks of their chins. Tom was speaking directly to Ricky, in a voice that didn't carry. From the way Ricky was glaring I figured it wasn't good.

Jordan touched my elbow and scooted along the wall toward some chairs. I followed, surprised to see Parker, the band's old drummer. His chair was tilted back against the wall, the front two legs in the air while he rested his feet on a wooden crate. He was watching Tom and Ricky with an amused expression, his arms crossed comfortably over his chest. He nodded at Jordan, and then at me, but went back to observing the band.

"Okay," Tom said, turning away from Ricky. "Here we go."

A smooth riff from Donny led them into the beginning of a song I didn't recognize. Probably a new one they didn't get to perform on Friday because of the bomb threat. Tom began counting out loud, leaning toward Marley, and she started to sing. It must've been the right place, because Tom went back to his mic and concentrated on guitar.

Marley didn't sound half bad that time. Wasn't Genna, obviously, but closer to good than she had been when we'd arrived.

I glanced beside me as the neighboring chair shifted, and Annie gave me a quick smile. I looked at Jordan, but he was immersed in the music—or in trying to forget that Genna should've been up there singing.

When the song ended, the tension in the room was heavy. Everyone looked at Tom, who stood with his hands still on his guitar.

"Okay," he finally said. "Let's take five."

The reflexive sigh from the band was loud enough to be heard, and the crisis was averted. For the moment.

"You here to help out?" I asked Annie.

She looked up at me, crossing one leg over the other. "Not really. I mean, I'll help if they need me, but they usually don't. Not for rehearsals."

"So you're just hanging out?"

She swung her foot back and forth. "Yeah. With Marley practicing and all..."

She broke off as Jordan got up from his chair and walked across the room to confer with LeRoy about something. They bent over to look at LeRoy's amp, their voices lost in the chatter of the rest of the band.

I looked back at Annie, remembering my suspicions about her and the bomb in the sound system.

"So how'd you get involved with the band?" I asked.

"Huh?" She swung her head toward me.

"The band? How'd you start hanging around with them?"

"Oh, I'm not sure, exactly. Marley was a fan, and started following the guys around, going to every concert she could, waiting afterwards to try to... Well, to see the guys." Her eyes flicked up at me.

"You don't have to spell it out," I said.

She squirmed.

"Which guys were interested?" I asked.

She let out a quick laugh. "None of them, really. Tom's married, you know, which I guess wouldn't stop everybody, but his wife's at all the shows. LeRoy's too religious, and Donny... Well, I'm not sure about Donny."

Allison, the girl at the bridal shop, knew more about Donny's tattoos than the casual observer, which made me think Donny hadn't always turned down female attention. But that was several years before.

"How about Ricky?" I asked.

"Ricky?" Annie looked surprised. "He was with Genna."

Like that would matter to a turd like Ricky. But I'd let the girl have her fantasies.

"You two kept hanging around anyway?"

Annie lifted a shoulder. "It was fun, talking to the guys about the music. I felt funny just doing the groupie thing, though, so I started finding little stuff to do. Jordan had me help sometimes, and that was fun. I've even thought about going back to school for it."

"Sound stuff?"

"Yeah. There are theaters here in Philly, too, where you can find work."

The band began drifting back into the practice area, and I watched Ricky saunter behind his drum set.

"So do you know how Ricky got in with the band?" I asked. "After Parker left?"

Her foot began swinging again, and I moved my leg so I wouldn't get whacked.

"I really don't know. By the time Marley and I started hanging around with the band Ricky was already in it. So I never heard the inside scoop."

I watched her face, tight and closed, and wondered why she was lying, because I was sure she was.

"Okay, Marley," Tom said, back in his spot. "Let's try 'Lust on Ice,' see how you do with that one."

Marley shuffled up to the microphone, her usual sexy bravado hidden behind self-consciousness and sniffles. I couldn't help but wonder why Tom was even giving the girl a chance. She was obviously no professional. Was it simply the fact that they needed someone immediately—like for Lucy's wedding? Or that a good female singer really is hard to come by? I couldn't imagine that finding one better than Marley would be too difficult.

Ricky clacked his sticks together and the song began. I knew it well enough I could mouth the words, even with Marley's uninspired performance.

The night is cold
And so's my heart
It's always numb
When we're apart
To be your girl
I pay the price
You always keep
My lust on ice.

I stole a glance at Jordan, who had taken a seat over by LeRoy. His eyes were hooded as he watched Marley, and I was shocked by the disgust I saw in his face. I thought Marley was an embarrassment to my gender the way she threw herself around, but she wasn't the only one who'd ever done it. I wondered if it was merely the fact that she was trying to replace Genna, or if there was something else behind Jordan's sneer.

The song wrapped up, and again we watched Tom. He obviously wasn't thrilled, but Marley *had* gotten through the song without crashing and burning, even if it wasn't up to Genna's quality.

"Pretty good," Tom said.

Marley's shoulders relaxed, if only a quarter of an inch.

"Let's do it again to be sure."

Ricky's mouth opened, but Donny threw him such a violent look the drummer shut up without a peep.

The song went a little better the second time, and Tom actually complimented Marley. "You worked hard today. I know it's not easy trying to fill in for somebody else. Thanks for helping us out."

Red crept up Marley's neck, and I was half afraid she was going to faint. She overcame it in a minute, and Annie joined her on the other side of the room.

"Now," Tom said to the guys, "I want to hit 'Expressway' before we stop."

Another new one, I guessed, since I'd never heard of it.

They started roughly, and repeated the beginning a few times before going on to the rest of the song. They stopped so many times to fix things I felt trapped in a disturbing déjà vu cycle. I decided to look for a bathroom.

I went out the closest door, the one Jordan and I had come in, and walked around the hallway, past the door on the other side of the room, close to where Marley and Annie were sitting. I found a ladies room in the back of the warehouse, and was using it when the outer door opened and a couple of people walked in.

"I'm telling you," someone said. It sounded like Annie. "Ricky better get his act together or Tom's gonna kick him out for sure, now that Genna's not around to mediate."

"He wouldn't," the other person said. Marley. "Ricky's so *awesome*. And he has some songs for the band to do. You should hear them. They're *amazing*."

A stall door a few down from me squeaked open and shut, and a lock turned. "They're not going to do his songs." Annie. "I mean, they didn't even do Parker's, and he was with them for *years*."

A sniff from Marley. "I'm sure Ricky's are lots better."

Annie made a loud production of unrolling toilet paper. "What is it with you and Ricky? You think you have to take Genna's place there, too?"

Marley made a sound of protest. "I'm not... Well, he is hot, you know. *And* he's a great musician. Besides, we've been... well...you know...the last couple months, anyway."

I tried not to breathe into the shocked silence.

"I can't believe you *did* that." Annie's voice squeaked. "You could've screwed up *everything* if Genna had found out. She would've had him kicked out of the band. And you'd be gone for sure."

"Which means you would be, too," Marley said, her voice mean.

No reply from Annie, except rustling and the sound of her zipper. "He doesn't really like you, you know," Annie finally said. "I heard him yelling at you backstage at the concert. He said he was going to wring your neck."

My mouth fell open. He'd been talking to *Marley?*

"He didn't mean it," Marley said. "And he feels different now. In a day or so he won't care if I French kiss him in front of the guys, let alone put my hand on his knee, like he was complaining about."

Silence.

"I don't care what you think," Marley added.

The toilet flushed and the stall door swung open again. "Whether you care or not, you'd better tell Ricky to start treating Tom with a little more respect or he's going to be out of a job. You know they only put up with him because of Genna. Heck, he only *got* the job because of Genna. You remember."

So she *had* been lying when she'd said she didn't know how he got hired.

Water splashed in the sink.

"Well," Marley said, "now that I'm going to be their female singer maybe *I'll* have some say in the matter."

Yeah. And I was going to sprout wings and fly back to the farm.

The outer door creaked open and shut and I was left alone.

On the way back to the rehearsal room I could tell things weren't going well. Instead of music, I heard yelling. I walked to the door I'd left, and peeked around the jamb.

"It's *you*," Ricky was saying. "Not me. Don't keep fucking pointing at me."

"Oh, it's *our* fault you keep losing the beat during the refrain?" Donny said. "It's the rest of us that are screwing up?" He snatched his water bottle from the floor and took such a long drink I thought he was going to drown.

LeRoy stood stock still, his eyes on Tom. I wondered if he was even breathing.

Tom faced forward, his back to Ricky. His hands rested on his hips, leaving his guitar hanging on his neck, and his head was bent so far down I saw the top of his head.

"It's not us, Ricky," he said. "It's you. It's you every goddamn time. You *know* how it's supposed to go. You've spoken it, we've gone over it. But when we actually do the song, I have to practically jump on you for you to play it right."

"You're never going to get it," Donny said. "You're a freaking liability."

Tom turned to stare at Donny. Donny stared back for a few moments before swinging the strap of his guitar over his head. "I'm done. I can't do this anymore today."

"Oh, that's great," Ricky said. "Now even the most faithful Tom Copper disciples are leaving."

"Shut up, Ricky," LeRoy said.

Ricky's face closed, and he jumped up from his seat, dropping his sticks on a drum head with a clatter. "I'm outta here. You can all just shove it." He stalked from the room.

The room was silent until a scuttling sound betrayed Marley's exit. Running off after the loser. Annie sat alone, her head bowed, her face shielded by her hand.

"What about his drums?" LeRoy said.

Tom looked at them. "Leave 'em. He decides to take care of his equipment, he can come back and get it." He looked around. "Where'd Donny go?"

I knew. He'd come barreling past me when Tom had turned to check out the drums. Now, I ducked out of the doorway and plastered myself against the wall in the front hallway, out of view of the rehearsal room. Tom was a nice guy, but I didn't think now was the right time to get caught in his sights.

I went out to my truck to wait for Jordan.

Chapter Fifteen

"So how much does Annie know about the sound system?" I asked Jordan.

We were driving back up from Philadelphia, Route 309 heavy with commuter traffic. I tried, mostly unsuccessfully, not to let it tighten my shoulders and make me want to scream with frustration.

"Enough," Jordan said. "She does the basic stuff I can delegate. Running to the storage room for parts, plugging things in, taping down cables."

"But not the more technical business?"

He glanced at me. "No. That's my job. Why?"

I slammed on the brakes to avoid rear-ending a Navigator at the turnpike exit ramp. When we were clear of the jam, I shifted up and moved into the passing lane.

"Cops talk to you yesterday?" I asked.

"No."

"They'll probably be calling again."

"Damn it, I didn't do anything to Genna!" His face went almost purple.

"I know, Jordan, I know. This isn't about her."

His color changed from an all-over shade to blotches of red. "Then what's it about?"

"The bomb."

"The *bomb?*" The confusion on his face supported my theory that he knew nothing about it.

"They found the bomb in the sound system," I said.

"*What?*"

"Detective Willard told me. It was in a speaker."

He stared at me for a few moments until his confusion turned to surprise, and finally to understanding. "Now it makes sense."

"What?"

"Why it shorted out at the concert. Remember, at the beginning of the second set we had that delay?"

"Sure." I'd been worried about Nick being gone for such a long time. But I didn't want to think about Nick. "How could they set a bomb in the sound system that you wouldn't find?"

He smiled grimly. "Pretty easily, actually. It's not like I was looking for something like that. A frayed wire, a disconnected plug…that's what I was checking."

I passed a sluggish wood-paneled Explorer, and pulled into the slow lane. "So how would they do it?"

He shifted in his seat so he faced me. "Well, there are a lot of self-powered systems these days where loudspeakers actually have amplifiers in them. Those amps have surge protectors with reset switches." He stopped. "You know which loudspeaker it was in?"

I shook my head.

He paused, pursing his lips while he thought. "If they put it in the first loudspeaker in the signal chain, it could short out the signal or the speaker until the reset button is pressed on that first box. The whole chain would be silenced until that was pushed. We had no idea what was causing the problem, so we just started pushing all the buttons on everything until we got the signal back. I don't know which one actually did the trick."

I swallowed. "You're lucky you didn't blow up in the process."

"Yeah. Yeah, I guess." He shifted back and looked out his window.

"So you don't think Annie could've done it," I said after a while.

"Nope. She's a good helper, but could never do much on her own."

"Not smart enough? Or just doesn't have the knowledge and skill?"

He grimaced. "Do I have to choose one?"

Rats. I'd thought I'd found a way to get the heat off Jordan. At least for the bomb.

"What more can you tell me about Tom and the guys?" I asked.

He set his elbow against the door and leaned his head on his fist. "Tom knows enough about sound he could do it on his own if he had time. LeRoy and Donny probably do, too. But Tom wouldn't set a bomb. None of the guys would."

"I wasn't suggesting it." A group of Harleys sped past us, their thunder shaking the windows of the truck. When they were gone I said, "What I really want to know is how the guys feel about Tom."

He looked at me sharply. "They love him. Everybody does."

"Even Ricky?"

He snorted. "Ricky doesn't love anybody. Except himself."

"But LeRoy and Donny?"

He hesitated. "What's this about?"

"I was thinking about what you said. About Tom being the songwriter. He also seemed to be the boss today, everybody looking to him to say when things were good enough. Is it always like that?"

"It needs to be. You can't have a good band if you don't have someone to keep things on track. And it should be him. It is the Tom Copper Band, after all."

"How come?"

"How come what? That it's called that?"

"Yeah."

He considered this. "I'm not sure. But it's been that forever. I always assumed he'd put the band together. And he is the lead singer."

I slowed to navigate a crowded downhill curve. "Donny didn't seem too happy at the end of practice. He looked pissed, actually."

"Why shouldn't he be? After hours of practice in that hot warehouse Marley still sounds like crap and Ricky's still an asshole."

Well, there was all that.

"Plus, I think he's…" He stopped.

"What?"

He wrinkled his nose, then rubbed it. "I think he's feeling responsible for the whole thing with…with Genna. And Ricky."

"What? Why?"

He sucked on his lips, then let out a breath. "He's the one who brought Genna into the band."

I looked at him. "Explain."

"He met her at…well, at a bar, back several years ago. Actually, like eight years ago or so. She was only nineteen. One of Tonya's friends." He paused.

"And?"

"And he liked her. She apparently liked him, too, at least for a little while. But by the time they were ready to call things off Tom had heard her sing, and he offered her a spot in the band."

"Bet Donny didn't like that too well."

"Actually, from what they all say it worked out fine. Genna and Donny were never so close as a couple that it caused a problem. They ended up being okay friends."

Uh-huh. I'd heard that before.

"And how did Ricky come into things?"

He blew out a huff of air. "You're not going to let that go, are you?"

"I would if you'd answer my questions."

He was silent as I waited for a darkened limo to pass before I pulled into the left lane and went around a little Fiesta that was blowing smoke.

"About a year ago Parker said he was leaving," Jordan said. "Just all of a sudden. Freaked the guys out pretty bad. Genna stepped in, said she'd just met a guy who played the drums. Thought they could give him a try."

"Ricky."

"Yup. They invited him to audition, and unfortunately he kicked butt. They were pretty psyched." He shook his head. "I think it was partly desperation, and partly Genna's influence, but he did seem like the answer at the time."

"And how long did the honeymoon last?"

He glanced at me. "You mean with the band?"

"Or with Genna."

"Not very long for either."

We reached Montgomeryville and had to stop at the light at the end of the expressway. I looked at Jordan, taking in his fatigue and misery. His color had now completely reverted to pale and pasty, and he sat slumped against the door.

"What're you going to do now?" I asked.

"You mean this evening?"

"Yeah."

He sighed, puffing out his cheeks. "Go home. Try to find something to eat. I don't know."

A flicker of guilt at the neglect of my farm shot through my mind, but I ignored it and hooked a thumb toward the theater complex across the road. "Still matinee prices. Want to take in a movie?"

His eyes slanted toward the list of what was showing. "Anything not depressing?"

I scanned the titles. "The newest Jack Black movie. Something about nuns, dogs, and hang-gliders."

"Not a romance?"

"Does it sound like it?"

He grinned. "Okay. Let's go." He sat up straighter in his seat. "And I'm buying the popcorn."

After dropping Jordan off at the North Wales train station to pick up his car, I headed home. He'd offered to treat me to dinner at the Olive Garden after the movie, which I would've been a fool to turn down, so it was close to ten before I got home. Tess was in bed and Lucy lounged in her pajamas, half watching *Boston Legal* while she wrote thank you notes for early wedding presents.

"Nick called," she said without looking up. "Wants you to call him back."

My stomach tightened. "Okay. Thanks."

"Where have you been?" She set down her pen and leaned her head back on the couch.

"With Jordan."

"Need supper?"

I shook my head and held up my doggie bag from the restaurant. "Jordan's treat. I think he just didn't want to go home and face reality any sooner than he had to."

She studied my face. "I'm glad you could give him some company."

"Yeah." I hesitated behind the couch. "Everything okay here? Nothing I need to know about?"

"Nope. Everything's good." She picked up her pen again. "Nick said you could just call his cell phone. He'll keep it on."

I took a deep breath, but didn't answer. Instead, I made my way to the stairs, Lucy following me with her eyes.

"I'll use the phone in my room," I said.

"Sure. Good night."

"Good night."

I went upstairs, where I got undressed for bed and brushed my teeth. The phone sat on the nightstand beside my bed. I looked at it for a while.

Then I turned out the light and tried to sleep.

Chapter Sixteen

Lucy joined me in the barn the next morning after getting Tess on the bus and helped with the last bit of mucking out. She didn't say much, but cast lots of curious glances my way. When I'd about had my fill, she finally spit it out.

"So what did Nick have to say last night?"

I stashed my pitchfork in the corner and headed toward my office. "Nothing."

It was true.

In my office I sat at my desk and turned on the computer. I'd been so busy worrying about non-farm crises this week I'd left the paperwork too long. I was going to be racking up late fees if I didn't get my ass in gear and pay the bills.

The door opened and Lucy came in. "I'm going to get started in the parlor."

I looked at her. Hadn't we just finished?

"The guys are coming to spray this morning," she said. "Remember?"

Nope. Hadn't remembered.

A glance at the calendar confirmed it. It was time for our yearly dose of bug spray, to keep down our barn's population of flies, spiders, and other various winged and multi-legged annoyances. It made a huge difference in our comfort level while milking, especially during the hot summer months. The cows' comfort, too.

I sighed. "I'll be right there."

"No rush. We have a little time till they get here."

After she left I took about a half hour to pay the piper, cringing each time I hit the "submit" button on the computer screen. I'd have to keep last night's movie and dinner in mind for quite a while—I wouldn't be doing that again anytime soon. Unless someone else paid again.

The phone rang as soon as I went off-line, and I snatched it up reflexively. It was only after I said hello that I realized it could be Nick.

"Stella?" A woman's voice. Good.

"Yeah, this is Stella."

"This is San. San Powell? Genna's sister?"

"Oh. Sure. Hi, San." I leaned back in my chair and stretched my feet out in front of me, arching my back.

San's voice was quiet, and timid. "I'm trying to find Jordan. Have you talked to him today?"

"Nope. You tried his house?"

"I did. I got his answering machine."

"Did you leave a message?"

"Yes. I asked him to call me."

So if he was there, he was screening his calls. And didn't want to talk to Genna's sister.

"You tried his cell, too?"

"Yeah. Not on."

Big surprise.

"Nothing else I can tell you, then," I said. "I haven't talked to him since yesterday, and he didn't give me his plans for today."

She sighed so loudly I heard it over the phone. "How was he?"

"Not good. But he'll make it."

"Did he...did he mention me?"

I pulled my feet back under me and sat up. "No. Sorry." Should he have?

"That's okay. If he...if he calls you, could you tell him I'm looking for him?"

"Sure. He has your number?"

"Yeah. He has it." She hesitated. "It was the same as Genna's."

Oh.

"Well, thanks," she said, and hung up.

A lot of help I'd been.

I pushed away from my desk and went out to the parlor, where Lucy was busy covering the water cups and feed bowls with plastic. I grabbed the tape and began securing the openings on the ones she'd done. She didn't say anything, but I knew she was dying to know what was going on with Nick and me. The tension of her unasked questions hung in the air between us, and I wasn't about to break it. I knew her curiosity wasn't from nosiness. She really cared about us. But that didn't matter.

The milk truck pulled up outside, and I breathed a sigh of relief at the excuse to get away. I could feel Lucy's eyes on my back as I left, and knew the respite would be a brief one.

Doug, the driver, didn't need my help, but I hung out with him anyway, discussing the weather, the cows, his kids' spring soccer. He didn't know Nick, or anything else about my personal life. Probably didn't even know Lucy was getting married that weekend.

It was pleasant.

But all too soon he was packing up his equipment to head back out on his route. I was standing outside, watching him get into the cab, when the phone rang. Once. Twice.

Doug looked at me.

"Lucy'll get it," I said.

She did.

Doug was driving out the lane when Lucy appeared in the doorway. "It's Nick."

I kept my eyes on the back of the milk truck, focusing on the happy, milk-drinking cow on the door.

"Take a message," I said.

Lucy didn't move.

"Please," I said.

"You're sure?"

I didn't respond.

She left.

I felt like shit. Almost ran after her. But didn't.

A minute later she was back. "I told him you were outside helping Doug. That you'd call him back when you could."

I nodded. Feeling even more like shit because Lucy had lied for me.

"The parlor's ready," she said. "The guys should be here before too long."

"Thanks. I'll watch for them."

She wanted to say more. I could feel it. But she walked away, toward the house.

I went back into my office and went on-line. Firefox opened, bringing me to the AskJeeves bar. I stared at the blinking cursor, my head aching. Finally, I typed in "multiple sclerosis," hoping I was spelling it right. I must've been, because I got thousands of hits.

The first on the list was the MS Society. I clicked on it, and got to a screen where there was more information than I ever thought existed. And more than I ever wanted to know.

But I read it.

I learned about symptoms, medications, support groups, charities, and prognoses. I saw photos, read testimonies, and studied diagrams.

I still felt like shit. But I also felt better educated.

I stood up and walked to the window, stretching my back. Lucy was in the garden, pulling weeds from her rows of peas and radishes. Probably picking lettuce for lunch.

Not that I was hungry. I wondered if Jordan was hungry yet.

I went back to the desk and clicked back on the AskJeeves bar. I typed in "Tom Copper Band," and again got thousands of hits. Within the first few was their official web site, and I took some time checking it out.

There was all the stuff you'd expect: reviews of their albums, praise from other musicians, dates and ticket information for upcoming events. The photo album contained pictures from their concerts, as well as shots of them with other high-profile musicians: Kenny Wayne Shepherd, Train, Aerosmith. Bands they'd opened for on the road.

A truck pulled into the lane, sending Queenie into a barking fit. I peeked out to see the bug spray guys unloading themselves and their equipment. Lucy was heading their way from the vegetable plot, slapping her gardening gloves together. She caught sight of me in the window and waved me back. She'd take care of the instructions. I was glad to leave her to it.

I sat back down at the computer and checked out the band's bio page, which explained their beginnings. A photo of them as youngsters, Parker included, looking cool and...well...hot. I wasn't surprised they'd had groupie girls following them everywhere. The text told about their start at Temple University. A bar band until they were discovered by—I blinked in surprise—Gary Mann.

They'd known the owner of Club Independence that long?

I sat back, thinking about how—*if*—that changed things. None of the guys had said anything at Genna's memorial service about knowing Mann that long, or the effort he'd put into the band. Not even Jordan had mentioned it. Why? Was it such a natural part of things they didn't need to? I kept reading.

The web site didn't say all that much about the relationship. Just that Mann heard the band playing at a school coffeehouse and had taken Tom and the guys under his wing. He'd gotten them gigs at his place during that time—a bar called simply The Bar—and helped them along the way to wider recognition, putting them in contact with their record label.

Nothing sinister. Just business. But still...

I typed "Club Independence" into the search line and found the club's web site. Seeing the façade of the building made me feel queasy, so I hit the "About Us" button.

A photo of Mann and Robert Baronne took up the left side of the page, accompanied by a paragraph explaining how Mann had hired Baronne, his long-time friend and business partner, to manage the finances of Club Independence. Former college pals, they'd participated in various ventures together over the years before landing in this one about a decade earlier.

So they really had been together for ages. No wonder Mann was looking ragged. Not only had Genna been killed in his club, but his best friend was missing.

Missing as in kidnapped? Or missing as in took off? I still wasn't convinced anyone was looking all that hard for him. Just Alexander, who was barking up the wrong tree, anyway.

I clicked around a bit more on the site, checking out the upcoming concerts and performances. The club had been closed over the weekend, after the bomb threat and Genna's death, so the police could investigate. I'm sure that was a pain in Mann's ass, having to either find a new venue for the folks to perform in or cancel the event altogether.

My mind stopped mid-thought when I clicked onto the photo album page and a picture caught my eye. Mann with another guy, each looking back over their shoulders at the camera, Mann holding a paper they'd obviously been studying. The caption said Mann was standing with George Walker, the head of Club Independence's security team, going over plans for an event. The security guy that had supposedly called in sick, giving Jermaine a night's work.

But he hadn't called in sick. I'd seen him with my own eyes. Wearing a B.B. King T-shirt and helping injured people to the ambulances.

Chapter Seventeen

"Go to the site's photo album," I said into the phone.

Jermaine grunted in the background. "My fingers are too big for this stupid keyboard. Keep hitting the wrong things."

"Yeah, yeah, cry me a river. You there yet?"

"Okay. Okay, I'm there. What am I supposed to be looking at?"

"The third picture from the top. See that guy with Mann? Where it says 'George Walker, head of security'?"

"Wait. Oh, there. What about it?"

"You recognize that guy?"

"Mann?"

"No, the other one. The head of security."

"Nope. But then, I wouldn't. The only reason I was at the concert was he called in sick. Wasn't there."

"But he was."

"What?"

"I saw him after the concert. Helping folks get to the EMTs."

"Really?"

"Really. So I guess he wasn't sick, after all. At least not at-home-in-bed-puking-his-guts-out sick, anyway."

Silence. "That's weird."

"I'll say. Any idea what's going on?"

"Nope. Unless Mann called him once the shit hit the fan with the bomb threat and all and he came over."

"I'm telling you, he didn't look sick. Looked healthy as a heifer."

"Don't you mean horse?"

"I don't raise those. Anyway, no ideas?"

"Nope."

"All right. Thanks."

"What you gonna do?"

"I don't know. I'll see."

I hung up and considered my options. I chose the easiest, and dialed a number I knew by heart. It wasn't long till Detective Willard was on the phone.

"Got a tip," I said.

"Let's hear it."

I explained the discrepancy I'd found. A supposedly sick head of security at the scene of a major crime, looking all too good for his alleged condition.

"Anything else you can tell me?" Willard asked.

"Mann knew Walker was there. Came running up to him, asking if he'd seen Bobby."

"Wait. You mentioned that before. Him asking about Bobby."

"Yeah, but at the time I didn't know who he was talking to. Makes a difference."

"Sure does. Thanks for calling."

"Anything to get Jordan off the hook."

"Well, maybe this will help. Not quite sure how, but I'll pass it along." He paused. "Anything else to tell me?"

"If you're meaning about Jordan, nothing I haven't already said. He didn't do it. Either thing. Any of them. How ever many crimes you're investigating."

"How ever many there are. I'll be in touch."

I hung up and went out to thank the bug guys, who were finished spraying. They were pulling out of the lane when the phone rang, its piercing jangle making me wince. Lucy, who was back in the garden, stood up and pointed at me. She wasn't going to lie for me again. I listened for one more ring and trudged into the house, where I took a deep breath before picking it up and mumbling, "Hello?"

"Stella!"

Not Nick. Ma. In a full-blown shriek.

"What is it, Ma? What's wrong?"

"It's Jordan! They called with the autopsy results."

My stomach plummeted.

"It wasn't accidental, like we thought."

Oh, God.

"They really do think someone did it, Stella. Someone *murdered* her."

I knew I should say something. Something to ease Ma's distress.

"Stella?" Ma said.

"How did she die?" Not that I really wanted to know.

"They say...they say she was beaten. But that's not what killed her. She could've been saved, if she'd been found sooner. If it hadn't been for the bomb threat that cleared the building."

I swallowed. "Saved? How?"

Ma's voice was steely now. "She didn't die from being beaten. She died because she bled to death. She was...whoever beat her either didn't know how badly she was hurt, or didn't care. Genna—" Her voice caught, and she cleared her throat. "Genna bled to death from a cut on her leg. That big artery you have in your thigh. They aren't saying how that happened, exactly..."

But it all came down to a cold truth. Genna hadn't been trampled. Hadn't died by accident. Genna really had been murdered.

"So where's Jordan?" I said.

A steadying breath. "I don't know. Our lawyer, your friend Mr. Crockett, he called to tell me. Said he had tried to call Jordan, but wasn't getting an answer. Jordan knows, I'm sure of it. I'm sure someone told him. And I can't bear to think where he's gone. Alone."

I knew where this was going. And I knew I'd say yes, because I had to.

"I'll find him, Ma," I said. "And I'll let you know."

I hung up as she was saying thank you, and sank into the kitchen chair, leaning my head against the wall. Someone had assaulted Genna, and was horrible enough to leave her there to die, possibly unconscious and bleeding out. Only one person came to mind with the arrogance and selfishness it would take to do such a thing, and I was sure Jordan had thought it, too.

Jordan didn't answer either of his phones, so I scrabbled around in the papers on the kitchen stand and found the number Lucy had given me for contact with the band. I dialed it and waited for Tonya's voice.

"Tom Copper Band." A male voice.

"This is Stella Crown, and I need to—"

"Stella? Tom Copper. What do you need?"

"Ricky's address. Or his phone number."

Silence.

"It's an emergency," I said. "Please."

"You think he did it," he finally said.

"What?"

"You think he killed Genna."

I took a deep breath through my nose and let it out. Tom had obviously heard the news about Genna's death. "Ricky is the first person who came to mind. But I'm not going after him. I want to stop someone else from getting to him first."

"Jordan."

I didn't need to respond. I could almost feel Tom thinking.

"I'm in New Jersey, on my cell," he said. "You can probably get there first." The phone crackled, like he was changing hands. "Tonya," he said, his voice muffled. "Find Ricky's number on here, give it to Stella."

The phone crackled some more, and beeped. "Stella?" Tonya now. "Here it is." She read off the number, which I scribbled on the same sheet as theirs.

"You know his address?" I asked.

"Give me a minute."

I heard a zipper, and papers rattling.

"Isn't the contact sheet in here?" she asked, her voice muffled now.

"Should be," Tom said. "Look in the blue folder."

More papers, then her voice again.

"Kimball Street," she said, and gave me a number. "He rents a townhouse there."

"Thanks," I said, and punched the flash button.

The phone in Ricky's place rang two, three, four times, before his answering machine came on. I cursed under my breath, stopping when I heard a beep.

"Ricky, it's Jordan's friend Stella. I think he's coming down—"

"Hello?" A female voice. Tentative.

"Who is this?" I said.

A pause. "It's Marley."

Of course.

"Where's Ricky?"

"He's not here. He should be back soon."

Damn. "Jordan could be on his way to your place," I said, then corrected, "Ricky's place. Don't let him in."

"What?"

"Just don't. I'll be there soon."

I slammed down the phone, snatched my keys off the counter, and sprinted out to the garden. Lucy peered up from where she bent over the rototiller, filling it with gas.

"Gotta find Jordan," I said. "Genna was murdered, and he thinks Ricky did it."

Her eyes widened.

"At least I think so," I said. And took off.

Chapter Eighteen

I showed no mercy to the other cars on the road. Flew by them right and left, cursing out loud at the slowpokes in the passing lane. I must've somehow been the recipient of divine intervention, not getting a ticket or causing a traffic pile-up in the process. I guess God hadn't noticed how long it had been since I'd been to church.

Once I made it to Philly I spent way too much time finding the damn street and the right block. Those one-ways were killing me. When I finally got in the vicinity, it wasn't hard to find Ricky's house.

A small crowd had gathered to watch as Jordan pounded on the door of the brick townhome. The numbers hanging on the doorjamb jiggled visibly with each thump.

I angled my truck toward the curb, filling up the space in front of an alleyway, the only space on the block. Hopping out of the truck, it didn't take me long to hear what was going on.

"Show your face, you bastard!" Jordan was yelling. He rattled the doorknob and kicked the bottom of the door. "I saw you in there! You come out, or I'm breaking down the fucking door!"

Neighbors stood on their front stoops, their expressions mixtures of amusement and irritation. No fear that I could see. From what I could gather, they weren't too sorry to see Ricky on the receiving end of trouble, but didn't necessarily want it on their quiet street.

I jogged down the sidewalk to Ricky's place and waited at the bottom of the steps. Jordan didn't notice me.

"Jordan?" I spoke quietly. Too quietly, I guess, because he didn't react to my voice.

I went up the steps and laid a hand on his shoulder. He spun around, his arm rising defensively.

"Whoa." I held my hands out in a gesture of peace, palms toward the sky. "Just me, brother. Take it easy."

He lowered his arm, offering me a view of his eyes, which were red and watery. The first show of tears I'd seen.

"He's in there," Jordan said. His voice began as a husky whisper but quickly elevated. "The goddamned prick killed Genna." He kicked the door again, not seeming to feel the impact.

I glanced at the many faces aimed our direction. Some of the amusement was still there, but I didn't think it would be long before suspicion took root. The last thing Jordan needed was some scared old woman calling the cops. Taking a deep breath, I turned around.

"Show's over, folks. Nothing here to see."

They didn't move. I took another look, gauging the mix of the on-lookers. Some older people, like I'd registered before, but lots of younger, too, with hard bodies and even harder faces.

I locked eyes with a young guy a couple of parked cars down, where he leaned on the hood of an old Mustang. His arms were crossed, riding high on his seriously muscled chest. His skin was almost as dark as Jermaine's, and a brand of a flaming goat graced his upper arm. I prayed it was the mascot from his high school, and not the symbol of some violent street gang. Or the Devil. A glance at the crowd showed they were looking at the guy, too. Perhaps for a signal to disperse. I could only hope.

A loud thump spun me around to see Jordan standing with his forehead against the door, his hands in fists above him, against the wood. His eyes, I could see, were still open, and fixed on some point beyond the physical structure in front of him. I had to get him away from here before he either went ballistic on the door or broke down completely.

I looked at the Mustang Man again and straightened my spine. "Please?"

He studied my face, his mouth upturned at the corners. His eyes danced as we stood staring at each other—probably with the knowledge that he could make or break this for me.

Finally, he shifted forward just enough he scooted off the car. A subtle jerk of his head sent several people scrambling for cover. The rest of the crowd let up a collective sigh, as if disappointed the entertainment had come to an end. Doors clicked shut all around us, and people went about outside business, watering petunias on their porches, picking up litter strewn by the curb. Mustang Man gave me one last look, raising his eyebrows, his eyes sparkling. I nodded my thanks, and he sauntered down the sidewalk, trailed by two other guys who could claim only a small percentage of their leader's charisma.

I guessed the guy ran the whole street.

Letting out my pent-up breath, I leaned against the doorjamb, about a foot from Jordan.

"Jordan. It's time to go."

His eyes closed.

"Come on, man. This isn't helping anything."

"But Genna…"

"We don't know that Ricky did anything."

That opened his eyes. "He—"

"—is an ass. I know. But that doesn't mean he killed her."

His eyes closed again, and his shoulders slumped.

"Come on, bro," I said. "If he did it, the cops'll get him."

He rolled his head back and forth on the door.

I pulled gently on his elbow. "Come on."

Using his upraised fists, he pushed himself off the door. Without the support, he swayed toward me. I caught his arms, his whole weight crashing toward me.

Using the wall as leverage, I eased him onto the step. His knees completely gave out halfway down, and he collapsed onto the step. I sank down beside him and put my arm around his shoulder, keeping him from keeling into the railing.

"She was getting out, you know," Jordan said.

"Genna? Of her relationship with Ricky?"

He leaned back into me, tipping his head up toward the sky. "All of it. Ricky, the band. She wanted to get married."

"To you?" I asked softly.

He nodded, his eyes filling again. "To me. Genna wanted to marry *me.*"

I tightened my arm around him, his pain evident in his words and voice. He cried silently for a minute or so before sitting up and swiping at his face with the heel of his hand.

"Ricky didn't know?" I asked.

He looked down at the step and dislodged a stone with his shoe. "He knew she wanted to quit the band."

"How'd he react?"

"Like you'd imagine. Completely freaked out."

"Why?" Although I knew. I'd heard it from Annie.

Jordan confirmed it. "Because the band only kept him on for Genna's sake. She was the only reason they considered him in the first place."

Exactly what Annie had told Marley at rehearsal, when I eavesdropped in the bathroom.

"Without her," Jordan said, "he had to know he'd be out on his ear."

"He didn't know about you?"

He sighed. "He knew about me. But he thought it was completely one-sided. My side. He had no idea how serious it had gotten."

Oh, he had more than an idea. I was sure of it.

But I didn't think Ricky was stupid enough to kill Genna. At least not on purpose. Because for *sure* he'd be done with the band then. Unless…if he got carried away and beat her up, he might not have meant to kill her, but figured she'd tell the others afterwards, so he left her to die.

I shook my head. It was all too horrible to think about.

"Jordan." I considered my words, not quite sure how to phrase the question. "Remember how people said they heard you and Genna arguing the night of the concert? What was that about?"

"Is it anybody's business?"

I looked at him, and he ducked his head. After a few moments he said, "She told me she wanted to quit the band, get married, have a family."

I waited.

"I asked why we couldn't do both. Why we couldn't pursue our music dreams with the band and be together." He stopped, rubbing his face with his hand.

"She didn't want that?" I asked.

He shook his head. "She was tired of it all. Tired of touring, of the songs, of the guys. Being around Ricky. And she didn't want to make the band choose between her and their drummer."

"Doesn't seem like it would've been a hard choice, seeing how they feel about him."

"No. They would've chosen her. But it was another excuse for her."

"You weren't ready?"

A strangled sound came from his throat. "I thought she was being selfish. I thought she needed to give the guys more warning, let them make the decision about the band. Show her she could have me *and* the music." He leaned forward, resting his face in his hands. "God, I loved her, Stella. I would've given it all up for her. I should've. I was an idiot."

"She knew you loved her," I said.

"Did she?"

Looking at Jordan, at the tension in his shoulders, I knew he would always wonder.

Chapter Nineteen

With Jordan practically comatose and me not knowing Philadelphia streets real well, I ended up somewhere I didn't recognize. I pulled to the side of yet another street that looked like all the others and poked Jordan's side.

"Whuh?" He blinked slowly as he turned his head my way.

"Have any idea where we are?"

He looked around. "What street are we on?"

"I don't know. Some freaking one-way."

He studied the area, then pointed out the front window. "Keep going."

"Where will that get us?"

"South Street."

"Where Club Independence is?"

"Yeah. I'll know my way home from there."

I stared out the front window.

"What?" Jordan said.

"You sure you want to drive by the club?"

He didn't answer, so I checked the mirrors and pulled out into the street.

"Jordan," I said when we were on our way. "Any reason you would've been arguing with Bobby Baronne at the concert?"

His face scrunched. "What? Why?"

"Someone told the cops they heard the two of you."

I expected a blow-up, but instead he closed his eyes and shook his head slowly. "I didn't argue with Baronne. Didn't kidnap him, either, if that's what you're wondering."

"I'm not wondering anything."

"Just the cops. Fantastic."

I stopped badgering him and drove. Following his mumbled directions, we soon came up on the club.

"Stop," Jordan said suddenly.

"What?"

"Stop!"

I swerved to the curb in front of Club Independence and we jerked to a stop.

"What is it?"

He kept his face averted from the building. "Will you see if anybody's here?"

I watched as his face grew pale. "Why, Jordan? Why would you want to be here?"

He shrugged and shook his head, apparently not sure himself. "I don't know. There's some equipment I need to pick up for Saturday."

But that wasn't the real reason. We both knew it.

"You're sure?"

"I'm sure."

I didn't know if we were actually in a real parking spot, so I looked around for some kind of marking. A sign by the curb read, "Independence Club Parking Only." I figured since Jordan worked there—at least sporadically—we qualified. I hoped the meter maids would agree.

"I'll be right back," I said.

He didn't say anything, but kept his eyes pointed away from the club. I opened the door without checking for traffic and about got the panel taken off by a Lexus, which screeched sideways, its horn blaring. Yanking my leg back into the cab I took a deep breath, hoping I wouldn't have a heart attack.

"Country mouse," Jordan said, his eyes lighting up a fraction.

I glared at him. "Oh, shut up." Scouring the street for cars, I jumped down from the truck and stalked to the doors of Club Independence.

All of the doors—a half dozen—were locked. I put my hands on my hips and studied the entryway.

"Over on your right." Jordan pointed beyond me to a small metal square on the wall. "It's a bell. Ring it, and if Mann's here, he'll answer."

I pushed the button with my thumb, holding it down long enough to annoy whoever was inside so they'd come see who was knocking. I hoped so, anyway.

A few minutes later, just when my thumb was hovering again over the button, the latch clicked on the closest door and Gary Mann peered out. He didn't look any better than when I'd seen him at Tom's place on Monday. If anything, his color looked worse after a couple more days of worry. His clothes weren't up to par, either. Dirty jeans, an even dirtier T-shirt, and smudges of grime marking up his cheeks and forehead.

"Help you?" he asked.

I glanced over my shoulder at Jordan, and Mann followed my eyes. Recognition lit his face, and he squinted at me. "I've seen you before."

"A couple times. I'm Stella Crown, a friend of Jordan's."

Jordan stepped down from the truck and slammed the door behind him.

Mann watched him, his expression softening only slightly. "What do you want, Granger?"

Jordan's jaw bunched, and he swallowed. "I need to pick up some stuff. That's all."

Mann closed his eyes and puffed out his cheeks, forcing air through his lips. "Okay, fine. Come on in." He held the door open wider, and I scooted by him before he could change his mind.

The lobby felt like a different space from Friday night, when I first saw the happy, before-concert crowd. Different, too, from the screaming, frightened mob. Concert posters plastered the walls almost from top to bottom. I hadn't noticed them on Friday night, with all the people. Mann advertised a variety of acts: magicians, dance troupes, plays. And, of course, bands.

"I've even done spelling bees and proms," Mann said, following my gaze.

"A multi-function facility," I said.

"You got it. That's where the money is."

"You ever have something like this happen before?"

His eyes shot to Jordan, then back to me. "You mean…?"

"The bomb threat."

"Oh. No. I've been in this business for thirty-some years, and there's never been trouble."

I raised my eyebrows.

"Well, there's been little things," he said. "Drunks and fights and graffiti and stuff. But nothing…nothing like this."

His eyes went blank again, and it almost looked like he was holding back physical pain.

"Have you heard from Bobby?" I asked. "Or his kidnappers or anything?" If there *were* kidnappers.

He blinked once, and his face sagged. But then he blinked again and was back to his old expression. "No. Now, is there something in particular I can do for you?"

I met his eyes, wondering again why he wasn't tearing up the police station for news of his missing partner. But I didn't think I'd be getting any more out of him about that particular subject. At least not yet.

"I need to grab some stuff from the stage," Jordan said. "We took a few things for rehearsal, but a lot of the concert equipment is still here."

Gary nodded. "It's all out there. I figured you'd be back to get it, and I don't have anything booked till Friday. I had to cancel the gigs last Saturday and Sunday, and the new act isn't moving their set in till Friday morning."

"So I can box up our sound equipment?"

"Sure."

Jordan avoided my eyes and headed into the auditorium. Mann didn't seem at all interested in where Jordan was going.

Kind of strange, if he was listening at all to the cops, who'd placed Jordan at the top of their suspect list for planting the bomb. For everything. How did Mann know Jordan wasn't going to set another one?

"Think you could show me something?" I said to Mann.

"Like what?"

I hesitated. "Where Genna died."

Mann narrowed his eyes.

"I don't really *want* to see it," I said. "But I think I *need* to."

"Because…"

"Because I'm trying to help Jordan deal with this whole thing, and I'd like to know everything I can." And maybe help out the cops in the process.

Mann's tongue worked in his cheek, and he jiggled the keys in his pocket. But finally, without another word, he turned and walked to the far end of the lobby, toward the door Nick and I had gone through when we followed Jordan, on our way to meet the band.

There was no tour guide patter this time. Just the clumping of our feet on the tile floor, Mann jingling his keys, which were now in his hand. We traveled through the maze of hallways, ending up at the backstage door, where we had first run into Marley and Annie. And where we'd seen Mann on our way out.

Mann opened the door and kept walking, but instead of leading me toward the green room, where the band had been hanging out, we curved to our left, through a fire door and into another hallway, this one doubly wide as the others.

"Storage," he said, waving his hand.

There were several doors in the space, and peeking through their small windows I saw boxes, shelves, and even one room that was completely empty. At the end of the hallway stood another door, with a red and white sign that read, *Do not open except in case of EMERGENCY.*

"Where does that go?" I asked, pointing at the exit.

He grunted. "Back alley. Our part's shut off by a metal garage door. It's where we load and unload big set pieces or equipment."

"So it's not really rigged to an alarm, like it says?"

"Sure it is. But I can disable it when I need to."

He stood by the second door on the right and hunted through his ring of keys. He slid one into the lock and turned the doorknob.

"Sound storage," he said.

I stepped into the doorway, but stopped at the sight. Cables, microphones, mic stands, amps, and even parts of an old drum set lay haphazardly around the room on the floor and metal shelving. A coat of black dust covered it all, and I couldn't imagine that anything in there could ever be used again. Those cops sure didn't scrimp when it came to checking for fingerprints.

"Here?" I said.

Mann stood in the hallway, his back against the opposite wall. "On the floor, right beyond the door, her head pointed that way." He indicated the other end of the room.

I looked down, now seeing a dark stain under the layer of dust, the black not as thick where fingers wouldn't have touched. "Is that—"

"Genna's blood," Mann said.

I stepped back into the hallway, bile rising in my throat. Why exactly had I wanted to see where she'd been killed?

"The door was shut," Mann said. "They didn't find her at first because the fire exit hadn't been used, so they assumed no one was in this section. Only after they'd cleared the main areas did they come back here."

"The band didn't exit this way?"

"No. There's a much closer door behind the stage. My security team took them right out the back. They were probably the first people out of the building."

At least the guys were. Genna was the last.

A sound from backstage made me jump, and I headed that way. "Can we get out of here? I don't want Jordan seeing that."

Mann closed the room's door and locked it, shoving his keys back in his pocket.

"You mind showing me backstage?" I asked. "Giving me a tour of the dressing rooms?"

He eyed me curiously, but gave a half-hearted shrug. "Can't hurt, I guess."

We walked out of the hallway and he led me around, showing me the room where I'd first met the band, and the little nook of dressing rooms surrounding it. I remembered Genna leaving in a huff after meeting us—probably still hurt at Jordan's response earlier that evening, when he'd said no to her proposal to run off and get married.

"If someone left the room that way," I said, pointing toward the door where she'd gone, "how would they get around to backstage?"

"Stage left or right?" Mann asked.

I considered this. Didn't stage folks talk about their sides backwards? When it's right it's really left, or some other dumb thing? I knew it was either right for the audience and left for the folks on stage, or the other way around. Freakin' theater crowd.

I stood in the same direction as backstage and pointed to my right. "That side."

"Stage right," Mann said. "Easy. You'd go out that door and simply walk across the stage to the other side."

"Even if there's an audience?"

"Sure. There are sound barriers that hide the actual back wall itself."

So Genna could've been in the wings overhearing Ricky tell Marley he was going to wring her neck if she didn't shape up. It would've become clear the kind of relationship Ricky had with the groupie girl, making Genna even more certain of her desire to take off with her new love.

We left the green room and found Jordan piling sound equipment onto a dolly. He glanced up from where he knelt, tucking a microphone into Styrofoam. His eyes were watery and red, and I realized too late that I should never have let him come back here. At least, not yet.

"Can we load some of this stuff into your truck?" he asked me, not meeting my eyes. "We'll need it on Saturday."

"The wedding?" Mann asked.

Jordan nodded.

"Sure," I said. "The bed's empty, and I've got some tie-downs."

He nodded again and began pulling the dolly toward the storage hallway. The place where Genna died.

"Jordan," I said.

He stopped. "What?"

"The truck's out front."

Mann looked at me, understanding, I was sure, my anxiety. "Yeah, Jordan, go ahead and take that out through the front. Use the ramp by the stage. Save you having to move the truck and all."

Jordan studied us both, obviously knowing something was up, but he changed directions and took the dolly toward the auditorium.

When he was gone, I turned to Mann. "So, Mr. Mann. How come your head of security was at the concert when he'd supposedly called in sick?"

His face went white, then red, and he began jangling those keys again. "What do you mean?"

I snorted. "Come on. I know why Jermaine Granger was called in to sub—or why *he* thought, anyway—but I also know I saw Walker after the concert. He wasn't in uniform, but he also wasn't sick. Looked healthy and strong, carrying injured folks to the ambulances."

"I don't think—"

"And he was talking to you, after you ran up to him, asking if he'd seen Bobby. I was there, Gary. I saw you. And him."

Mann closed his eyes and staggered backward, collapsing onto a folding chair that sat against the wall. He leaned forward, resting his elbows on his knees and hanging his head between them.

"You gonna faint?" I asked.

He shook his head.

"You care to explain?"

He shook his head again. "Not really."

"Humor me."

He sighed deeply and sat up, leaning his head against the wall and looking up at the rafters. "I can't—"

"A woman is dead, Gary. Don't you think it's time to tell the whole story?"

I waited, crossing my arms and standing three feet in front of him, staring down into his face.

"Bobby didn't kill Genna," Mann finally said.

I cocked my head. "You're sure of that?"

Mann's eyes opened. "He's not a killer."

"Okay. That's your opinion. But he wasn't kidnapped, was he?"

Mann looked away.

"Where'd he go, Gary?"

He shook his head. "I don't know."

"But he left on his own, didn't he?"

He was quiet.

"He ran away," I said. "With all your money."

His head dropped to the side, and after a while he looked at me. "I think he did."

His eyes closed again and for a moment I was afraid he was going to cry. I walked over and pulled another chair from the corner. I set it in front of him and straddled it, my arms across the top. "What happened, Gary?"

He took a long breath through his nose and sat up. "I went to get him last week. Friday morning, around ten or so. We'd been working late the night before to get ready for Friday's concert and I thought we could take a break at Starbucks, you know? But he wasn't in his office. I knew he was here, since I saw his car parked in back, and his office light was on, so I went in, looking for a clue as to where he'd gone. I was only in there for a minute, but it felt off. Wrong, somehow. I suddenly realized some of his things were gone from the wall. I didn't think much of it, figuring he must be redecorating, until I noticed exactly what was missing. The photo of him with Mick Jagger, a signed copy of *Abbey Road*. His framed poster of Christina Aguilera." He stopped and stood up, pacing across the space and back.

"I couldn't imagine what he was doing. I mean, he's my partner. My business manager. I'd know if he was going somewhere. At least I thought I would."

He looked at me, his eyes full of pain. "I checked in the back to see if his car was still there. It was, so I ran out to his house. I've got my own key, you know. And he's got mine. For checking in if one of us is out of town. Anyway, he wasn't there, but his suitcase was on his bed, partially packed. I couldn't think of any reason he'd be packing."

I could. "So you called Walker."

His shoulders slumped. "Yeah. I wanted him to keep an eye on Bobby that night, without Bobby knowing. That's why I had Walker phone in sick. Bobby took the call backstage, and Jordan heard him. That's how Jermaine Granger got the job."

God, it screwed up your life to trust people.

"So you really don't think he was kidnapped."

He laughed, but without humor. "No. I think Bobby is somewhere the sun shines all the time and he has no responsibilities other than to order his drink."

"One concert makes that much money?"

"Nah. And most of the take is through credit cards anyway. We get some cash, but not enough for... But that doesn't matter. From what I can see, Bobby's been taking more than his share for quite some time now." He smiled sadly.

"You think the Mafia had anything to do with it?"

His eyes opened wide. "What?"

"There was a big show-down on Friday night with the Mafia. Lots of shooting and dead guys. Think he was a part of it?"

He laughed again, and this time there was an actual smile—a small one—to go with it.

"No. Bobby wouldn't mess with them. *Real* bad guys. When it comes right down to it, he's a coward. I mean, come on. When he wants to steal massive amounts of money, where does he go? A bank? An anonymous house? Nope. His best friend. He knows I won't want to turn him in."

"And the bomb?" I asked. "He too cowardly to set it?"

He looked at me, the sad smile lingering. "It didn't actually go off, did it?" He sighed. "I don't think it was meant to."

I studied Mann's face, finding kindness in his sad eyes. "I'm sorry, Gary."

"Yeah. Me, too."

I pushed myself off the chair. "Guess I'd better go see if Jordan needs help loading that equipment."

"Sure. Let's go."

We walked quietly across the stage and up the aisle through the auditorium. Jordan was outside, leaning against the tailgate and waiting for help to load the sound board from the dolly. I looked at him for a moment before stepping up and taking a side. Between the two of us we easily got the big box settled in the truck.

"Thanks for the tour," I said to Mann, holding out my hand.

He nodded and grasped my fingers before turning to Jordan. "I'm sorry," he said.

Jordan took Mann's hand, but didn't reply before heading to the passenger seat of the truck. I sneaked a glimpse at Mann, wondering if he'd noticed the same thing I had.

The knees of Jordan's jeans were dirty, black with what could easily have been fingerprint dust.

Chapter Twenty

My stomach was growling furiously by the time I pulled into my drive. Jordan and I had stopped by the German-Hungarian club, where the wedding reception would take place, to put the sound equipment in the storage shed before I took him home. He promised he would call Ma to update her on his whereabouts and let her know he hadn't done anything stupid. I was glad I'd gotten to Ricky's when I had, so he could give an optimistic—and truthful—report.

Queenie met me in the drive, her tail wagging. It was nice to have at least one person who had no issues. Person. Dog. Whatever. Her friendship worked for me. I gave her some good scratching before stepping into the house.

Lucy was taking a break at the kitchen table when I got there, a sweating glass of that good lemonade in her hand.

"Got any leftovers?" I asked, sticking my head in the fridge.

"Chicken," she said. "Want me to make you a sandwich?"

"No, thanks, I can do it."

"Your loss. It'll taste better if I make it."

That would be true.

"All right," I said. "Might as well take advantage while you're here."

She popped up from the chair and got busy slicing her home-made bread and slathering it with any number of condiments and fresh veggies, besides the token protein. I took her seat at the table, putting my feet up on the chair across from me. It wasn't until I was settled that I realized how glad I was to sit and do nothing.

"So," Lucy said, "you found Jordan?"

"I did. Crisis averted. For now."

"Where was he?"

"Where I figured. In Philly, itching to knock Ricky's block off."

She looked up. "You stopped him?"

"If I hadn't, the cops probably would've. I'm sure someone had their finger on the 911 button."

Although I could've been wrong. Mustang Man might not have given the go-ahead for police involvement. If that was the case, it really was good I got there when I did.

Lucy shook her head. "Poor Jordan. If only he'd let his family share some of the burden." She looked at me in a way that I was sure was supposed to send a message.

"Telling everyone about your problems doesn't make them go away," I said.

She went back to the sandwich. "No, but it allows others to offer comfort."

"Fat lot that does when your heart's broken."

She looked at me again, and seemed about to say something.

"That sandwich done?" I asked.

She used a chef's knife to cut it into two thick triangles, bursting with tasty layers. "It's done." She brought it to the table and tossed a bag of chips down beside it. "Something to drink?"

"I can get it."

"I'm up. Want lemonade?"

I shrugged. "Sure. Thanks. You expecting a tip?"

She grinned. "Just your secrets, when you're ready to tell them."

She plopped a glass down in front of me and left.

Damn loving Mennonite woman.

I ate my sandwich, glaring at the fridge, which hadn't done anything except be in my line of vision. By all rights I should've been glaring at the phone, since I knew I should be using it to call Nick. But if I didn't look at it, it couldn't send me silent reprimands, right?

Right.

By the time I finished eating, I was beginning to smell whatever it was Lucy had stuck in the crockpot that afternoon. Even with that sandwich, the smell still made me hungry.

I put my dishes in the dishwasher and faced the phone, wicked as it seemed. Willard would probably appreciate an update, with the information I'd gotten out of Mann. That is, if that weirdo Alexander hadn't already paid a visit to Club Independence since I'd ID'd Walker, the security guy, as being at the concert.

Willard answered the phone himself.

"Gladys out for lunch?" I asked.

"Dentist appointment. They had an opening and moved her up in the schedule. I assured her I could answer the phone politely, if the rest of the gang was out of pocket. What can I do for you?"

"Your pal Alexander pay a visit to Gary Mann yet?"

"He's not my pal, and I have no idea. I just got your information about Walker to him a couple of hours ago."

"I think Bobby Baronne is your mad bomber. And he might've killed Genna, too."

Silence on his end. "Explain."

"He's been stealing money from the club for months. Mann doesn't know why. He just figured it out on Friday, when he discovered Baronne packing up to leave."

"To go where?"

"No idea. That's why Mann had his security guy, Walker, call in sick. He was supposed to keep an eye on Baronne, because Mann was sure Baronne was leaving and taking all the money with him. I saw where Genna was killed—"

"A room in a back hallway, right?"

"Right. With an exit to the back alley, where Baronne parked. I think she saw him taking off, and he killed her."

I could practically hear Willard's brain whizzing. "How would she know he was leaving for good? It's not like the hallway was off limits."

I let out a huff of air. "I don't know. Maybe she saw him carrying a bulging bag with money sticking out of it. You're the cop, you figure it out. I'm just the messenger here."

"A messenger with theories."

"So sue me. Will you pass it on to Alexander?"

"Sure. You think he set the bomb, too?"

"Why not? It seems too far-fetched to have a thief, a murderer, *and* a bomber in the building on the same night, unless it's the same person."

"You could be right. But we do still have those phone calls between Jordan and Baronne."

"Which, as I mentioned before, were most likely about arrangements for the concert. Come on, Willard, why would Jordan throw away everything for some guy he hardly even knows?"

"You're sure about that? That he hardly knows him?"

"Yes."

"Okay. Well, I'll throw your information in the mix. Thanks, Stella."

"You're welcome. Now go get the son of a bitch."

I hung up and looked at the clock. Time to make the doughnuts.

I met Lucy in the barn, where Zach had also shown up.

"You have other things you need to do?" I asked Lucy.

She looked at me. "You mean things for the wedding?"

"Or whatever. It is only three days away, you know."

"Oh, I know. *You're* the one who has something to do."

I waggled my eyebrows. "Did it."

She froze. "You got something to wear?"

"Not yet. But it's coming."

Her eyes narrowed. "What is it?"

"Geez. Have a little faith."

"It's not easy."

"So, you guys working," Zach said, "or am I in this on my own?"

"Smart ass," I said to him.

He smiled.

"You're serious about milking?" Lucy asked.

I waved her toward the door. "If Zach is here, I'm fine. As long as he keeps his mouth shut."

Zach had the gall to laugh at that.

"I mean it, buster," I said.

"Right," he said. "Like you're really as tough as you look."

I stopped in my tracks, watching as he walked down the aisle, slapping the cows on their rumps.

I used to be tough. At least I thought so. Until that damn love bug had bitten me in the ass.

I dragged the feed cart into the parlor and began throwing grain into the cows' bins. And prayed the phone wouldn't ring.

Chapter Twenty-One

The phone stayed silent, and I woke before my alarm the next morning. I got dressed and went downstairs to grab a quick breakfast and head outside.

Since I'd awoken a few minutes early, I walked to the back of the yard and gazed across the field, breathing in the morning air. Corn stalks pushing through the ground proudly displayed their now five inches of height in the early light. They would've been taller if we'd had any rain. Studying the sky, I couldn't see we'd be getting any precipitation in the day to come.

The developments beyond my fences shined in the dawn, their windows sparkling and their aluminum siding sending bolts of reflected light every which way, despite the dust. I'd managed to keep my farm, the land, the house. But the privacy I'd once known—years ago, now—was gone. There was probably some guy in a business suit staring out his kitchen window at me while he sipped his cappuccino, ready to begin his daily trek down to Philly. And here I was, this crazy farmer lady holding out so the developments couldn't creep one more foot in my direction. They were way too close as it was.

I ran through milking on auto-pilot, but kept the cows in their stalls, having scheduled the hoof-trimmer for that morning. We'd take the cows out one by one for the guy to check their feet, and let them go only when we knew they were healthy.

The trimmer rolled in around eight-thirty with his portable hoof trimming equipment. Lucy and Queenie met him on the drive, and I unlocked the paddock gate for him to pull inside the fence. I saw his hair first, a shock of white above his leathery face. His teeth were the next thing I could see through the windshield, since they matched his hair.

"Ms. Crown," he said, leaning out of the driver's window.

"How you doin', Al?"

"Can't complain, can't complain." He parked, his trailer just clearing the gate, and hopped down from the truck. He smiled, looking around at the barnyard and Lucy, who smiled back. "Your farmhand lady here tells me she's getting married this weekend."

"That's right."

"But she'll still be working here."

"Thank God for that."

He gave a hearty laugh and clapped me on the shoulder. "Shall we get started, then? I'm sure the last thing she wants to be doin' her wedding week is digging crap out of cows' hooves."

Lucy grinned. "There's worse things."

"Yeah?" he said. "Name me three."

Her forehead puckered, like she was really considering it.

Al laughed again. "Well, bring me the first victim."

I went into the barn and brought out Minnie Mouse, a rope around her neck to lead her forward. She did fine until she got to the mouth of the chute, where she balked. Couldn't blame her, really, for not wanting to walk into the claustrophobic tunnel. It seems like nothing—a little ramp leading up to a platform—but the sides are close and there's no space to move once the cow gets in. Not somewhere I'd enter willingly, that's for sure.

"C'mon, baby," I said. "In you go."

Al clucked his tongue, murmuring quietly under his breath, and Lucy spoke sweet nothings from Minnie's other side. Gradually Minnie's eye-rolling stopped, and she took a hesitant step into the trimming table.

"Good girl," I said. "Few more steps."

She got there eventually, and we locked her head into the equipment. When she was steady, Al pushed a button and the chute made a gentle flip, so Minnie was lying flat, like she was in bed. Her nervousness came through in her foot, which snapped back and forth like a whip, but Al was a veteran, and it didn't take him long to get her legs secured.

He took his time checking her over, cleaning manure and straw out from her hooves and checking for hairy wart, a contagious virus that produces a crack in the hoof. When he deemed her healthy, he ground her hooves to a comfortable level—the equivalent of clipping her toenails—and she was done. A push of the button turned her upright, and she was soon trotting happily away to the pasture, done with her yearly foot check.

Next.

"You hear the latest trimming story?" Al asked as we persuaded Ariel into the chute.

"Nope," I said.

He locked Ariel in and pushed the button, dipping her sideways. "Farmer down toward Lancaster hired a new fella for his hoof check. Guy ground twenty cows down too far before they realized what he was doing. Foundered 'em, right down to the flesh, almost. Farmer had to put 'em all down."

Lucy gasped. "That's terrible!"

"Insurance pay for it?" I asked.

Al shook his head. "Guy wasn't bonded, and don't have the resources to pay the damages himself. Farmer can issue a judgment against him, but you can't get something from nothing."

"At least he won't be killing more cows," Lucy said. "Nobody's gonna hire him after that."

Al absently flicked a wad of dirt in my direction, and I dodged it.

"You know the guy?" I asked.

"The trimmer? Nah. Guess I won't now, neither. Better not show his face 'round there again, I'll say. Or anywhere else, for that matter." He looked up at Lucy. "Whyn't you go get the next one, honey? I'll be done here in a jiff."

"You got it."

And so went our morning. Stories, cows who didn't want to go willingly into the chute, and, fortunately, only a few Al had to administer healing remedies to. As I watched Al work, I thought of Nick. Nick, who like some of these cows had something insidious inside him, betraying his body, changing possibilities for the future. I wondered if the doctors checking him out knew what they were doing, or if they'd screw up somehow.

"You all right?" Lucy asked.

I glanced at her, feeling my taut muscles, and realized I must've looked like I was in pain.

I jerked my chin. "Just thinking."

Al chuckled. "That can be a problem, can't it?"

I looked down at him. "That farmer down your way hired the crooked hoof trimmer on good faith, and the guy let him down. Betrayed that trust. When you get someone to take care of your animals, they need to follow through, not kill half the herd. The guy should be held responsible for what he did. Financially. Not just morally."

"Uh, okay," Lucy said. She watched me the way Tess had at the bridal shop, like I was a rabid raccoon who'd wandered onto the farm at night to raid the garbage.

"That's why you check references," Al said. "Kid hadn't hardly worked anywhere before. The farmer had heard he was trying to get started and wanted to help him out."

"Probably also wanted to save a few bucks," Lucy said.

Al snorted. "Ain't that right."

"Not that you quality guys charge too much," Lucy added.

Al smiled, and kept on cleaning. "This girl's good to go. Bring me the next un."

Lucy went to bring another cow while Al and I turned Mulan upright and freed her. Belle marched right into the chute like the matriarch she was, and didn't balk when the trim table laid her down.

"Like what's going on down in Philly," I said.

Lucy shook her head. *"What?"*

"At Club Independence. Bobby, the office guy and supposedly the owner's best friend, takes off with the club's money, leaving his friend to fend off the cops and the tax man. Plus, he probably set the bomb that evacuated the place during the concert."

"You mean he wasn't kidnapped?" Lucy asked.

"Gary Mann doesn't think so. He thinks Baronne's been stealing money for months, and finally took off on Friday."

"The cops know this?"

"I called Willard."

"What you talking about?" Al asked.

I looked down at his white head. "Friends. Betrayal. Like Lucy here, going off to marry another one of my best friends."

Lucy shook her head, but didn't say anything.

"How's that bad?" Al asked. "Sounds like a good deal to me. You yourself said she's staying on working here."

Lucy eyed me.

"Yeah," I said. "I guess." I watched a hawk circle in the sky, three smaller birds flitting around it, annoying the hell out of it, I was sure.

"But another thing going on in Philly," I said. "Jordan's in love with Genna, or was before someone killed her, but she was actually dating some other asshole who thinks he's a god and now has a groupie girl in his apartment. The same girl who's taking Genna's place in the band and has been screwing the asshole god-guy for months. Meanwhile, you've got the old drummer hanging around, even though tensions were high when he left because of the songwriting and how he crashed the band's van and got the lead singer addicted to painkillers. And all three of the original guys are about sick to death of each other from touring all these years. And don't forget Genna's little sister, who hated Genna's skanky boyfriend and was administering tough love, only to try it on the night her sister got murdered. I think she's got the hots for Jordan, too, who doesn't have a clue, being a guy. And speaking of guys, you've got one of the band members who seems to be in love with the wife of another band member, but everybody either ignores it or doesn't even notice."

I stopped when I realized Lucy and Al were both staring at me, their mouths hanging open and their eyebrows raised.

"Want me to explain?" I asked.

"No," they said.

Lucy trotted off to the barn while Al pushed the button and sent Belle on her way.

"In you go, Ella," Lucy said in a minute, giving the cow a smack on the rump. When Cinderella was lowered, her foot whacking the rails, Lucy came and stood beside me. "What about Nick?"

I scowled. "What about him?"

"I assume he fits into this whole anger theme you're spouting off about."

"Anger? Who's angry?"

Al looked up at me. "Nick Who?"

"Stella's boyfriend," Lucy said. "At least he was the last she talked to me about him."

"So you need me to update you?" I asked.

She shrugged. "'S up to you."

Yes, it was. And I wouldn't. "I'm going to get the next cow," I said.

I shut my trap till noon, when Lucy suggested we take a break for lunch. Al came into the house with us, where Lucy whipped up some grilled cheese sandwiches and tomato soup. I ate mine hunched over the bowl while Lucy and Al argued the finer points of sweet corn hybrids and which type of tomato they preferred to grow. I finished my lunch before either of them and went outside to sit on the step. Queenie trotted over and lay on the lower step, her head on my knees. I picked at a clump of hair behind her ear and tried not to think.

Somehow there just wasn't anything good to think about.

Chapter Twenty-Two

"Can you please go to the Biker Barn for me?" Lucy asked.

I opened my eyes and looked up at her from where I sat, my feet on the coffee table and my head on the back of the couch. Al had left twenty minutes before, having finished up with the herd and driven off with his machine.

"For what?" Even I could tell my voice didn't carry any enthusiasm.

"Lenny got the Harley napkins we ordered, and I want to wrap them around the silverware tonight."

"For Saturday?"

"Um, yes." She looked at me like I'd sent my brain off with Al.

"You're having fancy napkins and actual silverware at a pig roast?" I asked.

"It's a wedding reception."

"With a pig on a spit."

Her nostrils flared. "I'm not sure what's up your butt, since you won't talk to me about it. But if you're not going to share, then don't hold me responsible for how you're feeling. Now will you go or not?"

I ground my teeth. "Fine. I'll go."

She looked at me some more, and at my feet on the coffee table.

"Right now?" I asked.

"Now would be good."

I heaved myself off the couch and stomped out to the garage.

"You might want to take the truck," Lucy called after me. "Unless you think you can fit the boxes in your saddle bags."

I'd make them fit.

Twenty minutes later I entered the Biker Barn to the tune of the ringing bells on the door, and the smell of tobacco smoke. Bart glanced up from where he studied a catalog, his face lighting up when he saw me. He took the cigarette out of his mouth and stubbed it out in an ashtray.

"Hey, there. If it ain't the princess, come to make a social call. Bit close to milking time, in'nit?"

I dropped onto a stool by the counter and leaned my elbows on the glass top. "Evenings are Lucy's, and she's the one who sent me. I'm supposed to pick up some boxes of napkins or something you got from H-D."

"Oh, yeah, those. They're back here somewhere." He looked behind the counter, his braid swaying as he bent first one way and then the other, then stepped over to the swinging doors that led to the shop. "Len!" he hollered. "Those boxes of napkins?"

I heard Lenny's voice, but not the words, and Bart came back, passing me and heading toward the office.

"Can you carry them okay?" I asked.

It had only been eight months since Bart had been stabbed by an outlaw biker, almost losing his life. He still wasn't quite up to speed—especially in his endurance level—and he limped when he was tired, but he never complained. He was just glad to be alive. Alive with some new scars on his face that he loved to show off.

He came back and thumped two boxes onto the counter, ignoring my question. "You bring your bike?"

"Yeah. I'll squeeze 'em in."

"Well, don't squeeze 'em too hard, or Lucy'll have your head."

I grabbed them and hopped off the stool, heading for the door. Then I turned around and sat down again.

"Bart?"

He looked up from the catalog he was already back to studying. "Huh?"

"You know what you're wearing Saturday?"

He smiled. "Oh yeah. I got me a sweet outfit. Wait till you see it. It's kind of a tux, but it's got leather stripes down the pants and sleeves, and the shirt's got custom buttons. You won't be able to see most of my tattoos, but it looks sharp, anyway. Why?"

I glared at him. "No reason."

He shrugged and went back to his catalog.

"Bart?"

He sighed and looked up again. "What?"

"When you were hurt, how did you want people to act?"

He stared into my eyes and closed his catalog. "How do you mean?"

"Did you want people like Lenny driving you to physical therapy and shoveling your sidewalk?"

"It wasn't a matter of what I wanted. It was a matter of what I needed. There's a difference."

"But didn't it make you feel…"

"Bad? Stupid? Like a weak little dipshit? Sure it did. But it didn't matter. It had to happen. I couldn't do it myself."

I traced my finger along the outline of a watch under the glass counter. "How do you feel about all that now? About Lenny?"

His forehead crinkled. "What're you gettin' at?"

I took a deep breath and spun sideways on the stool, my eyes wandering over the assortment of leather jackets, chrome accessories, and Hogs. "I guess what I'm asking is, is Lenny still your best friend? Or are things different between you now? Now that he saw you like that, and you had to accept help from him?"

He paused before answering. "Things aren't any different. We get along just like we did before. We argue, we fight, we annoy each other." He smiled. "But now we do it with more feeling."

He came around the counter and sat on another stool. "You want to tell me what this is about? I sure as hell can't believe you're simply checking up on me and Len."

I chewed my cheek. "It's Nick. He's…He has MS." I snuck a look at Bart. He didn't gasp, faint, or otherwise show any sign of being shocked.

"How long have you known?" he asked.

"Since Monday."

He nodded. "Have you talked with him about it much?"

I slid off the stool and pulled a wallet off a shelf, opening it and feeling the soft leather. "He showed up on Monday to hit me with it, then left the next morning."

"How 'bout on the phone?"

I set the wallet down and picked up a key ring. "I haven't returned his calls."

"I see."

I heard his stool squeak, and he joined me at the display case. "You're wondering how to talk to him?"

I set the ring down with a click and wheeled on Bart. "He assumed I couldn't handle it. He actually said he wanted to give me an 'out.' He thinks I'm so..." I stopped and turned away, my vision blurring.

"He thinks you're so wonderful, he doesn't want to tie you down."

I shook my head, my throat feeling thick. "But what does that say, Bart? He doesn't think I can take it? I'm so weak that a little illness is going to stop me from loving him?"

Bart put a hand on my shoulder and turned me toward him. "It's not you, Stella. It's him. He's afraid of losing you. By giving you an option, a reason, you save him from rejection. You'd be saying no to the disease, not him."

"But I don't *want* to say no to him."

He looked at me. "You can deal with the illness? MS isn't really a 'little' problem. It's not something you can ignore."

I walked back to the stool and slumped onto it. "Jordan Granger just lost the woman he loved. She was murdered on Friday night. He'd give anything to have her back."

Bart watched me, waiting.

"I want to be there for Nick, Bart."

He nodded. "But it will be different from what you'd planned."

I closed my eyes, and opened them again. "The MS might not progress much. This might be his only episode."

"It might."

"But it might be something that has him incapacitated by the time he's forty."

Bart sucked on his lower lip, but didn't say anything.

"You think I can do it?" I asked. "That I'm strong enough?"

Bart gave a small, sad smile. "Stella, you're probably the strongest person I've ever met. Well, I guess you and Lucy are a tie. And if you love Nick, which I believe you do, you'll be able to overcome whatever this thing throws at you."

I hoped he was right.

"And you think he'll still love me?"

Bart laughed quietly. "That's not the question, Princess. The only love he's concerned with is what you feel for him, if you can still love him if he's sick and needing to be taken care of."

"God, Bart, what kind of person would I be if I couldn't?"

Bart put his arm around my shoulder. "You'd be someone who isn't you. Because your heart," he touched the front of my shirt gently with his index finger, "is bigger than that farm of yours. And he knows it. He just wants to make sure you know it, too."

I leaned my head against Bart's chin, his beard scratchy on my forehead. I hoped he was right. All I knew at that moment was that my heart was hurting like hell. And I hoped with everything in me that it would stop.

Chapter Twenty-Three

The boxes fit into the saddlebags without too much squishing. In fact, I figured I'd be able to push the corners out a little so Lucy wouldn't even be able to tell where they got dented. If she was upset I'd just make myself scarce after milking.

I was pulling my bike into the garage when a Jeep Wrangler drove up the lane, accompanied by Queenie's frenzied barking. I clicked the lock shut on the bike's floor bolt and went out to see who it was.

Tom and Tonya Copper stepped out of the red Jeep, Tonya reaching her hand down so Queenie could smell it. A familiar jolt of butterflies hit my stomach, seeing a celebrity like Tom Copper anywhere in my vicinity. I guessed I really was a country girl.

I walked into the drive, checking out the Jeep, its top down for the sunny spring day. "Howdy, folks. That looks like a fun ride."

Tom patted the hood. "It is."

"Long as I remember to put my hair in a ponytail," Tonya said, laughing. The bulk of her hair was tied back, but straggly wisps stuck out at all angles from her face.

"What brings you here?" I asked.

Tom waved his hand toward the outbuildings. "We were up in Sellersville, checking out the reception site for Saturday, thought we'd stop by and see your operation."

I looked at him, wondering what a well-heeled rock musician was doing checking out a small place like mine.

"I grew up on a hobby farm," Tonya said. "Just a few sheep and chickens and whatever, but it's fun to smell a barn every once in a while."

"Well, we've got plenty of smell," I said.

The screen door on the side of the house burst open and Tess ran out. She stopped short at the sight of our guests.

"Hey, Tess," I said.

She looked at Tom and Tonya. "Who're you?"

"Some friends," Tom said.

I waved at him. "That's Tom Copper. And she's Tonya."

Tess' forehead crinkled. "The rock star?"

Tom laughed. "Yeah, I play in a band. We came by today to see your place." He looked at me, apparently unsure if Tess was mine.

"Lucy's daughter," I said. "They live with me. Or will until next week, anyway."

Tess stuck out her lower lip, and I regretted my words. She rallied back, however, and grinned. "Want to see the babies?"

Tonya glanced at me. "Calves?"

"Yup," Tess said. "It's my job to feed them bottles in the evenings."

Tonya's face lit up. "Can I help?"

Tess clapped. "Sure! Come on." She grabbed Tonya's hand and led her toward the barn. I hoped Tonya was up for skipping.

"So," I said to Tom. "Want to tag along?"

"Why not?"

We followed at a slower pace.

"What are the different barns?" he asked.

I gestured toward them. "Feed barn. Garage. Tractor barn. Heifer barn." I pointed ahead. "That's the main barn, where we do the milking and the milk is stored till the truck comes."

"That one new?" He pointed at the heifer barn.

"Spanking. Just went up last fall, after the old one burned down."

He grimaced. "Lose a lot of cows?"

"None, actually. I was lucky."

We got to the barn and walked into the dimmer light, where Lucy was in the feed room preparing for the evening milking. "And there's the bride-to-be."

Lucy peeked out of the door and smiled. "Thought that was you out there. You need to see me?"

"Nope. We were up to the German-Hungarian club, checked out the set-up. Thought we'd see where you folks live, since we were so close."

I studied him, not quite believing the interest in the farm, or even where we lived. I mean, how many celebrity musicians took the time to visit their clients' homes? "How'd you find us?"

"Jordan. I called him to check in about this weekend, and he mentioned you'd been shuttling him back and forth from Philly, since you live up this way."

"Not exactly neighbors, but relatively close."

Lucy pushed the grain bin onto the parlor floor. "Want to help?"

Tom eyed the parlor and the cows' massive rumps aimed toward the aisles between them. "No, thanks. I'll just watch."

Lucy smiled, understanding, and began scooping feed into the cows' bowls.

"So would you like the grand tour?" I asked.

He took a deep breath and stuck his hands in his pockets. The interest obviously wasn't there. But something—and I wasn't sure Tonya's childhood was enough—had brought him to the farm.

"I won't bore you with details," I said. "We'll just walk around. Or we can sit and talk if you prefer."

His shoulders relaxed. "That sounds good."

I led him down the little hallway to my office and closed the door behind us. He stepped up to the window and peered out, but I wasn't sure what he was seeing.

"So what's up?" I said.

He turned from the window. "What do you mean?"

"I mean, it's clear you don't care about the farm. Why are you here?"

"Tonya—"

"Sure, her early farm experiences. That's nice."

He met my eyes.

"Why don't you sit down?" I said.

He did. "I'm not sure *why* I'm here."

I knew it.

"This whole thing," he said. "Genna, the bomb…"

"Bobby Baronne running off with the money."

Surprise sparked in his eyes. "Yeah. How'd you know?"

"Combination of things. But mostly Mann telling me his theories."

He leaned forward in the chair, his elbow on his knees. "You think Ricky killed Genna?"

I stared at him. "How would I know?"

It was his turn to look disbelieving. "Because, as I mentioned, you've been in Philly a lot, driving Jordan around. Somehow I have the feeling you don't usually spend much time in Center City, talking to rock musicians and club owners."

I pursed my lips. Couldn't argue with that. "I want to help out Jordan. Plus, his mother ordered me to."

"I have a feeling you would've done it, anyway."

I lifted a shoulder. He was right.

"So you think he did it?" Tom asked.

"Ricky?"

"Yeah."

I leaned my head back, studying the square tiles on the ceiling. "I hope so."

"What? Why?"

I looked at him. "There's no one else I would want it to be."

He was silent for a moment, his face tight. "Yeah. Me neither."

He pushed himself out of the chair and walked over to the wall, where I had some family pictures.

"You think it's true about Bobby?" I asked. "That he ran off with the money?"

He sighed and turned around. "Probably. It's been a long time coming."

"What do you mean?"

He looked at the long fingernails on his right hand, just right for plucking guitar strings, and used a nail from his other hand to clean one out. "Gary and Bobby have been together for years. Business partners, I mean. They first met up in college, where they started a band. Called themselves The Fever. They had a good run of it, but Mann quit when they were done with school. Said they didn't have enough talent between them to make it big. Decided he'd rather be involved by helping better bands build their careers. Opened his first club and started hiring in local talent."

"Was he right?"

"About The Fever?" He winced. "Having heard a recording from back then, I'd have to say yes. But Mann is a hell of a club owner. Gave lots of us our start way back when."

"At The Bar?"

He blinked. "You know about it?"

"It's on your web site."

"Oh. Right. I keep forgetting all that information is out there."

"So you think Baronne's been holding a grudge all these years?"

"A torch, maybe. He's always thought he could become the next Stevie Ray Vaughn."

"In his dreams, I'm assuming."

"Definitely."

"So you think he's run off to pursue these fantasies?"

He dropped back into the chair and ran his hand over his goatee. "There's no telling. But I wouldn't doubt it. I just feel bad for Gary."

"I take it you know Mann pretty well, having been around him all this time."

"I guess. He's helped us out a lot." He stopped, but looked like he had more to say. I waited. "He's made us an offer."

"Your band?"

"Yeah."

"A good one?"

He nodded. "I think so. He wants to make us regulars. Every Friday and Saturday night, with traveling gigs coming in during the week."

"You up for that?"

A flash of worry crossed his face. "I don't know. It's a big change. The other guys aren't sure we'd bring in enough money without the touring. I sometimes think—"

A burst of giggling came from the hallway, and the door opened, revealing Tess and a milk-splattered Tonya.

"What happened?" Tom asked.

Tonya laughed. "An overly enthusiastic calf. I couldn't keep the bottle in her mouth."

"It slipped out!" Tess said. "The milk sprayed all over her!"

Tom laughed, too, and got up from the chair.

"We've got some rags in the parlor," I said. "Or you can go in the house and use the bathroom."

Tonya looked down at her shirt and arms. "If you don't mind."

"Not a problem. Tess, why don't you show her inside?"

"Sure. C'mon, Tonya!" And dragging the woman by the arm, Tess took her away.

Tom watched them go. "Well, thanks for the excitement."

"Any time."

He glanced at his watch and the door.

"What were you saying?" I asked. "About what you sometimes think?"

A flurry of expressions flashed across his face. "Can't remember."

"About Mann's offer?"

"Oh. Nothing. It's no big deal."

Uh-huh. "All right. I'll walk you out."

We headed toward the front of the barn, and Tom stopped in the hallway. "Jordan going to be okay?"

I shook my head. "Don't know. I think so."

He sighed. "I figured he and Genna were going to end up together sooner or later. At least that's what Tonya was hoping."

He waited, as if expecting me to continue with the idea.

"I guess there's no telling now, is there?" I said, and walked outside.

Tonya came out to the Jeep a minute or so later, her face and arms clean, but her shirt still sporting dark splotches of wetness.

She ruffled Tess' hair. "Thanks for the fun."

Tess smiled. "You'll be there Saturday?"

"I will."

I stood on the walk with Tess and watched the couple clamber into the Jeep. "Thanks for stopping by."

Tom waved. "See you this weekend."

I held up a hand as they made a slow U-turn and headed out.

"That was fun," Tess said. "Except she doesn't know anything about cows."

Somehow I wasn't surprised.

Chapter Twenty-Four

I helped Lucy finish up the milking, wondering all the while why exactly Tom Copper had come to my farm. Thinking back on our conversation, it seemed the only thing he had initiated was the question of whether or not I thought Ricky had killed Genna. Tom agreed that he wanted it to be the band's new drummer, but never actually said he thought Ricky did it. Which made me wonder—which one of his friends did Tom Copper think murdered Genna?

"You done there?" Lucy stood at the barn door, one foot in, one foot out.

I set the pitchfork against the wall and looked over the newly limed aisles. "Yeah, I'm done."

"Then come on in for supper. I've got that cheesy tuna casserole that you like in the oven."

I wouldn't say no to that.

I had just heaped seconds onto my plate when lights flashed into the kitchen window and across the cupboards.

"That's Lenny," Lucy said, jumping up from her seat. "You go ahead and finish."

"I'm done," Tess said. "Can I come, too?"

Lucy looked at me, and I waved my fork. "That's fine. I can eat by myself."

I had to get used to it again, anyway.

They left, and I got up to pour myself another glass of milk. Glancing out the window at Lenny's truck, it seemed like there were more people than just him climbing out. There was a woman and…a wheelchair?

I stuck the milk back in the fridge and went to the door, where I looked out through the screen while a man lowered himself from the cab into the chair. I squinted, trying to see in the fading light outside. My head snapped upward when I realized who the man was. It was the guy from the concert. What was his name? I couldn't remember. Couldn't remember his wife's name, either.

The screen door slapped shut after I pushed my way through.

"You done with supper already?" Lucy asked, her head jerking my way.

"No. But I see we have more visitors than just Lenny."

Her eyes darted toward the couple, and she put her hands first on her hips, then in her pockets, and finally clasped them together in front of her stomach.

"What's going on, Lucy?"

"Oh, nothing. Nothing."

"Howdy, Stella," Lenny said. He stepped toward me and blocked the dusk-to-dawn light, casting his face in shadows. "I'm sorry to hear—"

He grunted as Lucy elbowed him.

"All right," I said. "I was going to finish my supper, but now I want to know what's happening."

Lucy's jaw tightened, and she looked at the ground.

"Stella?" The man in the wheelchair called me from the driveway. His wife stood behind him, trying to maneuver his wheelchair onto the walk.

I stepped forward. "That's me. Sorry I can't remember your names."

"Norm," the man said. "And Cindy."

"From the concert."

"Yeah. You saved our butts."

"Well, Lenny did."

Cindy cast a grateful glance toward our lumbering friend, but Norm tapped my arm. "From what I hear you helped clear the chair from the scene. So thanks for that."

"You're welcome. This the same one?"

"It is. We stopped in at the club on Monday and were able to pick it up. Just had to have a few repairs made and it was good to go."

"I'm glad. I was sure we'd wrecked it."

"Nah. These things are like tanks. At least the good ones are."

"Well, I'm glad you're all right. Now I'm headed back in to finish my supper. It's nice you came to see Lucy."

His face registered surprise, and Cindy made an "oh" kind of sound.

"What?" I said.

Lenny cleared his throat. "Norm and Cindy actually came to visit you."

"Me? Why?" I looked at the four of them, their faces showing concern and—God help me—pity. And it struck me.

"You have MS," I said to Norm.

"Last I checked."

I glared at Lenny. "Bart *told* you."

"Well. Yeah."

I closed my eyes and concentrated on breathing through my nose.

"We thought it might help for you to talk to Norm and Cindy," Lucy said. Her voice sounded tentative. Almost frightened. Which well it should.

"Oh, you thought so, did you?"

I turned to leave, but Norm clamped an iron hand on my arm.

"C'mon, darlin'. What would it hurt to talk to a poor old guy for a few minutes?"

I swallowed.

"One minute?" he said.

I shook my arm out of his grasp, but didn't move away.

"Good," Lucy said. "Why don't we go inside?"

Norm and Cindy looked up the walk toward the side steps.

"Why don't we just sit out here?" Norm said, a smile tickling his mouth. "It's a nice night, and I don't want to give my lovely wife—or Lenny here—a hernia trying to get me up there."

"I'll grab some lawn chairs," Lucy said. She scurried away toward the garage.

I stood silently, thinking with annoyance about my congealing tuna casserole, until she came back and unfolded a chair behind me. I felt like ignoring it, but decided that would just be stupid.

When I was settled, Cindy beside me and Norm at an angle to my left, I heard the screen door close. A twist of my head confirmed that Lucy and Lenny had gone inside.

"It's a bugger, huh?" Norm said.

I sat stiffly, my fingers clenched over the chair's metal arms.

"Not something you really want to hear about someone you love. That he has this disease."

"Not something you really want to talk about, either," Cindy said. "At least not at first."

My teeth remained clenched together, my throat tight.

"When we found out, we'd only been married a year," Norm said. "Were trying to get pregnant, too, while I worked at the Radnor Library. Custodian. And we were renovating an old house." He shifted slightly in the chair. "It started slowly. I'd get tingling in my fingers and toes, kept dropping stuff. Was tired all the time. Thought it was just I was working too hard. I finally went to the doctor when I went numb on my whole left side."

Cindy put her hand on Norm's, and he grasped her fingers.

"Didn't take the doctors too long to figure out what was going on. I thought at first I was going to die. You know, real quick. Took all kinds of tests. Was at the hospital all the time. But we got some good advice, and that kept us going."

He looked at me, waiting, I suppose, for a response.

"Docs told us I wouldn't die from MS. I'd just have to learn to live with it. Cindy, too. And they told us not to rush out and join a support group. Last thing we needed was a bunch of people boo-hooing about their disease and carrying on like they were gonna die tomorrow. So we waited on that. Finally did find a good group. More an informational group than anything. We compared medicines, had speakers, educated each other. Worked out well. We made some good friends there."

I took a deep breath and let it out through my mouth. I wondered where Jordan was. I really ought to check up on him and see how he was doing, make sure he wasn't falling apart.

"There are a lot of worries," Norm said. "Don't get me wrong. You worry your employer will find out and fire you and you'll lose your insurance. Course that's not really legal, but you never know. You worry about the tests. You worry about what people will think. You worry about having kids. So, you know, you don't make a general announcement about it, but people do hear. You find out who your true friends are. Lot of the morons act like they'll get it from you or something. The good ones ask questions and learn how to support you."

Jordan probably was at his house. Or he could be taking stuff over to the German-Hungarian club to get ready for Saturday. I hoped to God he wasn't down in Philly again, trying to get into Ricky's place.

"There are things you have to change. Like staying away from sick people. The meds you take lower your immune system. And of course there are the meds themselves you have to take. And the fall weather change is difficult. Makes your joints hurt, could bring on an episode. But really, there's not much you can't do, at least at first. You can exercise, long as you don't overdo it. You might want to avoid whitewater rafting, that kind of stuff. You can drive, except when you're seeing double, but that's just common sense. You can have kids, that's for sure. There's no chance of passing it on to them. We've got two in college, and they're doing just great."

I wondered if Jordan had talked to Ma yet. I hoped so, for her sake. Or at least let her know he was all right. She'd go nuts pretty soon if he didn't at least leave her a message.

"The biggest fear," Norm said, "is that you'll end up in a wheelchair, like me. But you know, I lived with it for a long time before ending up in my little vehicle, here. And medicine's a lot more advanced now. Drugs are better, doctors know more. Especially when it's caught early. And we've done okay, Cindy and me, even with the chair. Haven't we, honey?"

Cindy made an affirming sound, and patted their clasped hands with her other one.

"You know," Norm said, "they used to say you could live twenty-five years past your diagnosis. But anymore that's just not true. It's already been twenty-eight for me and I don't plan on passing away anytime soon."

I swiveled my head to the left in time to catch an intense look of love passing between Norm and Cindy, their faces tender and soft.

I unclenched my hands from the chair's arms, gave what might've resembled a smile, and stood up. I walked away and didn't stop until I'd reached the very middle of my property.

On my back between two rows of corn, I lay looking at the emerging stars and waited for tears to come.

But my eyes were as dry as the field around me.

And there was no telling the extended forecast.

Chapter Twenty-Five

By the time I got back to the house Lenny and the other two were gone. The house was dark, and I held the screen door so it wouldn't bang shut and wake Tess. She wouldn't be getting up early for the bus, since she was taking the day off to be at the wedding rehearsal, but there was no doubt she'd need her sleep to get through the stress of the next couple days.

I left my boots at the door and was tiptoeing through the living room when a movement on the sofa made me jump.

"Sorry," Lucy said. "Didn't mean to scare you."

"Why are you sitting here in the dark? Lenny's not here, is he?"

"No. I wanted to make sure you were okay."

"You can't do that with the light on?"

"It was peaceful."

I grunted and forgot about tiptoeing on my way to the upstairs door.

"Stella," Lucy said.

I paused, my hand on the doorknob.

"I'm sorry about Nick."

"Yeah," I said. "So am I."

I opened the door and went upstairs.

As soon as milking was done in the morning I went into the house to grab something to eat. The kitchen smelled of eggs and sausage, and I raised my eyebrows at the feast on the counter.

"Thought you'd enjoy a hearty breakfast," Lucy said. From the way she was looking at me, I could tell she wasn't sure how I'd be feeling toward her after the visitors the night before.

I sat down. "I am hungry."

She plunked a carton of orange juice onto the table and sat down across from me, bringing the food platters with her.

"You're gonna eat with me, too?" I asked.

She tried out a smile. "I need my strength today."

"Yeah. You excited?"

She paused, her fork in the air. "Excited. Nervous. Terrified." She took a bite of eggs and spoke around it. "But mostly just happy."

"And Tess?"

"Not up yet. Guess those school mornings really are too early for her."

We ate for a few minutes.

"Everything ready for the milk truck?" Lucy asked.

"Doug'll be fine. He's done it before."

We ate some more.

"You coming to the church with me, or driving separately?" Lucy asked.

"I'll go myself, since you probably want to go early and stay late."

"But you'll come in time to help with details?"

I looked her in the eye. "I'll be there, Lucy. Everything will be fine."

She set down her fork and lined it up with her napkin. "Yeah. I know."

The door to the stairs slammed and Tess came running into the kitchen, dressed in a cute purple outfit, her church sandals slapping on the hardwood floor. Only her hair had been forgotten, still a bed-mussed mess.

"We ready to go, Mom?"

Lucy held out her arms for a hug. "Just about. Want some breakfast?"

Tess gave her mom a quick squeeze. "Nope. We're having lunch at the church, right?"

"Well, yes, but not for a while."

"I'm not hungry."

Lucy turned to me for help, but I leaned back. "Oh, no. I'm not getting in the middle of this." I pushed my chair away from the table and got up.

"Stella," Lucy said, "I was wondering if you…"

The tone of her voice set off a rash of irritation up my spine. Because of her persistence or my own guilt, I wasn't sure. "No," I said. "I didn't call Nick."

I shoved my chair under the table. "I'll see you at church in a little while."

"Can I go with Stella, Mom? Pleasepleasepleasepl—"

"You'll have to ask her."

Tess hopped toward me and hung on my arms. "Pleaseplease pl—"

I couldn't help laughing. "That's fine. I need to take a shower, though. So you'll have to wait."

"That's okay. You take quick showers."

So I stumped upstairs, took my turn in the bathroom, and tried to figure out what was appropriate to wear to a wedding rehearsal. Jeans and a Harley T-shirt? Jeans and a flannel shirt? Jeans and…what?

I rifled through my T-shirt drawer and came up with a relatively new white one. It had quite a few wrinkles from being scrunched down in there for so long, but it would do.

Lucy was just leaving as I got downstairs, and though her eyes flicked over my clothes, she didn't say a word. Saving her energy for the wedding outfit, I guess. Which I really needed to check on. I'd left it up to Ma, and I assumed she'd keep up her end of the bargain.

I gathered up Tess and we headed to Sellersville Mennonite Church, where the Grangers had always attended, and where Lucy had gone since coming to work for me the last summer. Lenny wasn't a member of any church, but had made token appearances at Sellersville, now that he and Lucy were an item.

"Stella Crown, haven't seen you for a while."

Peter Reinford, the pastor of the church, welcomed me at the door with a smile and an outstretched hand.

"Well, I'm still alive," I said.

He laughed. "I would've welcomed Tess, too, except she ran past me at a million miles an hour."

"She's excited."

"I guess. You ready to be the maid of honor?"

How he said this without a burst of laughter was beyond me, but then, pastors are supposed to have some extra inner strength the rest of us are lacking. Or more self-control, anyway.

"As ready as I'll ever be."

"Come on in, then."

The foyer embraced me with the comforting smell of sloppy joes. A glance toward the kitchen showed me Ma in her splendor, organizing food and ordering workers around. Looked like her crew consisted of the church's kitchen committee, most of whom were probably relieved to have someone else running things, even with Ma barking orders at them. I suddenly felt lucky to only be in the wedding party.

"Stella!" Lucy's mother, Lois, strode toward me, hands outstretched.

I let her hug me, and stepped back. "Where's Lucy?"

She tipped her head toward the church's library. "On the phone. Something got mixed up with the flowers for tomorrow, and she's trying to fix it." She smiled. "It's good to see you."

"Yeah. You, too." I meant it. Lois and Ron Ruth were wonderful parents to Lucy, and even greater grandparents to Tess. They'd offered to stay and be with Tess for the next week, since she couldn't go to Lancaster and miss school, but Tess assured them I'd be enough. We'd see about that.

"Lenny here?" I asked her.

"Yup. In the sanctuary, helping with some decorations."

"How much time, Rev?" I asked Peter.

He glanced at his watch. "We won't start the actual rehearsal for, oh, another twenty minutes."

"Okay. I'll go see if I can help."

I went up the stairs to the main worship space, where Lenny was sitting on the front platform, trying to tie a bow with a wide ribbon.

"Having a good time?" I asked.

He glanced up, scowling. "I told Lucy my fingers were too fat for this." He held it out. "You try."

"Oh, no. Ribbons are definitely not my thing."

"Help me, then."

I turned toward the voice to find Jordan carrying some mic stands toward the front of the church.

"Hey, Jordan."

He jerked his chin, and I followed.

"Did San get a hold of you the other day?" I asked.

"Huh?"

"She called, trying to find you. It was…" I thought back. "Wednesday, I guess. Before…" Before all hell had broken loose and I'd had to go running to Philly to keep Jordan from pummeling Ricky.

"Oh, yeah. She left a message."

"You talk to her?"

He slid the microphone into the holder. "And you need to know because…?"

I held up my hands. "You're right. I don't. I just wanted to make sure you got the message."

He walked back toward the church's sound booth, and I tagged along. In the closet-sized room, he handed me a lapel mic, along with another mic stand. I backed out, giving him room to maneuver. Lenny, still trying to tie the bow, finally stood up and threw the ribbon on the ground. I tried not to laugh as he stormed down the aisle toward the fellowship hall, bellowing, "Lucy!"

Jordan pressed past me, and again I followed, this time to the piano at the front of the church, where he pointed at a spot for me to set the stand. He glanced around, and when he saw we were alone, said, "You know how you were asking me about Donny and Tonya?"

"Yeah. I was guessing they'd been together at some point."

He tore a piece of duct tape with his teeth, and bent to secure a cable to the floor. "Seems they were. Back in college. In fact, they were together when the Tom Copper Band was first formed."

"Wow. How'd you find out?"

"Asked LeRoy."

"So why did things change?"

"Seems Tom came to his senses sooner than Donny. All the guys liked the groupie girls back then. Including Donny, even though he had a girlfriend. Tom soon realized he liked Tonya's love for the music more than he liked the one-nighters, and basically stole her away from Donny."

"Ouch. How'd Donny take it?"

"Took him a while to realize it, actually, he was such a mess back then. And when he finally did, it about broke up the band. But somehow they got through it, and he and Tonya are good friends now."

Uh-huh. "Just like he and Genna were good friends."

"Well. I guess."

I shook my head. The rate Donny went, he must've had good friends all over the country.

"We about ready in here?"

Peter Reinford walked in, flanked by Lucy, Lenny, Tess, and now Bart, who flashed a grin. He'd opted for a button-down Harley shirt to go with his jeans.

"A white T-shirt, Princess?" he asked.

"Because she's so angelic," Lenny said.

Everyone got a good laugh out of that one.

"Belle's here," Lucy said, referring to Zach's mom, who was serving as the pianist. "I saw her in the lobby."

"I'll get her!" Tess said.

As she flounced away, Jordan took the lapel mic from my hand and helped Peter secure it to his coat.

"Doing sound already today?" Peter asked.

Jordan nodded. "Want to make sure we have everything we need."

Belle arrived, dragged by the hand, and made her way to the piano.

"Okay, everyone," Peter said. "Let's practice the processional. You can count music, right, Stella?"

And thus began the rehearsal from hell.

An hour and a half later Peter deemed it all "close enough for country," (which he said with a smile, since he had great affection for Tim McGraw, Faith Hill, and their kind) and sent us all to the fellowship hall for the rehearsal dinner.

I followed the pack, my stomach having rumbled during the entire rehearsal after smelling the food all that time. But when I got to the top of the stairs I froze.

Nick sat at one of the tables, waiting.

My stomach immediately switched modes, and I tried to remember exactly where the closest bathroom was. My eyes, however, were locked to his, even as I struggled to breathe.

"Stella?" Lucy stood beside me.

I ripped my eyes from Nick. "I didn't think—"

"He'd still come?"

"Well…"

Her face held a combination of kindness and steel. "He's my friend, too."

I looked back at Nick, who kept his eyes on me.

"Oh, God," I said, and stumbled backward into the sanctuary. I sank into a pew, where I leaned forward onto the back of the bench in front of me, resting my face on my hands. I concentrated on my breathing until I could do it without wheezing.

The bench creaked as someone sat next to me. A peek sideways showed me a pair of new khaki pants. Not jeans. I closed my eyes again.

"You want to talk?" Nick said.

"No."

I stayed sitting there long enough he finally got up and went away.

A little while later, my stomach was beginning to growl again. I sat up and weighed my options. The one I liked best had to do with me walking out of the church and never coming back. Realistically, though, I knew that would backfire. Instead, I left the sanctuary through a door at the front, which took me outside. I walked around to the back of the building, toward the kitchen. I knocked on the locked screen door.

One of the kitchen workers peered out at me. "Oh. You." She turned toward Ma. "Can she come in?"

Ma looked up from where she was scrubbing a crockpot in the sink. "I suppose."

The woman unlocked the door and I went through.

"You want leftovers," Ma said, "you'll have to help yourself."

I ducked out of the sightlines of the fellowship hall and found a Tupperware container filled with beef. I slapped some on a hamburger bun and took a bite.

"You know what you're doing?" Ma asked.

I swallowed. "About what?"

"That's what I thought." She thumped the crockpot upside down onto a towel and turned toward me, arms crossed on her chest. "You have a lovely man out there, who for some reason seems to think you're the one for him, regardless of the way you've been ignoring him."

"I—"

"Which," she continued, "affirms that the Lord moves in mysterious ways." She snapped her dish towel and hung it over the drying rack.

"Ma, there are—"

"And don't tell me you have your reasons. Whatever they are, they aren't good enough. So are you going to go out there and talk to him, or cower here in the kitchen?"

My choice would've been the cowering one if we hadn't heard a commotion coming from the fellowship hall. Ma took one glance toward the front door and lit out of the kitchen. I peered around the doorway, and stopped chewing.

Detective Willard and his non-pal Alexander from the Philly police stood in the foyer. Lenny barricaded their way to the main room and Ma was bearing down fast. I wasn't about to lay odds on the cops' success of entry.

I set down my sandwich, undecided as to what action to take, until Jordan walked down the stairs into the eating area. The look on his face was enough to make me overcome my...whatever it was...and head into the fray.

Reaching Jordan, I grabbed his elbow. "Don't worry. Looks like Ma and Lenny have got your back."

He shook his arm out of my grip. "But for what? How many times do I have to tell you that I didn't *do* anything?"

"You never had to tell me. It's the cops you have to convince."

He started to say something else, but stopped when Alexander somehow skirted around Ma and made his way toward Jordan.

I held out my hand. "No way, man. Not without his lawyer."

His smile reminded me of the snake Lucy had killed on my farm the day she came to interview. "Ah, Ms. Crown. A pleasure to see you again. But what makes you think we're here to talk with Mr. Granger?"

I raised my eyebrows. "Who else would there be?"

He looked around. "Well, you, for one. And maybe your boyfriend. At least I assume he's here somewhere. And even Lucy or her—" he glanced up at Lenny, who'd moved close enough to cast a shadow—"her rather large fiancé."

"You do realize you're interrupting a private event?" I asked. "A wedding rehearsal."

"Yeah," Lenny said. "*Mine.* And you're making it uncomfortable for my in-laws." He gestured toward the table where Lucy sat with her folks and Tess.

"Yes," Alexander said. "I do apologize for that. We have no intention of putting a damper on such a happy day."

Lenny made a kind of growl, but Alexander kept on with that smile.

"Can we all just stop," Jordan said. "I'll talk to the friggin' cops, if it'll get them out of here."

"No you won't, young man." Ma stepped between her son and Alexander. "Not until Mr. Crockett gets here. He's already been called."

She glanced at Nick, who was stowing his phone back on his belt. I wondered if Nick ever used his phone as much as everyone else did.

"I understand," Alexander said. "We'll wait for the respectable Mr. Crockett. Where should we sit?"

Ma glared at him and pointed to the table closest to the kitchen. "There. I'll feed you lunch while Mr. Crockett finds his way to the church."

Willard lit up at that.

"No, thank you, ma'am," Alexander said, patting his stomach. "Already ate."

Willard's face fell.

"That's all fine and dandy," Ma said, "but you're still coming over there." Where she could keep an eye on them.

Alexander followed Ma and her stiff shoulders across the room, and I stifled a laugh. "You can still eat, Willard. Even if Mr. Something-Up-His-Ass doesn't want to."

Willard allowed a small grin. "Well, gee, thanks. I think I will."

As he stepped away, I said, "So what does he want this time?"

Willard glanced toward Alexander, his face stony. "You know I can't tell you that."

"You do realize Alexander's on a witch hunt?"

"Of course." His expression was impossible to read. He shifted on his feet, ready to go grab some lunch. "You're keeping an eye on him, aren't you?"

"Jordan? Well, yeah."

"Making sure he's getting through this okay, and everything? Talking things out with him?"

I squinted up at him. He was sending some kind of signal, but I sure wasn't receiving it.

"You might want to ask him," Willard said, "why he was spending so much of his time in Robert Baronne's office last week. And the week before."

I stared at him. "Like I said earlier, he was getting ready for a concert. At Baronne's club."

"Would that include lunch with him? Multiple times? And at least fifteen phone calls?"

I didn't know. Would it?

He glanced at Nick. "We also got photos from Nick's phone, taken the night of the concert." He hesitated.

"And?"

"And there's a nice clear one of Jordan and Baronne."

"Let me guess. That argument you told me about."

"Actually, no. They look quite friendly."

Which would back up Jordan's claim that they had definitely *not* been fighting.

Willard's face turned thoughtful as he watched me take in the information, and I looked away. "Didn't you say you were starving?" I asked.

He left.

Why *was* Jordan spending so much time with Baronne? I couldn't imagine it really would be necessary, just to set up the concert. Especially since Club Independence had been on the band's schedule for years. It wasn't like it was a new venue. And Jordan hadn't said anything about becoming *friends* with Baronne.

I looked around for Jordan, but didn't see him anywhere.

"He's outside."

Nick had placed himself at my elbow, and I glanced at him briefly. "Thanks."

"Stella—"

"Later, Nick, okay? Please?"

He searched my face, then turned and walked back to his seat at the table.

I felt like a jerk, but I needed to talk to Jordan before the cops did. I found him sitting on the front steps, his elbows on his knees.

I sat beside him. "You okay?"

"Sure. I'm just great."

"Sorry. Stupid question."

He waved at me, like he was trying to shoo a fly. "No. I'm sorry. I'm just…" He took in a big breath, and let it out slowly.

"I know." We sat for a few moments. "They want to ask you about Bobby Baronne."

He sat up. "Again?"

"They seem to think you were spending a lot of time with him the last two weeks. More than you would've needed to."

His face tensed. "Now I have to explain my friends to them?"

"You do when that friend is suspected of running off with the money. Planting a bomb. Maybe killing Genna."

His head snapped toward me. *"What?"*

"What was going on, Jordan? It doesn't sound to me like he was your kind of guy."

"What are you implying?"

"Nothing. It just seems…out of character for you."

He glared at me and stood up. "Well, we sure wouldn't want that. Lord knows *you* never act out of character. Being Miss Loyalty and all. But, oops, you think I had something to do with it all. And, oops again, isn't that your boyfriend in there, who you refuse to speak to?"

"Jordan—"

"Forget it. And forget this whole sister act. I don't need you nosing around, making me hate myself more than I already do. So just…leave me alone." He stomped up the stairs, and back into the church.

Great.

The door opened again, and Ma came out and stood behind me.

"Well," she said, "I guess he gave you the boot. At least it took him almost a week to call you off. He rejected us immediately."

"Gee, thanks. That makes me feel so much better."

She snorted. "And in case you've been wondering, I did manage to whip something together for you to wear tomorrow."

I blinked. "I guess I hadn't been wondering too much. I just assumed you'd do it."

She smiled gently. "I suppose that's good."

"So where is it?"

She tilted her head toward the side of the church. "In my car. In the garment bag on the back seat. With a box of shoes."

I took a deep breath. "Thank you."

"You're welcome. And no complaining. I didn't have much time to work with."

"I won't complain."

"You'd better not. And you'd better be wearing it tomorrow. No matter what you think."

I took a deep breath and held it. Then let it out. "It's not like I have anything *else* to wear."

She laughed, a sound not common during the past week. "Then I guess you'll have to put it on. You don't really have a choice."

I shook my head. "No, I don't. Now, can you tell me what to do with the rest of my life?"

She laid her hand on my shoulder. "You say that, but you know you don't really mean it."

I couldn't help but wonder if she was right.

Chapter Twenty-Six

"Can we talk now?" Nick said.

We'd left the church in the middle of tying those damn bows in order to be back for milking. At least, it was a good excuse.

I reached a hand down to scratch Queenie, who'd greeted Nick with far more excitement than I had. "Gotta get started with the herd," I said. "You helping?"

He looked down at the gravel, hands on his hips. "All right."

"I need to change clothes."

"Yeah," he said. "Me, too."

Five minutes later we stood in the parlor, me pushing the feed bin toward him. He'd helped before. He knew what to do.

I turned on the Temple radio station, but instead of soothing classical music, they were playing some opera with big, wobbling voices. In Italian. Dairy farmers usually don't speak Italian. But even with my high school education I could tell what the lady and the dude were singing about, and it wasn't tiptoeing through the tulips. Just what Nick and I needed—passionate, star-crossed lovers who were probably about to keel over from a broken heart. Singing all the while.

I changed the radio to Philly's lite rock station. The songs might be about love, but at least they're quieter.

Two and a half hours later we left the barn.

"Now?" Nick said.

I sighed. I was tempted to put it off until after we ate, but realized he was reaching his breaking point. "Okay, Nick. Now."

We walked out into the corn field, Queenie trotting along happily beside us, oblivious to the tension. The stalks were a little taller than when we'd come out on Monday, but didn't have nearly as much growth as if there'd been some rain.

"You're avoiding me, obviously," Nick said when we'd reached the center point. "You about fainted when I showed up at the church today. You didn't return any of my calls all week. You even went so far as to have Lucy lie to keep you off the line."

I looked up at the darkening sky. What did that old sailor's tale say about colors around the moon? "I'm sorry. I didn't know what to say."

"I guess not. But I thought you'd at least want to find out some about…the disease."

I choked out a laugh. "I know plenty. Not only did I do my own research, but Lucy and Lenny sicced a couple of folks on me who had their own testimonials. Remember that couple from the concert? The guy in a wheelchair? Well, there's not much I don't know at this point."

He was quiet for a long time. "So the reason you didn't call was because you're not sure if you can live with this. With me."

I turned to him. "No. The reason I didn't call is because *you* thought I couldn't live with it."

He opened his mouth to say something, but I held up a hand. "Let me finish. You gave me an out. Said something about understanding if I didn't want to have to deal with it. Well, let me tell you. After all I've learned about the illness, I know for sure it would be hard. It's something you—I—would have to deal with every day, whether or not you were in the middle of an episode."

I heard my voice catch, and I turned away from him to look again at the sky. "After reading and hearing about the disease I'm pretty sure I could handle it. But you know what I'm not sure I *can* deal with? I'm not sure I can get over the fact that you thought this illness could make me stop loving you."

I looked at him, his expression frozen in the waning light, and said, "Do you really think so little of me?"

This time it was my turn to walk away.

Chapter Twenty-Seven

Halfway back to the house Queenie—who'd chosen coming with me over staying with Nick, proving *some*thing, though I wasn't sure what—took off running toward the house, barking. I looked ahead and spotted Jordan's white truck in the drive. Super. I was trapped between the two men in the world who thought I was unworthy of trust. Well, there could've been more. They were the two I knew about.

I kept walking until I reached the truck, and Jordan jumped up from where he sat on my side steps, petting a now quiet Queenie.

"What?" I said. "Come to chew me out some more?"

He closed his eyes and shook his head. "Sorry. I was…" He threw up his hands.

"Okay." I took a fresh look at his face and was startled at the wild look in his eyes. "Something happened."

He nodded tersely. "Donny called me. Ricky's disappeared."

"So? The band's better off without him." I stopped. "Except they're supposed to play at the wedding tomorrow."

"Who cares about the wedding?" Jordan said. "He's running because he killed Genna."

I looked at him. "You really think so, Jordan? *Really?*"

His nostrils flared. "Yes."

"I know we *want* it to be him—"

"It *is* him."

"Fine. Why are you here? What am I supposed to do?"

"Come with me to find him."

"Find him? What about the cops?"

"The cops aren't going to look for him. They think I did it. The bomb, too."

I sucked in a breath. "They said that? Today?"

"They didn't have to. Why else would they be so worried about me spending a little time with Bobby?"

I pinched my lips together. He was right. "Where do you think he is?"

He shrugged. "That detective said he's not at his place, or his folks. They live in State College, anyway. Not near here."

"Have they checked Marley's house?"

"Marley's? Why would they check there?"

I shook my head. "Are you completely blind?"

"*What?*"

"Do you have her phone number?"

"I don't know."

"Check."

He pulled his cell phone from his pocket and started scrolling. "Here. I think this is it. I needed Annie one day and got Marley's number to call her there."

"So call and see if Ricky's there."

"She's not going to answer if I call."

That damn Caller ID again. "We'll call from inside."

Lucy was in the kitchen, her face scrubbed clean and her hair pulled back in a ponytail. She turned when we walked in, her eyes immediately flicking to Jordan, then back to me. "Where's Nick?"

"In the field."

Her eyes stayed locked on mine. "What's wrong?"

I chose to interpret her question as if it were about Jordan's presence. "Ricky's missing," I said. "Jordan wants to find him."

She shifted her gaze to Jordan. "Missing how?"

I answered. "Donny called and said he was gone."

I saw the information register, but she was smart enough to realize there was more at stake than her wedding reception.

"So what are you doing?"

I shrugged. "Trying to find him." I plucked the phone off the wall. "Number," I said to Jordan.

He read it off his phone and I punched it in. Marley answered with her usual tough-girl voice.

"Stella Crown," I said. "I'm looking for Ricky."

A pause. "So?"

"Is he there?"

"No."

"You have any idea where he is?"

"Why would I?"

I gritted my teeth. "I thought you were friends."

"Well, we are. But I have no idea where he is."

Good friend. "All right. Thanks." I hung up and turned to Jordan. "He's at Marley's."

"She told you?"

"No. She said she doesn't know where he is. She's lying."

"How do you know?"

"It's not rocket science."

He looked blank.

"It's more like the sixth grade sex talk."

"What?"

He was hopeless. "Never mind."

I looked into Jordan's still-wild eyes and considered the options: let Jordan go after Ricky by himself, pretty much guaranteeing a ride home in a cop car; or leave Nick to think I really had abandoned him.

Shit.

I looked at Lucy, who regarded me with resignation.

"Go ahead," she said. "I'll tell Nick."

I kneaded my temples with my fingers, wondering not for the first time how my life had gotten so complicated.

"You know where Marley lives?" I asked Jordan.

"Sure. I've picked Annie up there when she needed a ride."

A look out the window showed that Nick still wasn't back, or even in sight.

"Thanks, Lucy."

She didn't respond.

I felt like the biggest ass in the world.

Outside, I called Queenie to me.

"Good girl," I said. "Take care of Nick while I'm gone."

At the mention of Nick's name, Queenie's ears perked up.

"Go," I said, shooing her.

I watched until she was out of sight, then held out my hand to Jordan. "Keys."

He rounded the truck to the driver's door. "I don't think so."

"Come on, Jordan. You haven't been sleeping, or eating, probably, and you're not—"

"I'm fine. Get in."

He slammed the door and started the truck. I jumped in, figuring he'd leave me if I didn't. At least if I was along I could help him watch traffic.

He did better than I expected, only hitting eighty on the Northeast Extension, until we got clogged up on the Schuylkill. Could've been worse. As it was, we had to slow to about thirty. Jordan was surprisingly calm for all the tailgating, and flipped his rearview mirror up to keep the headlights from blinding him.

Once we got to the city, Jordan navigated the streets with a comfort I'd never had there, especially in the dark, and we were soon parked in front of a fire hydrant on Bainbridge. Jordan was gone before I could point out the possibility of getting a ticket.

I jogged up the sidewalk after him, catching up as he pounded on the door of a run-down townhome a block or so down the street. A vision of the crowd at Ricky's flashed through my mind, and I couldn't help but wonder if there was some version of Mustang Man who would emerge from the shadows.

The door flew open, and Jordan's arm froze mid-swing. "Annie?"

The girl's face was streaked with tears, her eyes pained above red cheeks.

Jordan stepped toward her. "What's wrong? Annie?"

She jerked out of her stupor and crossed her arms over her chest. "They're leaving. I told them they can't just—"

"Who?"

"Marley and Ricky."

I reached out to grab Jordan's arm, but was too late to keep him from storming into the house. I followed.

"Ricky?" he yelled.

The front room was a disaster. Boxes, stacks of CDs and DVDs, clothes strewn over the furniture. If Marley was hoping to leave soon she had her work cut out for her.

She came into the room, her arms loaded with pillows and blankets, but stopped at the sight of us. "I told you Ricky isn't here."

"Yeah," I said. "I know."

But suddenly—surprise—Ricky's voice came floating in from another room. "Who's here?"

And then he was standing in the doorway. This time I was quick enough to get a hold of Jordan and keep him from pummeling Ricky. Or getting pummeled by him.

Ricky sneered at us. *"You?* What do *you* want?"

Faced with him, Jordan went silent, his body trembling under my clenched fingers.

"So," I said. "Where are you folks headed?"

Ricky swiveled his eyes toward me, then jerked his head at Marley, who walked past him back into another part of the house. "Where we'll be appreciated."

I snorted. "And where would that be?"

Ricky raised his chin. "New York. We're starting our own band."

I held back a laugh. "You and Marley."

"Yeah. So?"

So good luck with that.

"Any idea just how expensive it is in New York?" I asked. "And how many people there are trying to make it?"

"We'll be fine."

I looked at him. He really believed that. That they'd be fine.

I let my eyes go past his shoulder, the direction Marley had gone. "Come on, Jordan. Let's leave these people to their packing."

He yanked his arm from my grip. *"What?"*

"Yeah," Ricky said. "Get lost."

Jordan lunged toward him, his hands going for Ricky's throat. They slammed against the wall, sending a framed photograph of Ozzy Osbourne crashing to the floor.

Annie screamed.

Jordan got in a few punches before I was able to drag him off Ricky, whose fist slammed into Jordan's nose, sending a spurt of blood across Jordan's face and the drummer's shirt.

Marley ran into the room, almost tripping over the three of us.

She screamed.

"Jordan," I said. "Get it together."

He swung his foot and connected with Ricky's stomach, sending Ricky retching against the wall.

"He killed Genna," Jordan yelled.

I got my arms around Jordan's shoulders and dragged him further away. "We don't know that."

Marley practically fell on top of Ricky, holding his head against her chest. "Ricky didn't do anything," she shrieked. "He didn't kill anybody."

Jordan went suddenly quiet, his shoulders relaxing in my grip. A tear made its way slowly down his cheek to his chin, where it mixed with the blood from his nose. "I loved her."

I leaned my head against his, trying to send comfort through my encircling arms, rather than restraint. "I know, Jordan. I know."

Annie watched the four of us with wide eyes, backing against the far wall, her arms still crossed on her chest, as if protecting herself from the craziness she'd just witnessed. Her head shook slowly back and forth, her mouth working as if there were things she wasn't saying.

"Now, come on, Jordan," I said. "There's nothing for us here but more trouble." I pulled gently on his shoulders, and he sagged against me. I led him toward the door.

I'd gotten the door open and we were halfway through it when Ricky called to us. I looked back at him, while Jordan had already set his sights on the street.

"I loved her, too," Ricky said.

My eyes met his. And no matter how much I resisted the idea, I believed him.

At least, I believed he *thought* he loved her.

I pushed Jordan gently through the doorway and shut it behind us, leading him down the steps toward his truck.

When we were out of the townhome's sightlines, I yanked Jordan's elbow. "Come on."

He blinked and held the front of his shirt against his face, trying to wipe blood from his nose and lips. "What?"

"I think I know why Ricky's so sure they'll make it in New York."

He stared at me. "Huh?"

"Who do we know that just got away with tons of money? And has dreamt for years of having his own band again?"

A light began to shine in Jordan's eyes. "Bobby Baronne."

"Exactly. And I think I know where he's been hiding."

Chapter Twenty-Eight

We found a narrow passageway leading between a couple of the houses, and were able to jiggle open the weak gate at the opening. The path led us back to a dark alleyway behind the row of decrepit buildings. I tried to block out the smell of rotting garbage, and prayed we wouldn't run into some crazy crackhead looking for his next fix.

Jordan was on a mission now, and I had to keep moving so I wouldn't lose him.

"Does that look right?" he asked.

I counted from where we'd come in. Four places down. "That's it."

The fence around the tiny back yard had more holes than I'd fixed on my entire property, and I guessed they weren't from snowplows. We had no trouble finding a trail through it. Where we did have trouble was picking through the junk and moving quietly toward the house. In a way I was glad it was dark so I couldn't see exactly what I was stepping on.

"There," I said, pointing at a lighted window. "See if you can make out anything."

A crooked blind blocked a full view of the room, but Jordan stood to the side, one eye closed as he peeked in. He shook his head.

I stepped up and leaned sideways, trying to see through a sizable crack in the shade. When my eyes focused, I jumped back, knocking into Jordan.

"What?" he whispered.

"Ricky's right there, talking to somebody."

He leaned over and peered in the crack. "Asshole."

"Yeah. But can you see who he's talking to?"

He shook his head.

I stepped up, flattening myself against the building, and squinted my eyes, trying to focus through the tiny line of vision. I could see something…an elbow? Couldn't tell.

Jordan stepped back from the window, gesturing me away from the house. "There's a suitcase on the bed. It has men's clothes in it." He put his hands on his hips and let his head drop. "It's him, isn't it?"

"I think so."

"So Ricky had him plant the bomb?"

I shook my head. "I don't think Ricky had him do anything. I think he did it all himself."

Jordan's head came up. "You think *he* killed Genna?"

I grunted with frustration. "I don't know."

His jaw clenched, and the fire began to reignite in his eyes.

"You got your phone?" I asked.

"Yeah."

I held out my hand. "Hand it over."

"Who—"

"Let's have the cops come get him."

His eyes flashed. "We'll get him ourselves."

I looked pointedly at the blood on his shirt. "You think?"

His jaw clenched, and a battle was being fought on his face. Finally he relaxed. "I guess you're right."

"Thank you. Now may I have your phone?"

He placed it in my hand, and I stepped away from the house to again dial a number I knew by heart. An officer answered.

"Police department. This is Officer Stern."

A cop I actually knew. "Stella Crown here," I said. "Can you please have Detective Willard call me at this number?"

"Ma'am, I can hardly hear you."

I faced away from the house and said it again, a little louder.

"Oh, Ms. Crown. Can I help you?"

"Just have Willard call me here." Jordan supplied me with his number and I repeated it to the cop.

"The detective's at home," Stern said.

"I know. It's an emergency."

"Shouldn't you call 911?"

"It's not that kind of emergency."

She paused, obviously not sure what to do.

"Please?"

"All right. I'll call him. But it might be me calling you back."

"Fine." I pushed the off button and held it out to Jordan. "Put this on vibrate so Ricky and Baronne don't hear it."

Two minutes later, the phone shuddered in my hand. I answered. It was Willard.

"We found Baronne," I said.

"What?"

"He's hiding out with Ricky and his new girlfriend—the dark-haired girl from the band. Marley. They're planning on skipping town."

"Where are you?"

I gave him the address.

"I know it's a lot to ask," he said, "but can you please let the police handle it from here?"

"That's why I'm calling."

"Okay. Good. I'll get on the horn to Alexander and you should be seeing someone soon."

"Thanks, Willard."

"I think I should be thanking you."

I gave Jordan the phone and we hunkered behind the fence, our eyes on the house. Realistically, it would probably be at least ten minutes till anyone official showed up. Willard had to find Alexander, who then had to relay information to the rest of the force. I wouldn't think they'd hurry this, since they knew exactly where Baronne was.

A few minutes later I heard scuffling, and I peeked out from my hiding place to see the shapes of two cops coming down the alley, backs bent to keep their heads below the fence. I stepped out, so they'd see where we were waiting. The cops swung toward us, hands going toward their belts.

I held my hands up. "I called it in. We're staying out of the way."

"Crown?" one of them said, squinting in the darkness.

"That's me."

He stepped closer, revealing himself as a middle-aged guy, a slight paunch above his belt. I squinted and could just make out the name Ganno on his name plate. He nodded shortly, gesturing the other cop ahead of him. "You need to leave the alley," he said to me.

"Yeah," I said.

"I mean it. We've got the bomb squad and SWAT heading this way, and you don't want to get in the middle of it."

When I didn't move, Ganno's face went stony, so I pulled Jordan from our spot and tugged him down the alley, away from the house.

Ganno watched as we left, then turned to pick his way into the yard to his partner. As soon as he was out of sight, we crept back to the fence, where we saw the cops positioned by the back door.

The sound of cars parking in front of the house sent a chill up my spine, and I pressed closer to the fence. Jordan breathed heavily beside me, his fingers clutching the wire.

The back door burst open, sending the younger cop plunging backward down the steps. Ganno lunged at Baronne, who barreled down the stairs and over the fallen cop. Baronne avoided Ganno's grasp and ran across the yard, stumbling on junk and rocks as he made his way toward us. The young cop rolled over, yanking his gun from his belt and pointing it at Baronne.

"Freeze!" he screamed. "Police!"

Baronne launched himself through the gate, a huge shape in the dim light. He stopped for a split second to check out his options, and I threw myself at his ankles. He fell heavily to the ground, and Jordan rushed him, landing on his chest and pinning his arms to the ground.

Before I could react, Jordan was up and raising his fist. I threw myself forward to grab his arm, and latched my fingers around his wrist, scraping my nails across his skin.

Jordan, halted mid-punch, reared back as if to throw me off, but caught himself before following through.

Baronne, seeing an opening, scrambled out from underneath us. I grabbed his ankle again, landing him back on his face. This time Jordan got Baronne's arms and twisted one behind his back.

The cops from the back yard burst from the gate, guns out.

They hesitated only for a moment as they read the situation, until the younger one came to cover Baronne.

"I thought you left," Ganno said to me.

"Yeah," I said. "I know."

"Get off him," the other cop said.

I got up. Jordan kept Baronne's arm twisted at his back. Painful, if Baronne's expression was any indication. His head was turned sideways on the ground, his cheek squished forward, and his eyes bulged.

"Let him go," the young cop said to Jordan.

Ganno was on his radio, calling in the take-down.

Jordan stared at Baronne's face.

"You killed Genna," Jordan said. His voice was barely over a whisper. "After all I told you."

Baronne tried to twist his face upward, only to be rewarded with a push on the head from Jordan.

Baronne spat dirt from his mouth. "I didn't do anything to her. She was alive when I left."

"You killed her!" Jordan said, his voice now loud with desperation.

Ganno put a hand on Jordan's shoulder. "Let him go, son."

I stepped toward Baronne and squatted down. "What do you mean, she was alive? When did you leave?"

His face was red with pain.

"Jordan," I said. "Let him go."

"But—"

"Do it!"

He gave Baronne one last twist and dropped the arm. Baronne pulled it under himself and cradled it against his chest while the younger cop's gun stayed leveled at him.

"When?" I said to Baronne. "When did you see Genna?"

He closed his eyes for a moment, then focused them on me. "The end of the second set. I was…heading out the back exit."

"That back hallway?"

"Yeah. But she wasn't in there. She was just at the door leading into it."

"What was she doing?"

He glanced at Jordan. "Crying."

Jordan opened his mouth, then turned away to lean his hands against the fence, looking as if the cops were about to search him.

"Was anyone with her?" I asked Baronne.

He shook his head. "Not that I saw."

Ganno pulled Baronne's arms behind him, making the man wince with pain, and snapped on the handcuffs. Between the two officers, they got him to his feet.

"And the bomb?" I asked.

He looked at me, then pointedly around the alley. "You see my lawyer anywhere?"

I snorted. "Not likely."

"Then it's not likely I'll be talking anymore, is it?" He swiveled his eyes toward Jordan, opened his mouth like he was going to say something, despite his bravado, but shut it again.

Footsteps sounded from the back yard and down the alley. More cops appeared, SWAT gear covering their bodies and faces.

"Time to go, Baronne," the younger cop said.

They started toward the clump of cops.

"Hey, Ganno," I said.

He looked back over his shoulder. "Yeah?"

"Aren't you forgetting something?"

He looked blank.

I pointed at Baronne and smiled. "You're welcome."

Chapter Twenty-Nine

The police station was cold. Not winter cold. Just...cold. I hugged myself to ward off the chill, whether it was real or in my head. I'd been sitting there about an hour and a half, and my muscles were stiffening.

Willard had been waiting at the building when I arrived, having run down to the city after my call. Not there as a major player in the actual proceedings, he sat with me in my interviews, offering support as he could.

I knew there was a reason I liked him.

The Philly cops had finished with me pretty quickly, wondering mostly how I'd smelled out Baronne's presence at Marley's, and what exactly went down in the house when Jordan and I first got there. After they'd gone over that three or four times, I got a visit from Alexander the Slime. He greeted Willard with professional detachment, then walked me through everything I'd just told the others, as well as everything I knew about Baronne, Ricky, and Marley, as well as the band, Genna, and the bomb. I didn't have a whole lot to tell him he didn't already know. He finally realized he'd sucked out all my knowledge of the situation, and set me free.

I'd lost track of everyone else. A glimpse of Ricky was all I'd seen when we got to the police station, and he wasn't looking any too happy. I assumed Marley was there, too, the complicit little bitch. I hoped she'd learned something from the whole mess, including what happens when you steal a woman's loser boyfriend less than a week after she dies.

But then, Jordan was really Genna's boyfriend. Wasn't he?

Jordan—Genna's boyfriend or not—finally stumbled out of the interview room, his face gray with fatigue and grief. He walked right past Willard and me without even a glance in our direction. I followed him out the door, not sure where he was going, but certain he shouldn't be walking around the streets of Philadelphia alone. When he reached the curb, he stopped and looked up and down the street.

"Know where we are?" I asked.

He sighed, raising his shoulders, then dropping them. "No."

"Okay. Stay here." I watched his face, but got no response. "Jordan? You'll wait for me?"

"What? Oh, yeah."

I went back into the police station. "Give us a ride to Jordan's truck?" I asked Willard.

"Glad to."

He got directions from the first cop he found and dropped us off close to Marley's place, where the townhouse still bustled with activity. Cops looking for evidence and money, I supposed. Willard said he wanted to see what was happening, and that he'd be in touch.

I turned to Jordan and held out my hand for his truck keys. He didn't argue this time.

"You gonna make it?" I asked when we were in the cab.

His lips twitched, and he nodded.

"Good. Now help me get out of this place."

With his guidance we made it back to the Schuylkill without any problems, and at this time of night the traffic was like another highway might have during the day. Which meant we could drive the speed limit without having to brake every two seconds.

When we'd gotten a few miles down the road I glanced at Jordan. "So what were you telling Baronne?"

He blinked. "What do you mean?"

"You know what I mean. What was that about 'how could he do it' after all you'd told him?"

His mouth pinched shut, and he studied the dashboard.

"Jordan."

He shook his head, but said, "I'm not proud of it, okay? He…he duped me. Said he wanted to learn about sound stuff. Once we started talking, we had fun. At least I *thought* we were having fun. Talking about the business, the band, and stuff. It's not often I find someone actually interested in the *technical* part of the whole music scene."

I flicked my brights at a truck coming the other way, and its lights went to the lower setting. "What did he want to know about the band?"

"What I saw in them, how they worked together, what it was like touring."

I remembered what Tom had said about Mann's interest in having the band as a headliner for Club Independence, and wondered if Baronne was using that as his ticket to get out of town and on with his life. In a strictly illegal, backstabbing way, of course. "Was he especially interested in Ricky?"

Jordan considered it. "I don't know. He did ask me about him."

"About how he got along with the other band members?"

"No, not really. More about how I thought he played. If he was good or not."

So Baronne already knew Ricky was on the way out with the band and wondered if he'd be worth recruiting for himself. I guessed he'd decided he was.

"How much did you tell him about sound?"

Jordan made a growling sound. "Like was it enough he'd know where to put the bomb?"

"Well. Yeah."

"It was enough."

We were silent for several minutes, and I negotiated the merge onto the Northeast Extension.

"But why the bomb?" Jordan said. "He already had the money. Why would he want to kill people?"

I checked my mirrors and pulled over to pass a slow-moving truck, its hazard lights blinking. I put on my turn signal and the truck lights flashed. I settled back in the right lane, my brain fizzing with a new idea. "What if he didn't *want* to kill anyone?"

"Huh? Why plant a bomb if you're not going to set it off?"

"Look at what he accomplished. He cleared out the whole place with that phone call. Ruined the concert. And he got away."

"Yeah," Jordan said, "but why wouldn't he have planted a fake one? Why set one that really could go off, if he didn't plan on detonating it? In fact, why plant one at all?"

I considered the question. "He planted a real bomb. But something changed his mind."

Jordan lifted a foot and rested the sole on the dashboard, leaning his head back on the seat. "What? What would change your mind if you were set on bombing something?"

I lifted a shoulder. "Maybe he realized once he got away that he didn't need to bomb the place. He was free."

"But he made the bomb threat. Put the whole evacuation in motion."

"Maybe he was afraid the bomb would go off even if he didn't want it to."

"But he had the remote, right?"

"Right. But couldn't something still set it off?"

Jordan swiveled his head my direction. "I don't know anything about bombs. Remember?"

"Yeah. I know."

I flipped on my turn signal and coasted off the Lansdale exit. I paid the toll, not quite able to smile at the tollbooth operator, and made it to my street in record time, the commuters at home in bed for once instead of clogging up the roadways.

"I still don't get why," Jordan said.

"Why what?"

"Why plant the bomb to begin with? Let's say he never planned to detonate it, or even if he did. Why? Why not just take the money and run to New York to start his new band?"

I pulled into my lane and swung the truck in a U, leaving the nose pointing toward the road. "How about revenge?"

"Revenge? For what?"

I took a deep breath. "Baronne and Mann were friends. Best friends. Musicians. And Mann didn't believe they'd ever make it as a band. He gave up on it long ago, without even trying to work things out with his partner." I unlatched my seatbelt, and it slapped back into place. "Perhaps Baronne couldn't forgive that. That lack of faith."

Jordan shifted in his seat. "You sound pretty convinced about that theory."

"Do I?" I could feel Jordan's gaze on the side of my face, and my eyes locked on Nick's Ranger, sitting like a thorn in my driveway. "I guess I've learned something about that in the past week." I opened the door and stepped out.

Jordan scooted over to the driver's seat and held the door open to look at me. "Learned something about what?"

"About what happens when people don't believe."

The flash of pain in Jordan's eyes sent my heart to my throat. "Jordan, I wasn't talking about—"

"Yeah, yeah," he said. "I know." He slammed the truck's door shut and sped out the drive.

Chapter Thirty

The first thing I thought when I woke up Saturday morning—Lucy's wedding day—was, *Holy cow. It's raining.*

The raindrops tapped on my roof, and I stumbled out of bed to peer out the window. The dusk-to-dawn light illuminated the steady, feathery rain, and I felt a confused tumble of gratefulness and irritation. Could God not wait one more day to send it? Or was this God's way of telling us something profound, that I wasn't getting?

Nick was sprawled on the sofa in the front room, the afghan on the floor, along with his shoes. He hadn't even bothered to take off his jeans. I studied him, listening to the rain pound the metal roof above that section of the house, and wondered if it was the last time he'd be sleeping on my sofa. I left him, not sure I had any chance of choking down breakfast.

Lucy was already in the kitchen, leaning on the sink, her nose inches from the window. I grimaced, not sure I was ready for the tears I was sure I'd see because of the rain.

But she turned around smiling. "Isn't it beautiful?"

I stared at her, my mouth hanging open. "Huh?"

"The rain. We need it so badly."

I stared at her some more.

"What?" she said.

I shook my head. "Nothing."

She pushed herself off the sink. "I thought I'd help with milking this morning."

"Lucy—"

"I want to."

I gave a half-laugh. "Well. Okay. It's your wedding."

The news reported the arrest of Bobby Baronne, saying only that he'd been found safe and sound and holding much more money than he should've had. A mug shot blinked onto the screen, showing an exhausted and down-trodden middle-aged man with stringy long hair and a big nose. Baronne didn't look like any rock star now.

Ricky and Marley weren't pictured, but it was told that Baronne was being harbored by two adults who were also being held for questioning.

Good for them.

I called the police station, only to be told that Detective Willard wasn't in. I left a message to have him call me, and the cop promised to relay it. I guessed I had to leave it at that. Willard's family wouldn't be too happy if I called their house at five-o'clock in the morning.

After a light breakfast, which I managed to eat despite my worries, Lucy and I headed out to the barn at a trot, trying to dodge the raindrops. Queenie met us in the parlor. She knew where to hang out in a rainstorm.

I squatted down and rubbed both sides of her neck. "Thanks for taking care of Nick last night."

"You're welcome," Lucy said.

I looked up. "I was talking to Queenie."

Lucy's eyebrows rose.

"But thanks to you, too."

She continued on to the feed room.

"He mad I left?" I asked.

Her voice drifted around the corner. "Actually, no."

I wondered what that meant.

Lucy appeared with the feed cart. "He didn't seem to even notice you were gone. In his own world. Went right to the front room, and hasn't come out yet."

I blew my bangs off my forehead. "Your folks at the hotel in Kulpsville?"

"Yup. Seem happy there. No stepping over anybody to get to the bathroom. Except each other."

"You'll be in a hotel tonight."

She blushed, and I couldn't help but chuckle. The woman was at least forty and had been married before. What was the blushing about?

"You all ready for today?" I asked.

She smiled again. "Yes. Can't wait."

"Even with the rain?"

"Don't they say rain on your wedding day is a good omen?"

"I guess."

She paused, a hand on her hip. "I would think rain after a drought would be even better. Lenny and I must be in for a lot of good years."

I grabbed the bucket and ran warm water into it.

A lot of good years. We couldn't always count on those, could we? As Lucy knew too well, after losing her husband Brad.

"Besides," Lucy said. "We can use the hall at the German-Hungarian Club if we have to. It might be a little smoky, but we'll survive."

Milking went quickly and smoothly, Lucy and I working together without having to talk. By eight-thirty I was practically pushing Lucy out the barn door.

"Will you go, already? I'm feeling guilty here."

She laughed. "All right, all right. It's just…I'll miss the girls." She patted the rump of Ariel, the first cow in the row.

"Yeah, yeah, send 'em a postcard."

She hesitated in the doorway. "You'll be getting ready soon, too?"

I froze, my pitchfork in a lump of dirty bedding. Ma had handed me the garment bag after the rehearsal the day before, and with everything that happened I hadn't even unzipped it. It was hanging unopened in my front closet, where I'd stashed it before milking with Nick.

"You bet," I said to Lucy. "My outfit is all ready for me."

I didn't mention I had no idea what it looked like.

Her face softened. "Well, good. I can't wait to see it."

Me, either.

By the time I finished up in the barn, she and Tess were in clean clothes, ready to head to the church. Lucy's wedding gown lay in plastic over her arm, while Tess already wore her dress, an adorable light green thing with all kinds of frilly stuff.

On her, that style looked good.

They left, and I found Nick in the kitchen, where he cradled a cup of hot tea in his hands. His hair was wet from a shower, and he wore pressed, dark gray pants and a light blue shirt that I knew would bring out the color of his eyes.

"Morning," I said.

He blew on his tea, the steam rising past his face. "Morning."

"We driving to the wedding together, or separate?"

He took a sip of his drink. "Whatever you want."

Oh, great.

"I have to leave as soon as I'm dressed," I said.

He spooned a sprinkling of sugar into his tea. "I'm ready whenever."

"Then I guess we can go together."

He nodded. "All right."

"All right."

I turned and left the kitchen.

Grabbing the garment bag and shoe box from the front closet, I felt a pang of anxiety. Not about the clothes, exactly, but about the entire day. Too many issues at hand, besides what I would be wearing.

Swallowing my worry, I took the clothes and went upstairs. My closet door stood a few inches open, and I hooked the garment bag's hanger over the top. It was the moment of truth. I pulled down the zipper.

Tears sprang to my eyes as I took in Ma's creation. Not only because it was beautiful. Or black. Or unfrilly. It was just…me. I showered quickly, put on the outfit, and went downstairs.

Nick's reaction when I stepped out of the stairwell affirmed my feelings, and I had to smile. He looked more animated than he had since before he got sick, his eyes traveling up and down Ma's original design. Well, up and down *me*.

The two-piece outfit was made of some kind of black material. Shiny and flowing. Silk, maybe? I didn't know. The top was sleeveless, with a V-neck pointing to a row of shiny black buttons down the front, and did wonders for the fact that I had no cleavage to speak of. The shirt ended at my waist, just covering the band of the pants Ma had fashioned. The flat-front slacks had flared legs, long enough and wide enough to accommodate the dressy black boots Ma had gotten. They weren't Harley boots, but soft black leather above low black wooden heels.

"Wow," Nick said.

I felt like a million bucks.

We made a quiet trip to the church in my truck, listening only to the rain on the windshield and cab roof. From previous experience I knew the awkwardness we felt would only be heightened by songs we might hear on the radio. So I left it off.

We stepped into the church, shaking the rain off our shoulders, and were greeted by Tess and a smiling mother of the bride. She held her arms out, and again I let her hug me.

"Oh, Stella, good morning. You look wonderful."

Unspoken was the worry Lucy had shared with her about what I'd show up wearing.

"Thanks, Lois. You look good, too."

"And Nick," she continued. "It's so good to have you here."

I glanced around the fellowship hall while they greeted each other, taking in the podium with the guest book, and other members of Lucy's family who'd arrived early, having come from Lancaster. I wondered if Jordan had made it yet, or if he was still recovering from the night before.

Something tickled my ear, and I heard, "Rrrow."

Bart stood beside me, glorious in his special tux, as promised.

"Talk about hot bridesmaids," Bart said. "You know how they always say the best man and bridesmaid get together?" He waggled his eyebrows.

I snuck a peek at Nick, expecting a light joke about how I was already taken, but he purposely avoided my eyes. Bart noticed this, and made an apologetic face.

"So where's the bride?" I asked.

"Downstairs in the nursery."

"The nursery?"

"Attached to a bathroom. With mirrors."

"Oh. Right."

Lenny clumped down the stairs from the sanctuary, huge and black in his tux. His red mane had been tamed somewhat, and his beard combed into submission. He looked kind of like a kid playing dress-up, and I resisted the urge to pinch his cheek.

He took the final step onto the floor and froze, his eyes bulging at the sight of me. His mouth dropped open and he slapped a hand over his heart.

"I know," Bart said. "Our princess cleans up pretty good."

I slugged him lightly on the shoulder. "I'm going to see Lucy."

"Good idea," Lenny said, grinning. "Put her mind at ease."

I stuck my tongue out at him and left them snickering in the foyer.

I knocked lightly on the nursery door, and, at Lucy's summons, entered. She stopped in the middle of pulling on her pantyhose, and I turned in a circle, holding out my arms. A slow smile stretched across her face.

"Wow," she said.

"Exactly what Nick said."

She lifted an eyebrow. "Well, that's good."

"So it's okay?"

"It's perfect."

"Good. Now, how can I help?"

So I did the girly thing and helped with her dress, a simple, off-white sheath. I held the mirror so she could see the back of her hair, and scootched back her sleeves while she washed her hands. The photographer came by to snap our photo, and before we knew it, Peter Reinford, the pastor, was there, telling us it was time.

He left, and I looked at Lucy. "You ready?"

"I'm ready."

I reached for the door, but she laid a hand on my arm. "This doesn't change us, does it?"

I opened the door. "Why would it?"

Tears welled in her eyes. "I just wanted to be sure. Because you know I love you, even if we won't be living with you anymore."

"Yeah," I said. "I know." I pulled a tissue from a box on a bookshelf. "Here. Don't let your mascara smudge up your face."

She laughed and dabbed her eyes with the Kleenex. "Okay. Let's go."

We passed the sound booth on the way up, and I did a double-take at the sight of two people in the cramped space. Jordan lifted his head and caught me staring at the woman beside him. San. Genna's sister, who'd been desperate to find Jordan.

And who'd originally wanted him for herself.

Jordan's face was unreadable, and I didn't have time to find out what San was doing here. Well, other than the obvious.

I shoved it aside to think about later, since I needed to keep my mind on my job. Which right now was supporting Lucy, not figuring out who had killed a woman I'd met briefly in a green room.

The wedding was a lovely affair, with everything moving along smoothly except for Lenny knocking over the unity candle with his elbow. At least it hadn't been lit yet.

Peter presented a short but meaningful message, and Lenny gave Lucy a kiss that seemed longer than usual for a wedding smooch. After the presentation of "Lenny and Lucy Spruce," the new couple headed back down the aisle, Tess skipping between them, her hands in theirs.

Bart and I followed, and a quick glimpse of the outside showed that the rain had stopped and the sun was peeking through the clouds. I guessed we could have the outside reception, after all.

Lucy and Lenny got situated near the stairs to greet guests as they headed out to the reception, so I quickly told Lucy and Lenny congratulations before the hordes arrived—made up of such various groups as bikers, church folks, tattoo artists, family, and farmers—and waited for Nick, figuring we'd drive to the reception together.

When he emerged, however, it was from the elevator, with Norm and Cindy, the couple who had come to give me the MS lecture the other night.

I turned away and stalked outside, where I breathed in that wonderful smell of spring rain. People began to stream by me, heading for their cars, and I stepped to the side so I wouldn't get run over.

I felt a presence at my shoulder and looked over to see Willard.

"Sorry I didn't get back to you," he said.

"I figured you were busy. Or sleeping."

He grunted. "Both."

"So what's the news?"

"Ricky and the girl—"

"Marley."

"Right. Marley. Anyway, they've been released on unsecured bail."

"Meaning what?"

"They've been charged with hindering apprehension or prosecution, as well as obstruction of justice. But they're out without having to pay bail money as long as they show up for their hearing."

"You trust them on that?"

"Not my call. But they seemed sufficiently frightened by the experience. Especially the girl."

"Good. And Baronne?"

"Still in custody. Bail will probably be set at fifty to a hundred thousand dollars. And he can't use the money he stole to make it. They seized the cash they found with his belongings, and froze his bank account."

I took it all in. "Did he say anything?"

"About what?"

"The bomb? Genna?"

He rubbed his face, which looked tired, even if it was clean-shaven. "He hasn't been charged with Genna's murder."

"So they believe him that he didn't kill her?"

"There's no evidence to say he did."

"And the bomb?"

He laughed quietly. "Now there *is* evidence for that. Fingerprints, bills of sale for components, his own confession. Not the sharpest tack in the box."

"So if he had killed Genna, he would've made a hash of it."

"Most likely."

I shook my head. "He say *anything* about Genna?"

"Oh, yes. Apparently she was waiting backstage, close to the exit door."

"Crying," I said.

He shot me a sharp glance.

"That much, he told me last night," I said.

"But did he tell you what *else* she did?"

I raised my eyebrows. "No. What?"

He smiled sadly. "She convinced him not to blow up the building."

Chapter Thirty-One

"So Genna saved us all?" Jordan said.

We stood in the yard at the German-Hungarian club, the grass drying quickly in the sun. Clusters of talking and laughing people sat at tables and circles of chairs, eating roasted pork and real mashed potatoes, reminding me of the "memorial service" at Tom's house, except this event was *supposed* to be a party.

Across the yard Tess was giggling, hiding behind Tonya while Donny tried to tickle her. From the natural way Tonya and Donny were smiling and laughing, it seemed they really were friends, much to my amazement and skepticism. I guessed the possibility of healed relationships was real, after all.

I'd driven Nick to the reception, then left him to find a seat while I pulled Jordan to the side, San following like a puppy. She stood beside him now, clutching his elbow, her eyes wide with new-found grief at this news of her sister. That Genna had somehow kept Baronne from detonating the bomb.

I kept my eyes on Jordan, his nose slightly swollen from the pummeling Ricky had given it. I said, "Apparently Bobby saw Genna crying and asked what the problem was."

"Surprising he even noticed," Jordan growled.

"Yeah, I know. But he did. And she let it all out. Her wanting to quit, her..." I glanced at San. "...wanting to marry you, the problems with the band. Baronne got the idea that the band was about to self-destruct, and knowing how Mann was counting on them for his headliner, figured that was even better than blowing up the building."

"Was he really going to kill the entire audience?"

I shook my head. "He'd planned all along to call in the bomb threat and have the building evacuated. He was going to wait until everyone was out and then detonate the bomb. Put Mann out of business for good, without hurting anybody."

Jordan frowned. "Except the building was never completely empty. The bomb squad was in there by that time."

"I know. So his decision to let it go saved some lives. And saved himself an even worse sentence than he'll get now."

San sniffed. "You mean *Genna* saved them."

Jordan patted her hand. "Genna saved them." He looked at me. "So she really was alive then. Between sets."

I nodded. "She was."

Jordan closed his eyes, and I could see pain etched into his face in the crow's feet that had appeared during the past week.

"Jordan?" We looked down at Annie, there to help with sound. "The guys are wondering if you're done setting up."

Jordan opened his eyes. "I'm coming."

Gently, he peeled San's fingers from his elbow and headed toward the band. I watched him go, following his path toward the platform put up just for today. Tom Copper stood in front of the stage, his back toward us as he checked out the space. Donny had joined LeRoy, and they stood in their usual places, setting the mic stands at the correct height. Parker heaved a drum onto the stage and hopped up, making me think his complaints about aging were a bit stretched.

Beside me, San watched Jordan as he followed Annie toward the stage.

"So, San," I said, "you still thinking of a relationship with Jordan? He's a great guy."

She smiled sadly. "No. It...wouldn't work. Every time he'd look at me, he'd be thinking I should be Genna. That he'd had her first. I'd just be the runner-up. The kid sister who tried to take her place."

I didn't say anything. She was right. Which meant that if San had sneaked into Club Independence and killed Genna, she was only now realizing her mistake.

But I didn't really think she'd murdered her sister.

Leaving San on her own, I wandered toward the band.

"Glad to see you have a drummer today," I said to Tom.

He glanced over at me. "Yeah. We figured Ricky would pull one of these someday. I'm just glad he did it here, and not in Idaho or some god-forsaken place. It's not like we could find a replacement just anywhere."

"Park looks excited."

Tom smiled. "Yeah. He misses the music, even though he won't admit it."

I watched as Jordan and Annie unrolled a black swath of carpet and laid it on a trail of cords.

"Think he'll be joining you full-time again?" I asked Tom.

"Parker? Nah. He might like it once in a while, but not as a full-time gig again. In fact..." He hesitated, and I looked at him.

"What?"

"We're probably going to be taking some time off."

I stared at him. "What do you mean?"

He sighed loudly, shoving his hands in his front pockets. "We've been thinking about it for a while. Ever since Genna admitted she was considering quitting—"

"Wait. You knew?"

The corner of his mouth twitched. "She told Tonya. You know. Being best friends and all. And Tonya told me. You know. Being my wife and all."

"So all along, Genna thought it was a secret, but it wasn't?" Jordan had thought so, too.

"Aw, I don't know. She had to figure Tonya would tell me. But we acted like it was a secret. We never talked about it." He shook his head. "I should say the guys and I never talked about it *with Genna*. But we've been talking without her."

"About what would happen if she quit."

"Sure."

"And what did you decide?"

He took his hands out of his pockets and ran his fingers through his hair. "We never got a chance to decide anything. We thought we'd have time. We thought she'd tell us, and give us a chance to find somebody else, if we wanted to. But..."

"Yeah," I said. "It didn't exactly turn out that way."

We were quiet for a minute as we watched Jordan and Annie cover another section of cables.

"So we're going to take some time off," Tom said. "Do our next round of commitments with Parker, and then call it quits. We're tired. LeRoy has a gal in his church choir who's got her eye on him, and he's not sure she'll wait much longer."

I laughed.

"And," Tom said, "Tonya's pregnant."

I looked at him. "Congratulations."

"Yeah. Thanks. That was the final straw for me. The road's no place for a kid. And I don't want a child staying home and growing up without me ever being around. Not fair to anybody."

"So the gig with Club Independence?"

He shrugged. "I told Gary we might do the occasional concert. It's in town, we all live here. But just for fun. Not as a regular act every weekend or anything. At least not for now. We're just...*I'm* just...family is where I have to put my energy right now."

I looked at him, at his face. He was at peace with it. With this decision to put his career on hold. To put it in what he considered its proper place.

"So that's why you let Marley sing," I said.

He glanced at me. "What?"

"You knew it was just for a couple gigs. You didn't want to find somebody really good when you knew you were breaking up."

His lips twitched into a sort of smile. "She was cheap."

A scream shattered the peaceful hum of the reception, and I jerked my head around. Annie stood with her hands raised, screaming as Ricky sat on Jordan, hammering him with his fists. Tom and I raced over, pulling Ricky off and getting his hands secured.

Jermaine suddenly appeared, his security-guard personality overriding his family one, and hauled Ricky away from all of us, wrenching his arm behind his back. I wondered if Jermaine had taught Jordan that move, seeing how Jordan had used the exact same one on Baronne the night before.

I squatted by Jordan and sat him upright. Blood dripped from a cut on his lip. Good grief. The second injury in as many days. "Get me something for this," I told Annie. It took a moment for my words to register before she sprinted off.

"Where'd he come from?" I asked Jordan.

He shook his head and felt at his face with his fingers. "Don't know. I was working, and suddenly there he was."

"Here." Annie thrust some of the Harley wedding napkins toward me, and I pressed one on Jordan's lip. He took it and looked at it, grimacing at the blood before putting it back on the cut.

"It's *his* fault," Ricky yelled. All eyes shot to him, and the finger he pointed at Jordan. "If it wouldn't have been for *him*, I'd still be with the band. I'd still have...I'd still have Genna." He sobbed once. "*He* pressured her into it, saying Marley could take her place. That it would be fine. It was all because of *him*." He sank against Jermaine, a pathetic specimen, wearing the same clothes he'd had on the night before, his hair now a disaster, the spikes not so much stylish as clumps of greasy black.

Jordan stared at him, dropping the napkin from his mouth. "I never did. I never would've..."

"I know," I said. "I know you didn't."

"Marley's a *terrible* singer."

Annie gave a bark of laughter, then clapped a hand to her mouth, her eyes filling with tears. She turned and ran away.

I watched her go, arms flailing, her feet stumbling on the grass. Finally, she disappeared behind the storage shed.

And something in my mind clicked.

I got up and began walking where the girl had gone. Footsteps padded behind me.

"Where are you going?" Jordan asked.

"To ask some questions."

"To *Annie?*"

We rounded the corner of the shed and found the girl sitting on the ground, her back against the wooden siding. She stared at her feet, not even looking up as we approached. I sank beside her, sitting on my heels.

"You knew Genna was leaving, didn't you?" I asked her.

She was silent, biting her lip.

"You heard her and Jordan arguing at the concert. Genna saying she wanted to quit."

She closed her eyes, and Jordan sucked in a breath. *"She* told the cops about Genna and me fighting?"

"But you didn't want Genna to leave, did you, Annie?" I said. "You knew Marley couldn't take her place. At least, not permanently. And if Genna left, that meant Jordan would be leaving, too."

Jordan was breathing through his mouth, the gist of my questions beginning to hit him.

"Your place with the band would be gone, wouldn't it, Annie?" I said. "Marley would go off sulking when she realized she'd never get her dream, and Jordan wouldn't be there to ask for your help. You'd be alone. And you don't do alone, do you?"

She pulled up her knees and dropped her head onto them.

"It was an accident," she finally said.

"An accident."

"She was there, at that back hallway, and I needed to get to the storage room to get a new cable. It was between the two sets, and the sound system wasn't working. Jordan sent me..."

Oh, God.

"So Genna was there," I said. "And you fought?"

She rolled her head side to side on her knees. "I asked her to get out of the way. Said I needed to get to the storage room to get something for Jordan. She followed me back, to see if she could help." She stopped her head and glared at Jordan. "Since it was for *him.*"

I waited, but she didn't continue. "So what happened?" I asked.

"I told her I'd heard her and Jordan fighting. That I knew she wanted to leave the band. I told her she couldn't. She *couldn't.*" She lifted her head and banged her fists on her knees. "Things would never be the same. Marley would never get the singing job, and I would..."

"You'd be lost."

"Yes," she whispered.

"So you hit her?" I said.

"No. *No.* We were at the storage room. I needed to get in the door. It was open and she was blocking it, telling me I didn't know what I was talking about. That it was none of my business. That I'd find a way to fit in. I pushed her to the side, and...and she *tripped.* She fell backwards, onto that old drum set. She went...she got this look on her face, and I saw it. One of the stands for the drum heads had gone right through her leg. It was sticking out the front. I...I tried to help. I yanked it out from the back, but that just made her bleed like crazy.

"She looked at me. She wasn't even scared. She was just...mad. She yelled at me to go get Jordan. Or somebody who could help. I just...I grabbed the mic from the shelf that I was supposed to get, one of the old kind with a cord sticking out of it, and I...started swinging it. I hit her, and I...I probably would've kept hitting her, except I heard the first song of the next set starting. Jordan had been able to fix the sound without me, after all."

She went quiet.

"So you left her there."

She dropped her face into her hands. "She was still alive. She was okay. I thought she'd...I thought she'd just come out. But then we had the bomb threat, and I...I forgot about her."

"You forgot."

She met my eyes for a brief moment, then looked away, her guilt almost visible in the air between us.

I glanced at Jordan, and his face had gone white, his eyes glassy. I stood and pushed him down so he was sitting on the grass.

I stepped out from behind the shed, keeping an eye on the two of them, and saw Lucy, her face hard with anxiety. Lenny stood beside her, his arm around her shoulders. I caught Lucy's eye, and she knew immediately that I needed her. She was at my side in a few long strides.

"I need Willard," I said.

She turned without question to go find him.

"And Lucy," I called after her.

She stopped.

"Tell Ma the time has come. Her son needs her. And he won't turn her away this time."

Chapter Thirty-Two

The Tom Copper Band was playing now. Tom crooned a ballad. One of their best. I tried not to listen, but couldn't close my ears.

The love I feel
Is not my own
It's not my heart
I'm not its home
But hold me close
You'll know it's true
The love I feel
Is all for you

The party was back in full swing since Willard had discreetly removed Annie from the reception. Besides the murder, she'd also admitted to lying about Jordan and Baronne fighting at the concert. She'd wanted the heat on someone else, and since she'd already decided Jordan had caused all the problems, she was glad to sic the cops on him.

Problems? She had a lot of them. And they weren't Jordan's fault.

Ricky left the reception with a little more noise, but at least he was gone. Ma, along with Jermaine and his family, had taken Jordan home.

My heart ached.

I sat alone at a table, my hand gripping a lukewarm glass of lemonade. I'd tried to smile. I'd tried to remember it was Lucy and Lenny's wedding reception. I'd done the dance with Bart, and with Lenny.

But all I kept seeing was Jordan's face.

A hand fell on my shoulder, and I looked up at Nick. He tilted his head. "Care to dance?"

I stood up slowly, my eyes not leaving his. We stood there for a few moments, not touching, not speaking.

"Jordan really loved her," I finally said.

He nodded. "I know."

"But he let everything else get in the way."

Nick looked over my shoulder. "Stella, I—"

"I love you, Nick. I've loved you ever since you stepped onto my farm last summer. It took me a while to realize it, but I know it now." I reached up and placed a finger on his chin, forcing him to look at me. "I need to know if *you* know it. If you believe it. Because I won't live the rest of my life having you doubt me."

Tears welled in his eyes. "I don't doubt you," he said. His voice was husky. "I just want you to have what you want, not some guy who—"

I placed a hand over his mouth. "Nick, you are who I want. Even if that means... *Whatever* that means."

He leaned forward, his forehead resting on mine. "I love you, Stella. So much."

"I know," I said.

And I did.

To receive a free catalog of Poisoned Pen Press titles, please contact us in one of the following ways:

Phone: 1-800-421-3976
Facsimile: 1-480-949-1707
Email: info@poisonedpenpress.com
Website: www.poisonedpenpress.com

Poisoned Pen Press
6962 E. First Ave. Ste. 103
Scottsdale, AZ 85251

6 X 5/12

X